A BRANCH IN SPRING

A Branch in Spring

A NOVEL

Lara Meredith

LARA MEREDITH

Printed in Canada, First Printing, January 2022
ISBN 978-1-7775807-3-5

A Branch in Spring is a work of fiction. Characters, businesses, places and events are a product of the authors imagination or used fictitiously. Any resemblance to events, places, or persons dead or living, is completely coincidental.

For my amazing husband, Garry, who makes all things possible.

Chapter 1

By the time the hum of her cell phone lifted the hairs on the back of her neck, Rayna was one trestle bridge outside of Talsburg, comforted by the three hundred miles of track that now stretched between her and New York City.

She pressed the off button until the screen went dark before tucking the phone into her coat pocket. It was the second story she'd killed at the last minute, and higher-ups at the newspaper would be livid, cursing her as their heads hit the glass ceiling. Thanksgiving weekend or not, they'd be wanting an explanation, and a good one, something she didn't have.

While some were concerned that she'd left the big city, others would be troubled when she arrived back in the small town. Rayna was beginning to question her decision to run home and wondered how it was possible to feel relief and disappointment at the same time.

She pushed up her sleeve, revealing a delicate gold watch. They were thirty minutes from Fallencrest Station. She snapped her laptop shut and removed a red USB from the side port. The tiny flash drive seemed far too small to hold every disturbing story she'd reported on, and another waiting to be written. That one unnerved her the most. Ominous details she'd secreted away, images she could easily erase—but never forget.

Without warning, Rayna's heart raced, and her thoughts became muddled. Everything seemed to swirl around her as a collage of images came in and out of focus: the emergency exit sign, the glaring pot lights, and the red memory stick. But as quick as the spell had cascaded over her, it was gone.

Left shaken, Rayna concealed the USB in a gum wrapper and zipped it into a hidden compartment inside her laptop case. She removed an official-looking document from the side pocket and set it on her lap, scanning the page with a furrowed brow.

Crossing the last overpass, Rayna smoothed the crimped corners of the document as she cozied up to the glass for the breathtaking view. Beneath a pink sunset, the valley below rolled with color, lush green trees which once lined the tracks now shocks of red, ocher, and burnt orange. Rayna smiled as she stared down into the bowl of autumn soup, with white church steeples floating in the broth of fall leaves. A procession of weather-beaten homes backed onto the tracks spewing streams of smoke from their brick chimneys, while eager children rallied around piles of crusty foliage—a beautiful image that spoke to her of love and family, of new beginnings and second chances.

Between the sway of the train and the mesmerizing view Rayna found it easy for her thoughts to stray, and visions of Westcott Farm and Stable began playing against the blur of colors flashing by in the distance. Her family homestead dominated the landscape in Talsburg, renowned for being one of the finest horse-breeding stables in Pennsylvania. Twelve miles of pristine white fencing circled the grand estate. To most it represented a life of privilege, an opulence they'd never know, but to Rayna, it was a refuge. A faint smile graced her lips.

Untwisting her thoughts, she buried her hand deep within the mounds of chestnut curls that feathered about her perfectly arched brows and fell to her mid-back. Rayna separated a lock and pulled the desired piece over her shoulder, twirling the strand until primed to perfection. In one proficient move, her nimble fingers coaxed the silky wisp into a flawless knot that tightened when she pulled on the end. With a light pinch, she studied the Windsored tress before letting it fall.

Passengers rustled when the hot wheels scraped against the steel tracks, unleashing a thunderous roar that whiplashed from one end of the car to the other. She wiped a fresh film of condensation from the window, disappointed the unsettling but recognizable sound had shattered the trance she'd lulled herself into. She caught a glimpse of the last level crossing, but darkness would hide the remainder of the route.

Rayna glanced around as she rummaged through her messy purse, the back of her hand sliding against the satin lining until she found the silver pen. Relieved, she rolled the cool barrel in her palm for several seconds, clicking the end sporadically. With her chin thrust forward, she steered the pen toward the document and signed on the dotted line, Rayna Lynn Westcott. She sat motionless staring at the black ink, with its dramatic strokes, deep slant, curly cues, and flare to end all. She was a simple country girl with the flamboyant signature of a Hollywood starlet.

The matronly passenger beside her marveled at the signature in disbelief. "Dear, anyone who can sign their name like that … shouldn't need to take the train." She removed a cinnamon candy from a crackling package, motioning for Rayna to take one.

"No, thank you." Rayna cringed at the attention the noisy packet had drawn. She forced a smile before returning the document to her bag, while the friendly passenger turned her attention to a rumpled newspaper strategically folded to reveal a half-finished crossword puzzle.

Rayna did a double take when she noticed the front section tucked between the passenger's hip and the arm of the seat. The bold caption screamed from the page, *Talsburg Cold Case Remains Unsolved.* It was official; her father would be none too pleased. With that thought, moist heat surged beneath her sweater, but when she flapped her neckline, the cool air produced an instant shiver.

Determined to rest for the last peaceful moments of the trip, Rayna spread her cloth coat over her legs and tucked the soft collar under her chin. With little to see beyond the blackness, she focused on the rhythmic sway of the train, the hint of cinnamon drifting throughout the cabin, and the simple lock of hair that had innocently found its way back to her hand.

Chapter 2

Two hours after leaving New York, the train parted the low-hanging fog hovering over the historical Fallencrest Station. The sky had turned dark slate, and with it, the leaves surrendered their jewel tones for muted night shades.

Rayna squinted, trying to see out into the darkness as the interior lights bloomed, but the glare from her reflection hindered the view. She smiled when she finally spotted Beaker stretched out on a long bench beside the terminal entrance, a white Stetson tipped over his eyes.

"Bet it's chilly out there." She reached for her bag. "I'll be needing this." Rayna exchanged goodbyes with the friendly traveler before heading for the exit.

Inspecting her light gray coat in the windows as she followed the aisle, Rayna pressed her palm against her hip, turning to sneak a peek from several angles. The cinched waist gave the illusion of curves, and her hunch about the mid-length jacket had been spot-on; the style took inches off her height, a tall order for any coat. She adjusted her blush pink scarf, and when she didn't see anything disagreeable, at least not in her reflection, she nodded with approval.

Whoosh! When the door slid open, Rayna's knee-high boots struck the wooden platform, rousing the sleepy figure.

"Hey, Brat." He walked toward her, flashing a playful grin, and hooked her bag over his shoulder. "You've got that look on your face. Go ahead … say it."

She gave him a curious stare. "Did you fall asleep on the bench?"

"I might have." He bumped his shoulder into hers. "You got a problem with that?"

"I'll never figure out how you manage to nod off all over the place. It's like you have a switch on your back that flips off the second you lean against a hard surface."

With a defiant smirk, he pointed at her. "That's good."

She turned to get a look at him. One of the few men who matched her in height, it made the tiny line interrupting his left eyebrow all the more noticeable. "My father doesn't expect you to kill yourself. You look tired."

"Don't you worry about me. It's a waste of your imagination."

"I'm just saying."

"Tell me something. Who do you annoy when you're not here?"

"All right, then." Pulling out a white envelope, she slipped past him and headed for the mailbox on the platform. Rayna fed the letter into the slot, dangling it for a moment before letting it fall from her fingers. As the envelope left her hand, she whispered to herself. "You're all in now, Rayna Westcott." She quickly rejoined Beaker on the platform.

With hat in hand, he patiently watched her every move. Revered as her family's most trusted employee, it was a well-earned distinction judging by the last seventeen years. Her father often said that taking Beaker in when he was only fifteen had turned into a blessing for both. It went a long way in explaining why Beaker had never become bitter. With all his misfortunes, his smile had endured.

Despite her best efforts and a coating of expensive styling products, Rayna could feel her hair frizzing as the damp air seeped into every shaft. She gathered it at the nape of her neck and pulled it over one shoulder, trying to control it, as she admired his shaggy brown waves. "I'm loving the hair, Beaker."

"Why, thank you. I give all the credit to Drive-Through Hair Cutters." He slipped the Stetson on his head and bent down to pick up a small acorn off the platform. "How the heck did this get way up here?" He offered it to her with the care afforded a priceless jewel.

"Aww … my favorite reminder of home." She inspected it before tucking it into the front pocket of her jeans on the way to his black truck.

Rayna never failed to appreciate the scent of spearmint and fresh soap that trailed Beaker. And she'd learned to accept him calling her Brat, even though it still annoyed her. At times his relentless teasing made her feel like a teenager, and to her chagrin she'd suddenly start giggling and acting like a schoolgirl. She hated that. Barely a year older, he'd never seemed young to her—ever. It often made her sad when she thought about it.

Beaker opened the passenger's-side door and shamelessly pushed a rolled-up take-out bag and a stack of newspapers off the seat to make room.

"Hmm … I think I know where the acorn came from." She shook the shearling lapels of his jacket and mockingly watched as if she expected to see others fall out.

"Hey, hey, hey! Watch the coat. It's vintage."

"Vintage? Really, Beaker?"

"Okay … it's old."

She flared her nostrils and took a deep, exaggerated breath followed by two quick coughs. "Oh, it's vintage, all right."

"Be nice!"

She gave a knowing laugh while surveying the dusty truck. "I bet you haven't washed this rig since the last time I came home."

"When was that?"

"Fourth of July."

She waited as he worked the math in his head. "Seriously, Beaker? That's terrible."

"You got a problem with my truck?" He lifted a shiny lock of her hair and playfully tossed it up into her face. "You're such a brat."

"Beaker!" She backed away, laughing. Without taking her

eyes off him, she slid her finger along the top of the dash and with a critical glance inspected the harvest.

"What're you doing?" He shook his head. "Yeah, it's dusty. It's a man's truck."

"I never heard that excuse before."

He opened the door further and motioned for her to climb in. "Listen. It might be dusty, and messy, but this rig is finely tuned and in perfect condition. Safety is always my priority. The problem is … you're just getting spoiled from riding in those big-city limos."

"Unfortunately, the limos I take … are actually called taxis." She feigned disgust before jumping into the messy cab.

Their drive home marked a perfect end to the day. She was grateful for Beaker. He looked out for her family and made their lives easier, and it meant the world to Rayna when she found herself pacing around her apartment in New York, or tossing in bed at night, trying not to fret. Regardless of what tragedy unfolded, Beaker always made her feel certain the sky would still be hovering over them the next morning. She'd often counted on that.

The smell of freshly turned soil wafted into the truck as well-lit tractors circled the fields. With three days of rain on the forecast, exhausted farmers would be working well into the night, marking the last few hours of the fall season.

Before long, the truck left the back road and pulled onto the white, crushed-stone driveway. Milk paint coated the plank fencing that bordered the laneway, and the branches of the tree-lined passage created a tunnel. A welcoming haven waited for her at the end. For now, the city was a distant memory. She was home, and for some reason—she felt safe.

The truck had barely stopped when Beaker jumped out and set her bag beside a white pillar on the top step. He looked around the grounds, as if seeing Westcott Farm for the first time. "I don't often see the place from this vantage point." He stretched his arms out and filled his chest with the cool air, then made his way back down to the driveway.

"Harland showed up here late last night. Drunk!

"Oh …" She took a deep breath and slipped her baby fingernail between her whitened teeth.

"Spewing the usual threats, about ruining his life and being sorry one day. It was sad, actually. As many times as I've watched him carry on, I'll never get hardened up to the sight of a grown man crying."

She listened intently, imagining the mayhem.

"Trent was able to haul his father off the property fairly quick this time—once Charlotte managed to calm him down."

Rayna rolled her eyes and folded her arms at the mention of Charlotte's name. *Of course she would be the only person capable of defusing the situation.*

"Whoh …" Beaker smirked at her off-the-cuff reaction. "How long are you planning on letting her jerk your chain."

"Don't you worry about it." Rayna tried to hide her irritation, and her embarrassment that Beaker had called her out. She ran his comment through her head, wondering.

As far as Harland was concerned, her feelings were the complete opposite; she'd always had a soft spot for him. At times she felt like she was more on his side than her father's. "Was he okay by the time he left?"

"Yeah, he was fine. "Before I forget, nice work on the Grainger story."

"The family's not too happy about it." She swished some gravel around with her foot. "My father's worried it might unearth trouble."

Beaker's head snapped back as he laughed. "Denver Westcott has never spent a day of his life worrying about what might happen. Anyway, you did some great reporting. The version they tried to spin over there never sat right with me. It needed a second look." He stared off before adding, "Grainger was a dangerous man, and the world's a safer place without him. The sooner the truth comes out, the better."

Rayna folded her arms across her chest, her shoulders creeping toward her ears. "The fire, and then the accident right after, are without a doubt, the most terrifying events to ever happen around here." She shuddered at the thought.

He glanced up at her while digging a heel in the gravel. Silent.

"Beaker, you know more about what happened on the Grainger farm than you're letting on."

"Could be … but if I did, I wouldn't share it out here—in the dark. That would be way too creepy." He pinched the back of her neck, sending an unexpected tingle down her spine.

"Beaker!" She growled in frustration.

"What?" He walked back to his truck with a satisfied grin.

"They opened the cold case based on my excellent investigative skills. You're kidding yourself if you plan on keeping that secret for long."

With a mischievous grin he pulled on the door handle, and in one swift movement he'd hauled himself into the cab of the truck and spoke through the open window. "Call down to the barn tomorrow. Let me know what time you want to ride. I'll have King ready to go."

"Count on it." She nodded. "But not too early! Thanks, Beaker." As the tires rolled along the crunchy gravel, she called after him. "I will figure out what you're hiding, mister!"

His hand flashed from the open window.

Rayna's tranquility vanished when the dusty truck drove off into the fog. Minus the driver's-side taillight, it resembled a motorcycle driving too close to the side of the road.

"Seriously, Beaker!"

Chapter 3

The stately front porch sat all but empty this time of year, the wicker furniture and glass tables already stowed away in anticipation of the wintry weather about to move in on the small town. Two welcoming planters sat on either side at the base of the porch stairs. Filled with fall greens and birch branches, they gave no hint of the embellishments about to invade them in just a few short weeks.

With its usual splendor, her mother's signature wreath hung prominently on the black, oversized front door. This season, a ring of orange mums, mixed with purple sprigs twisted amongst white snowberries, hung from a simple sash of cream lace.

To most, the fancy garland was merely a welcome ornament. But to a Westcott, it became a reminder that—as a family, they could survive the unthinkable. For Rayna it provided comfort; the first sign that all was well. If a wreath hung on the front door, Rayna knew that *everything was exactly as it should be.* They'd gone an entire year without a wreath once, but following a decent amount of mourning, her mother vowed they'd never know another season with the front door barren—and she'd held to it.

White pine lined the route home, but when the Westcotts built the new homestead they'd brought in a dozen oak trees to shade the Georgian-style porch that spanned the entire front of the house. They were enormous now, providing cover from the road, and this time of year, an abundance of falling acorns for fodder and entertainment. She stood at the foot of the staircase relishing the gift of silence, the open space, and the scent of autumn leaves mixed with fresh country air.

Rayna had lain in bed many a night visualizing every detail, longing to be home and wishing she could turn back time. Bittersweet memories crowded her thoughts, one painful image after another: collecting fireflies in glass jars, Halloween treats in plastic pumpkins, and a chaplain's car sitting in the circular drive on a powdery winter morning.

She could almost hear Cole's voice in the wind as it rustled through the trees. 'Three more sleeps until Halloween, Rayna. I'm going to be an ace fighter pilot, like in World War II!' Pain drifted in like burning flames, and heat filled her chest with a feeling she dreaded. *Heartache.*

"Hi, sweetie, I thought you would never get home." Rayna's mother sashayed across the impressive porch and joined her on the driveway. She had a gentle stillness about her, every movement purposeful, and her layered caramel-blonde hair perfectly offset her tiny frame. "Did you enjoy your trip?"

"Scenic! Love taking the train this time of year."

"Yes, the colors are glorious. Your father and I shared a beautiful ride today. We were gone longer than planned. I had to really focus to get the chili on in time."

"Just focus? You didn't have to rush around like the rest of us?" she teased.

"There may have been a little rushing." Her mother blushed.

"I can't wait to break out on the trails with King in the morning and get into the slow cooker tonight." Her voice softened. "Mom, if I came home to canned soup and crackers, you'd never hear me complain."

"I know, but I've made a pot of chili for every homecoming. I have no interest in changing the tradition anytime soon."

"I'm just saying."

"I can't explain it, but … the smell of warm spice wafting out of the kitchen all day reminds me you're on your way home, and it makes the waiting tolerable. Sounds silly, I'm sure."

"Doesn't sound silly at all." Her father's towering frame

emerged from the fog and moved toward them with giant strides. "Larissa, darling." He picked up her mother's hand and touched the back of it against his cheek before kissing it lightly and guiding it back to her side.

Rayna always sensed her parents' relationship had a special quality, an intense connection. She could feel it. Through all the years they'd spent together, life never changed them. She was still his sweet Larissa, and he … well, he was *Denver Westcott.*

"Hi, Daddy." She kissed his cheek.

He gave her a warm smile before walking up the stairs ahead of them and picking up her bag.

Rayna's mother shivered. Her white cotton blouse, folded below the elbow, was no match for the damp air. "You managed to beat the worst of the fog."

"How's Daddy? Beaker told me what happened last night."

"He just starts to forget about the entire mess and then something happens to remind him."

"It's been a horrible two years. I wish we could turn back time and get our families back together. I'd give anything to have things the way they were, but I know that's not possible."

"Your father knows what needs to be done."

Rayna's eyes darted to meet her mother's as she pondered the cryptic remark. There were days when it seemed like she was on Harland's side, as well.

"It's a chilly night, sweetie." She stared up at the foggy sky.

"Yeah, it is. Daddy still upset about the Grainger story?"

Falling back a few steps as they walked toward the stairs, Rayna's mother folded her arms across her chest and spoke under her breath. "The case brings up events that no one wants to relive." She rubbed her arms. "I'm sure your father would have preferred you not cause problems where we sleep."

Convinced he'd have a change of heart when she surprised him at dinner, she nibbled on her baby fingernail and committed to her plan.

"If I were you, I wouldn't mention it tonight," she

cautioned.

Well, you're not me. Rayna reached in her handbag and squeezed a tissue-covered box for reassurance.

"Just a suggestion," her mother piped in one last time for effect.

Rayna stiffened as she considered the warning. Her mother usually had the last word, mainly because Rayna found it difficult to present a stronger argument. But since Rayna's thirtieth birthday she'd been trying to take control of her life, pulling away gently when she had the opportunity or when something was important enough. It had only been a few months; it was still too early to decide how that was going to go. The process of fighting for her independence involved trial and error. And it didn't help that her mother was usually right.

"You should've seen Beaker's messy truck tonight. I had to share the seat with a week's worth of unopened mail." Rayna laughed before looking down at her feet. "My new boots sat on top of an empty food wrapper, a stack of newspapers, and whatever else he tossed off the seat to make room for me." She brushed her palm across the toe of her suede boot and used her fingernail to pick at the heel, checking for scuffs.

Her father's eyes narrowed before commenting. "He had a blown taillight."

"Oh! Did he?" Rayna opened her eyes wide in mock disbelief.

"I'll speak to him in the morning." He set her bag inside the door as Rayna and her mother caught up to him.

If she had to pick a single talent her father prided himself on, it would be his ability to recognize trustworthy men to run the farm. There wasn't a good man within ten square miles in need of a job thanks to Denver Westcott. Most of the hands being family men, he paid a living wage and provided health benefits, a rare blessing. But he often expected perfection. If anyone was careless with something he valued or let him down, he took it hard, and the misdeed wasn't easily forgotten. Rayna could read the disappointment on his face, and worried about how much of it she could take credit for.

Chapter 4

The Westcotts were considered Talsburg royalty. The sheer majesty of the estate was quick to put most people in their place, its grandeur a visual reminder of the family's wealth and stature within the community.

The front foyer boasted a dark, circular oak staircase with white risers, and white balusters cascading onto a light marble floor, collecting in a swirl at the bottom. A black "W" inlay marked the center of the grand room, and a shimmering chandelier of teardrop crystals rained from above. But, despite the trappings, a welcoming glow managed to radiate from the grand entrance way, the lighting only a small part of the charm the homestead cast over all who entered.

Her mother pointed to a fireplace in the family room, visible from the front hall.

"Your father and I added a few photographs to the mantel."

"None of me, I hope."

"What is it with young people nowadays." She smiled at Denver, and he shook his head.

Rayna found it impossible to resist and veered off toward the blazing embers. "Meet you in the kitchen."

An elaborate stone fireplace took up most of one wall. Her mother loved the open hearth, so her father refused to convert it— no matter how much work it took to haul logs and sweep ashes. A parade of picture frames, two rows deep, lined the rustic wooden mantel, displaying a patchwork of family history: faces of loved ones suspended in monumental moments, candid shots memorialized, and unremarkable photos of beautiful smiles that were no longer. Rayna's eyes darted back and forth until she spotted Cole waving from the cockpit of the abandoned Lancaster Bomber they used to fly after school. The picture could've been taken yesterday; the afternoon still so clear in her mind. Their seventh birthday.

Cole was looking right into the camera lens, and it gave the illusion of him staring back at her. Unwilling to look away, she stood there, powerless, cherishing every second of the optical delusion. His smile so full of life, unaware of the cruel irony to come. Rayna labored to draw each breath, but her gaze continued, gently resting on every picture, every face, before resting in defeat on the hardwood floor.

With a quick spin, she turned her back to the rolling flames. There'd be more than enough time to feel sad. Rayna forced a smile of her own and rushed toward the savory aroma drifting from the kitchen.

"Mom, everything looks amazing." Inhaling the scent of fresh-baked pumpkin and chili spices, she tucked a chair in close to the table and set the small, tissue-covered box on the seat next to her.

As with all her mother's rituals, the harvest table waited, pre-set, and ceramic bowls of steaming chili cooled beside the slow cooker. Her mother removed the toasted garlic bread from the oven, and with a smile, delivered the feast on a wooden serving tray that boasted their family insignia. She set the platter in the middle of the table beside three half-filled wineglasses.

"It smells delicious." Rayna leaned in closer to the dishes.

Her father reached over and touched her mother's hand. "I snuck a taste earlier. I have to say, it's probably the best batch you've ever made."

Her mother blushed. "You don't have to say that."

"Honestly, it *is* the best. I know you're always concerned it might bother my stomach so it can be a little wishy-washy in the flavor department at times … but today it's perfect. Just a nice bite to it."

"I think there was a compliment in there somewhere." Her mother adjusted the cutting board and carved the garlic bread into thick slices.

Rayna could barely wait for the right moment to retrieve the modest acknowledgment. It wasn't a gold statuette, but a plaque could be displayed on the wall and that was all she cared about. She unwrapped the tissue, beaming as she set the award in front of her father.

"Oh dear!" Her mother's palm pressed against her chest as she eyed the wooden plaque with its silver inscription plate.

Rayna's voice cracked as the words tumbled out. "It's for the Grainger story, Daddy. I want you to have it. You can put it with the others."

Surprised, he stared at it in silence.

"Isn't that a cute, little thing." Her mother reached over and polished the silver square on the front with a napkin.

Taken aback, he hesitated before lifting the plaque, smiling. "Nice work, Rayna, but this would get lost in with the others. Bring it back to the city with you. It will inspire you to go after the big one."

Rayna's heart sank. Obviously, it didn't compare to the trophies that lined the Westcott display cabinets, but to her it was 'the big one' and she was proud of it … until now. Without any arguments—to her disappointment, she scooped the award off the table. But, as she did, the weight of it shifted in her hand and she watched in disbelief as the plaque crashed onto the table, hitting the three wineglasses sending shards of glass everywhere.

"No!" She reached for the award, wiping the wine off the silver inscription before using her napkin to sop the wet mess off the tablecloth. Fragments of glass sparkled on top of the deep brown beans. It was all ruined.

"Larissa, careful!" Her father pulled her mother's hand out of harm's way. "Let me get this."

"Ugh … Mom. I'm so sorry. You had to rush around to get it made in time, and now … I've spoiled everything." Their disappointment was palpable.

"It was an accident." Her mother tried to reassure her as they picked up pieces of glass off the tablecloth and dropped them onto the serving tray beside the bowls. "There's leftover roast beef in the fridge. I'll throw together some sandwiches."

Rayna was devastated. "Mom, I …" *Stupid plaque.*

"Don't you give it another thought."

Her father picked up the pieces, continuing to guard her mother's hands from getting involved. "Your mother's right." He tipped the tray, dumping the ruined meal into the garbage bin, the glass shards smashing together as they hit the bottom.

If she hadn't been sulking, and so interested in the plaque, they'd be enjoying the beautiful meal her father had been looking forward to and her mother had slaved over. Deep down, she couldn't wait for the meal to be over and disappear into her room. In the meantime, she helped her mother make the sandwiches and tried to put the incident out of her mind.

With a long face she enjoyed the roast beef, while her mother periodically offered a little humor as a distraction to lighten the mood. Thankfully, it worked. Her parents shared the latest small-town news and Rayna followed suit with tales of her adventures in the city. The stories came easily, and the laughter came often, but the clock in the hall promptly struck eleven, to everyone's regret.

I'm turning in. Leave you to your girl talk." Rayna's father kissed them on the cheek before heading upstairs to bed.

Rayna poured another cup of steaming tea and lifted a warm slice of pumpkin pie from the baking dish, eating it right out of her hand, like a cookie. Her mother dropped the dishes into a sudsy bath as they chatted.

"I hope Daddy isn't too hard on Beaker about the taillight."

"He should be concerned. The visibility is horrendous tonight. I have always trusted your father to be fair and to do the right thing, and by now, you should too."

"True." Rayna stood in front of the picture window, sipping tea and soaking up the view, mulling over the earful Beaker would surely suffer at the snap of dawn. Her father, well-respected for being fair but notorious for being rigid, would have a new vehicle-maintenance chart put into action by lunchtime the next day. She hoped Beaker wouldn't think she had anything to do with it.

She stared out at the pasture in silence, while her mother wiped away all traces of her disastrous homecoming meal.

The estate glowed with clusters of garden lights strategically sprinkled across the property. Three stone buildings connected seamlessly with the gray board-and-batten clad stables; their interiors dimly lit for the evening. Each featured a notable set of double barn doors flanked by imposing wrought iron coach lanterns, glowing brightly but strictly for drama.

"I love sitting by this window at night. I miss it when I'm—"

"Listen. When you're home, the rest of the world does not exist. At least that's how I look at it." She picked up Rayna's mug and set it in the sink. "I never hear you mention the lawyer, the gentleman you keep bumping into." She waited for details, but Rayna failed to offer any. "Have you gone out on an actual date yet?"

With her serenity breached, Rayna tried to downplay her reaction while her heart jumped into her throat. "No. And we won't be."

Her mother gave a pitiful look that all but begged Rayna to reassure her.

"My life is wonderful, Mom." She paused, determined not to utter a single word that carried the power to worry her mother. "I'm super busy right now, that's all." She noticed a stack of photographs on the deep windowsill. "Are these for the Winter Ball?"

"Yes, they are. What do you think?"

Rayna flipped through them before fanning them out on the

kitchen table. "Nice pictures." A paper clip held a couple of typed pages to the back of one. "What! It's going to be in the old hangar. No more waffling?"

"The airport won in the end. It felt right."

"Mom, I love this venue! It captures the essence of the event."

"I'm relieved you agree. The goal is to raise enough money to refurbish the Lancaster, so having it at the hangar makes sense. It will offer a few challenges, but I think it will look dramatic." She leaned over Rayna's shoulder, offering a faint hint of her signature scent. "I asked Charlotte if she could take a few pictures. I was pleasantly surprised when she dropped these off an hour later."

Rayna bristled at the mention of Charlotte's name. "Just a thought, but … Charlotte and Trent Jackson stand to benefit from the fundraiser. He needs the money to finish the restoration. So, it wasn't all that selfless of his wife."

Rayna's mother shifted the subject, pointing to the notes attached. "The wording of the invitation is giving me a headache, and it's no exaggeration to say I've spent at least ten hours working on it."

"Leave it with me. I'll look it over." She raised her eyebrows sarcastically. "I'm no Charlotte, but I'll do my best."

"Rayna! I wish I understood what you have against that girl."

Me too. She lowered her head. But people became blinded by Charlotte's charm, and it made them vulnerable to her deceitful ways. Rayna wondered why she was the only person capable of seeing right through her. And Charlotte knew it, too.

"It's been two years. Keep in mind, you were close friends once."

"Huh …" Tired, Rayna closed her eyes and massaged her temples. "No, Mom. Charlotte's friendship had more to do with convenience. Hanging out with me came with plenty of advantages— beautiful hand-me-downs and getting better access to Cole. She would drop our plans the very minute a more exciting offer came along … or the second she walked through the front door and realized Cole wasn't home. During the three years he spent in the air force she contacted me once—the night before he arrived home. That's the kind of friend Charlotte was."

She was getting a little tired of her mother's perpetual cheerleading for Team Charlotte. Rayna was convinced, if she knew half the things Charlotte had put her through, she'd be just as angry, but Rayna didn't have the heart to toss her under the bus.

"People don't change. Charlotte's the same selfish, manipulative person she was as a teenager. The only difference is she grew up, and over the years she's learned how to hide it better."

Her mother stood stock-still, listening, shock registering on her face.

Rayna knew her issues with Charlotte had little to do with her mother and tried to move past the awkwardness by forcing a smile. "I'll have this tightened up by tomorrow night." She tapped the pages.

"That quick?"

"You forget I work at a newspaper. I make my living *turning a beautiful phrase.*" Rayna smiled as she drew invisible words in the air.

"Are you still in that horrible department?" Her mother shook her head in silent revulsion. "What do they call it?"

"Major Crime. And that's all I'm going to say about that tonight."

"Do you find many opportunities to turn a *beautiful phrase* in the crime department?"

"I do my best." Rayna pushed the stack of pictures across the table and turned away.

"I'm sorry. You know I'm supportive of whatever you choose to do with your life."

Rayna thought about how much her father enjoyed reading

her investigative reports, and how proud she'd been to tell him one had been published in every major news outlet across the nation. He wouldn't approve of her mother encouraging her to walk away from an opportunity to produce great reporting, and Rayna wasn't sure she wanted to. He'd never commented on a single fluff piece from her stint at the magazine. No, he valued serious writing. But his cherished approval came at a price.

"Enough about that." Her mother wiped her hands on a tea towel.

"All right then." Rayna envied her mother's ability to change her train of thought or wash a problem away by drying her hands on her apron or a nearby tea towel.

She gently touched Rayna's furrowed brow. "Careful … you'll end up with frown lines."

Ouch! Thanks, Mom. "It's a terrible habit to break." She pressed on the dime-sized spot while she studied her mother's brow. "You're lucky. You always look so serene." *And no one will ever point out your frown lines.*

Her mother hung the wet towel over the handle of the oven door. "Are you riding tomorrow?"

"I'm going to call down to the barn, have King tacked up by midmorning. You should come with me."

"I would love that. Did you have a ride in mind?"

"The usual. Take the Maple Ridge trail and stop at the garden, ride past the airport, and take the back road home."

"Sounds perfect." Her mother covered the pie and visibly braced for disappointing news. "When are you planning on returning to New York?"

"Saturday evening. Right after Thanksgiving." She leaned against the granite counter. "But I have two weeks, and I plan on enjoying them."

Her mother nodded.

Left alone in the kitchen, Rayna poured another cup of tea and stood in front of the farmhouse sink, eating a second helping of pie she didn't need. With one ankle tucked behind the other, she leaned against the cool porcelain skirt while she worked on the pie and thought about the cold case. In secret, Rayna agreed with her mother; she, too, had second thoughts about causing trouble. Getting back to the city before they reopened it would've been too much to wish for. Now it was destined to hang over her like a brewing storm cloud. Seconds later, she searched her empty hands for the pie.

She brushed her fingers together, knocking the crumbs into the basin, recalling the burned-out remains of the Grainger barn. A pile of smoking black rubble and white ash. There hadn't been a charred beam left standing. The acrid smell remained buried deep within her nostrils, surfacing with a vengeance when the memories replayed in her mind. Images that fueled many nightmares and infinite sleepless hours, even still.

Chapter 5

Cursing herself for wolfing down an extra slice of pie Rayna climbed the circular staircase, pinching a tiny roll that hovered above the waistband of her jeans. "Ugh, ten extra minutes of planking before bed." When she determined no amount of exercise could make it disappear overnight, she threw her hands in the air. *To heck with it!*

Reaching the landing, her last step hung in mid-stride when she spied the streak of light stretching across the floor like a pathway. Perched on the top stair, she tightened her grip on the rail, and after a brief hesitation folded her hands behind her back and followed the bait.

Shuffling her feet in the doorway, a mental debate played out in the back of her mind. She stared at the faint red glow from the clock radio. Once again, the glint of light had managed to find its way into the hall. She marveled at the squadron of model airplanes dotting the ceiling. Suspended on fishing line and positioned in dramatic dives and spiral maneuvers, it was easy to see the vivid imagination of a young boy in love with flying.

Before long, she found herself standing in front of the overstuffed bookcase, running her finger along the treasured collection that represented a life of curiosity, *How to Build a Model Airplane*, *The Life of a Bush Pilot*, and *Timber Frame Construction.* Scanning the shelves, she stopped at the spine of a tattered book and pulled it loose, *The Illustrious History of the Lancaster Bomber.* With a heavy heart, she slid it back into the case.

Moving from shelf to shelf, she randomly tipped books forward until a makeshift jacket crafted from a brown paper bag caught her interest. Prying it free, she heard a rush of air escape her pursed lips. "Rayna and Cole, Tales from the Haunted House, by R. L. Westcott."

The modest little book of thirty-pages followed a simple format, with a solitary sentence under each colorful work of art. A sensible plan for an eight-year-old—nine, maybe. She remembered coloring the cover, the black, haunted house and two stick figures running under a navy sky. Each clutching a flashlight in one hand and a jack-o-lantern in the other, the image captured the excitement of their favorite holiday.

Squatting by the bedside lamp she read it through, the story's simplicity warming her heart. Even by adult standards it captured the elements of a well-developed tale. Rayna set it on the nightstand and continued to scan the room, in search of forgotten memories.

A handmade shelf displayed a mason jar overflowing with acorns. A small tag was secured to the rim by a piece of jute: In case you get homesick. She retrieved Beaker's tiny gift from her pocket and squeezed it tight. Next to the jar, a barnwood frame held a photo of Cole and Trent pushing her and Charlotte on the tree swing by Raspberry Cottage. Guarded, even then, Rayna seldom let people close enough to hurt her. Everyone wanted to be friends with a rich kid. Even Charlotte had proved she shouldn't be trusted.

A slender cardboard tube stood on the floor, leaning against the dresser, the seal at both ends still intact. She scanned the white, printed label: Benk and Shell Architecture. It was by far the saddest reminder in the room. A lifetime of plans arriving three weeks too late.

Deep in thought, she stretched out on the rumpled bed, every wrinkle a telltale sign that her broken heart wasn't the first to lay there. The movement of the small planes, imperceptible while standing, became mesmerizing to a body without motion, adding the tiniest bit of life to the still room—drifting left then right, left then right. Within seconds a wave of twilight carried her into a dream state, and for a moment, Cole didn't seem that far away.

The images were fuzzy at first; collecting acorns in the front yard, as they'd done a hundred times as children. Even in her sleep she could hear them rolling around in the orange plastic pail and feel the warmth of the sun on her face as it flickered through the leaves. When she walked toward him, Cole held his closed palm between them and slowly opened his tiny hand, revealing a sparkling crystal. In silhouette, the sunshine poured over his shoulder, dancing upon the dazzling jewel. She'd never witnessed anything so beautiful. When the sun disappeared behind the trees, she realized that, no longer a child, her brother stood before her as a grown man.

Her fingers unfurled and the acorn rolled onto the mattress, drawing her from her sleep. With the dream fresh in her mind she tried to make sense of it, yawning before getting up and smoothing the quilt.

Rayna added the acorn to the already brimming glass jar, where it was swiftly rejected, sending acorns everywhere. They peppered the floor while she fought to contain them, catching one in the air and another after the first bounce. She turned her ear to the door, certain she'd woken the entire house. *Quiet.* She gingerly restocked the jar.

Hanging on the wall opposite Cole's bed, an inspirational poster of an airplane, flying into the horizon, caught her attention: If you can dream it, you can do it. Cole's dream had killed him and living hers had left her feeling dead inside. Would she ever have the courage to dream again?

Rayna picked up the handmade book from the nightstand and returned it to the shelf. She rubbed her watery eyes, which only managed to skew the lines on the gray plaid wallpaper. Taking one last look around the room, she retreated to the safety of her own floral-covered bedroom.

Chapter 6

Fried bacon with a hint of hickory coaxed Rayna from her toasty blankets by midmorning. Never one to sit at the table, she curled up in the dove gray gingham-covered nook in front of the kitchen window. Rayna enjoyed a plate of scrambled eggs with a side of melon as she watched a couple of fillies run circles around a broodmare grazing in the nearest field. A few of the farm hands were running about, trying to rally them up and escort them back to the barn. Rayna placed her bet on the spirited horses to show the farm hands which team was really born to run.

After dropping the dishes in the sink, she wrapped three crispy bacon strips in a paper towel, filled a thermos with black coffee, and headed straight for the barn to bridle King.

With every breath, Rayna noticed her body seemed to gain energy and her thoughts became sharper. Fresh, cool air filled her lungs as she strolled between two stretches of white fencing that ended at the main stable. A small silver airplane hummed along in the clear blue sky, escorting her in lockstep. There'd be more than a few pilots taking advantage of the weather, and her brother would've certainly been one of them.

She nibbled on the salty bacon and sipped from the steaming cauldron, but the plan to save a piece of bacon for her riding companion failed when the temptation turned out to be too great and the walk just a few minutes too long. Before she knew it, half of the last strip vanished as well. She cursed herself until she reached the stone entrance.

It was eternal spring in the stable. She often looked for

excuses to spend time there. The continuous chirping of swallows in the rafters, and the gentle breeze whistling through the stalls, mingled to produce a peaceful white noise; an irresistible combination following three chaotic years in the city. And it was much more fun dodging the dozens of pest strips spiraling down from the rafters than a moving crowd, any day.

The heavy smell of hay and loam permeated the air, and mixed with the combination of sweet beet greens, grooming products, and medicinal preparations, it was quite tolerable. But it never escaped her notice that a freshly mucked stall smelled anything but, an odor she'd never get used to.

Mornings in the barn were hectic, especially right before lunch. Horses moved in every direction, from the stalls to the pastures, through various grooming stations, and back again. Rayna automatically fell into the rhythm, and in no time at all she, too, found herself walking at a fair clip.

The breezeway was well lit and wide enough for large animals to comfortably pass each other. Glass cabinets lined the main center aisle, and every medal, ribbon, and trophy ever awarded stood prominently displayed in a showcase. Larissa Dawson's name donned many of the earlier trophies, but Westcott Farm and Stable laid claim to the rest. Making her way along the corridor, Rayna eyed the impressive hardware. Some of the statues were three feet tall, and most of the silver bowls were large enough to sit in. She hated to admit it, but her father was right; her measly plaque would have easily gotten lost in the sprawling cabinet. But it still hurt.

Every horse had a distinct appearance. They were black or various shades of brown or mushroom, some exceptional for their size, others for their unique markings. One or two didn't need a bit in their mouth to take you on the gentlest ride you ever experienced, but a few were considered wild or stubborn, like Bandit, she'd snatch a paperback out of your pocket and chew it up in front you, just to let you know who's boss. But, as different as each of them were, they all neighed and stomped their hooves on the wooden planks in protest when she passed. The sun was up, and the odds were good they'd soon be freed from their dreary quarters. And they all seemed to know it.

"Mornin', Rayna." A wrinkled farmhand shouted, juggling a bucket of oats and a watering hose without missing a step.

"Hi, Harvey. You're looking after that shoulder, I hope."

"Shoulder's great, now, thanks to Mr. Westcott."

"Good to hear." She continued walking through the breezeway, more concerned about the prominent hump on his upper back. She watched him wince, knowing it had to be painful. It was all she could do not to go over and take the tools out of his hands and sit him down against a heating pad.

"Hi, Gord. Any colts?"

A burly character grunted as he straightened. "Good morning. Yeah, two. They're both at the far end, the stall beside the lounge."

"Great, I'll be heading over there after my ride. How's the new baby?" She hesitated. "Girl, right?"

He smiled. "Yup. Lil' lass is doing great. As perfect as a spring tulip."

Rayna envied the spark that lit up a person's face when their children were mentioned. She had no intention of ever settling down. She could only imagine, but the mention of living in Paris one day probably cast the same silly look across her face.

The local radio station droned on twenty-four seven in the tack room, the announcer updating the price of wheat and soybean futures every hour, whether you were interested or not. Their itinerary had already been posted on the blackboard. Her mother had beaten her to the stable. Rayna lifted the heavy English saddle off a beam and wiped the shiny leather with a white cloth. She gathered the rest of her equipment before tucking a carrot inside her vest and continuing on to King's stall.

She preferred King over the others. At fifteen hands high he was considered average size, but being less spirited than most made him more predictable. The rich brown, quarter horse gelding was gentle and forgiving. You could make a mistake or two and he'd let you get away with it, more so than a more temperamental mount.

King jostled from side to side when she pushed the wooden gate of the small cubicle open. Like her, he too was anxious to break out into the open. Nine hundred pounds of confined, restless motion demanded respect. Rayna proceeded with caution. It may have been the treat in her pocket, but he greeted Rayna with excitement and appreciation. She spoke to him in a whisper, brushing his shiny coat and combing his flowing mane with her fingers. All the while his knowing, round eyes were hard at work melting her heart—and the last of her vigilance.

A small amount of heat poured in from the overhead furnace duct. Mixed with the small beams of sun shining through the window, it was enough to warm her hands and face if she kept moving. She tossed the heavy English saddle onto King's back and tightened the leather strap, buckling it in place. The bit gave her the usual trouble, but within minutes Rayna had him tacked up and ready to go.

"Hey, Brat. You in a great big hurry this morning?" Beaker spoke in a soft voice from outside the stall, his arms resting on the top rail with leather gloves in hand. "I told ya I'd get him ready to go."

Rayna looked over her shoulder with a warm smile. "Actually, I wanted to spend a little quiet time in the barn." She fussed with the bit. "Thanks for not springing up on us."

He walked into the stall. "I passed Larissa. She'll have Aragon bridled and on his third lap around the pasture before you're even in the saddle." Beaker took the reins and systematically gave King the once over, tweaking the bridle, checking hooves for debris, and looking for loose connections. Instinctively lengthening the stirrups, he threw her a knowing smile quick to add rose coloring to any bits the chilly air had missed. He gave a hard pull on the girth, tightening the strap and moving the buckle two full notches. Within minutes he handed the reins back to her. "There, you're all set."

"Thanks, Beaker." She led King from the stall, and they walked toward the exit at the end of the passageway. Anyone else might've been insulted, but as much as she loved to ride them, Rayna never had the same comfort level with the impressive animals her family seemed to enjoy. Beaker understood that. Out of the blue, she found herself wondering why some nice girl hadn't scooped him up. She'd never known him to have had a serious girlfriend. *He's certainly good-looking enough, in a rugged sort of way.* It surprised her that the entire scenario had never occurred to her before.

When they reached the exit, a heavy clomping and rustling sound drew their attention to a towering dark shadow moving in from along the right side of the building. Soon after, Larissa appeared in the doorway dressed in black riding attire, with complete command of the heaving, midnight stallion beneath her. Blocking most of the daylight, they dwarfed the double entrance.

Aragon, large by anyone's standard, strutted over a thousand pounds of notoriously difficult demeanor. Larissa considered him a loyal companion, but truth be told, there wasn't a champion on the estate who dared to pull anything over on her. She had a reputation for being able to rein in the wildest charger on the property, and at the time, that was Aragon.

With steely composure, Larissa masterfully pulled on the leads, forcing the massive animal to face the opposite direction, his right side now flanking the exit in a hail of dust. In one grand spectacle, she summoned the stallion to rear into the air, where he dominantly flashed his mane and snapped his tail, before slamming back down on all fours with a thud. She backed the magnificent champion away from the doorway and into the open, all the while a demure smile gracing her tiny face.

No longer the risk-taking show jumper that had once caught her father's eye, her mother had never lost the skill and agility of a champion rider. She exuded a confidence to be envied, and Rayna couldn't help feeling proud and humbled by the impressive sight.

Denver moved forward through the group of onlookers, his smile growing with every step he took toward Larissa. With a critical eye, he rubbed the full length of the back of Aragon's hind legs. He spoke briefly and Larissa nodded. Without a word, he worked his way back through the group, which quickly dispersed when he reentered the barn.

"You ladies have a nice ride." Beaker gently held a section of King's mane twisted in with the reins as Rayna mounted, then he was gone.

"Riding the big guy, I see." Rayna leaned over and patted the side of Aragon's neck.

"Look at that sky, it's going to be a beauty."

"Daddy looked worried about something."

Her father was renowned for having the sharpest equine instincts within a thousand miles. The best in the industry believed he could smell sickness and had x-ray vision when it came to the stock. Few things escaped Denver Westcott. If he was concerned, there was good reason to be.

"Your father thought he noticed a little stiffness in Aragon's back legs. He asked me to keep an eye on him, and to be extra careful on the Maple trail, maybe avoid the last hill. He wanted me to let him know when we're back safe and sound."

The 'safe and sound' part didn't sound reassuring. Rayna took a moment to settle into the saddle and test her equipment□and her nerve. Her mother waited patiently, putting Aragon through a few diagnostic maneuvers, walking him forward and backward. When Rayna signaled that she was ready, they leisurely rode away from the barn.

Deep in the field they broke into a lively gallop that escalated into a mock competition. Pretending otherwise would've been pointless; King offered little challenge for Aragon, and she was no match for her mother's skill. But the facts never stopped them from reveling in the ritual. Rayna squeezed her thighs firmly against the horse's flanks and pressed her heels hard into the stirrups. The first ride being both terrifying and exhilarating, she'd decided long ago she would never sacrifice a fraction of one experience to heighten the other.

The edge of the forest waited for them, ablaze with color. Even from a distance she could tell something magical was happening and Rayna couldn't get there fast enough. The sun was shining through the leaves, transforming them into florescent shades of amber and ruby, and the gentle wind sent them swirling through the air like pieces of stained glass. They stood motionless, watching as a thousand falling leaves tried to fill in the narrow path ahead of them.

"Mom, it's … stunning." They basked in the kaleidoscope before them.

"Breathtaking. Another hour and we would have missed all of this." She watched Rayna take in the shimmering sight. "I have never seen the path into the woods look so inviting. Perfect timing."

Perfect timing? Rayna found herself questioning. Was everything that happened in life just random? What path was she meant to be on? Or had she missed it? Was it all a matter of timing? Her world was spinning, her thoughts were spinning, the leaves were spinning. *Enough!* She stared at the passage into the woods, where a foot of leaves piled across the opening. For now, she'd have to settle for the adventure at hand, the only path that lay before her.

Without another word, they ducked to clear the low-hanging branches as they entered the wooded access in single file. The team brushed the crispy topping aside with their hooves as they entered the colorful forest.

Chapter 7

Light flickered through the leaves as Rayna and Larissa traveled along the trail through the Maple Woods. It narrowed in spots and dipped in others, but it was a comfortable path, well-worn and reliable. Other than a few splashes of unexpected beauty it held few surprises, and they handled the familiar path with ease.

Before long, the horses emerged from the trees with their precious cargo. They'd been shaded in the woods, and the first glimpse of sunlight hit Rayna's eyes like sharp needles. She slipped on a pair of slate blue aviator sunglasses, and her mother followed suit, but Rayna was sure it was for entirely different reasons.

With the cool air from the forest behind them, they took a moment to enjoy the warm sun in the low clearing. They followed a winding stream that briefly meandered out of the woods then twisted its way back in, resting long enough for their companions to enjoy a cool drink before walking the horses up a grassy knoll.

When they reached the top, Rayna laced the reins between the pickets of a cast-iron fence. Her mother unsnapped Aragon's saddlebag and withdrew a small paisley satchel, matching gardening gloves, and a cellophane package of flowers. With calm resolve, they wove their way through the granite markers before stopping side by side. They stood motionless, staring at the marble headstone.

Denver (Cole) Westcott
Loving Son of Denver and Larissa

Loving Brother of Rayna

Their arms linked while an autumn breeze blew softly through the silence. Rayna tried to make sense of the moment. *Sorrow has no use for words. It is a silent tear dispersed on an invisible arrow, piercing one heavy heart and then the other.*

It was a beautiful monument ... if such a thing existed. The stone was two feet high, grayish with deep, dark lettering. There was an image of a Lancaster Bomber engraved in the top right corner. The call letters were faintly visible. Lucky KB420. Two manicured emerald cedars flanked a perfectly tilled garden in waiting, covered with a thin layer of cocoa bean shells that still held a hint of chocolate.

With familiar skill, her mother wiped the granite with a cloth she pulled from her satchel: first the shiny front, then the sides, and finally the top ledge. She pulled pieces of grass that crept up the stone and removed any weeds threatening to take over the lawn. Wasting no time, she cleared away a limp bundle of purple flowers tied with a spotless white ribbon. She sprinkled the garden with water from an old galvanized can that hung on a rusty spout nearby.

Rayna's heart broke as she watched her mother perform her ritual of cleaning and grooming. A stranger would've thought he died yesterday. That level of care and dedication usually waned after the first year. The love and respect she was witnessing was both sad and inspiring.

With the grooming complete, her mother unwrapped the bundle of purple anemones and laid them gently at the foot of the stone, taking great care to arrange the new white ribbon to sit at the base of the flowers and on the top of the stems. She stood back, admiring her handiwork.

"Looks beautiful." Rayna bent down and touched the moist petals.

"Yes, it does look nice."

"Daddy come here much?"

Her mother fiddled with the ribbons. "No. We all have our own way of grieving."

She could never understand how her mother had managed to tend the garden every week for the last three years. Watching her fuss over the smallest details, adjusting the tails of the ribbon and picking tiny brown needles from the shrubs, she wondered if tending the site gave her mother an element of relief, if it made the separation bearable in an odd sort of way.

"You've invested a lot of time keeping this place up. Most of the other sites here look neglected." She walked a few feet closer to the neighboring stone to read the lettering. "Kinda sad that people move on with their lives after they lose a loved one. You want people to move on, but□"

"Not forget," her mother added.

"Yes, but not forget. The other sites, they look … gloomy, to be honest with you."

Her mother closed her eyes and pressed on her temples. "When Cole survived the Middle East, and his stint with the air force ended, I thought we had escaped all of this." She stared at the marble stone. "To lose him on a sunny afternoon, flying over American farmland …" She sighed. "After dodging missiles in the air force, to be knocked out of the sky by a bird strike …"

"Mom, don't."

She gathered her gardening tools and looked around. "We should head back."

Rayna agreed. She hated the thought of her mother spending too much time at Cole's graveside.

At high noon, the full, overhead sun promised a warmer ride home than the earlier trip through the woods. Physically, Rayna had finally relaxed and settled into the saddle, but her thoughts were all over the place as they stood before the gradually sloping lawn that led down to the North Road. It was a beautiful spot beside the cemetery, offering a panoramic view, which was heartbreaking in itself.

Rayna studied the modest Talsburg airport before leaving the top of the hill. A small plane taxied between the two hangars and headed along the tarmac toward the lone runway. With no control tower, it would take off and land unassisted. She found it ironic that she could stand by Cole's grave and see the airport. She wondered how often Trent Jackson stood at the airport, looking up at the cemetery, missing his friend.

They descended the hill on foot, and for a good mile they walked the horses along the North Line. Between patches of bulrushes and tall, wild grass growing in the ditch, Rayna caught the odd glimpse of the back of the farm.

Years before, the township renamed a few of the local roads in honor of their oldest inhabitants, if they still resided there. The North Road was honorably designated Jackson Line, but the locals never referred to it by the new name. Trent never seemed to care one way or another, but it never failed to irritate his father. Quick to snap when he felt disrespected, Harland often took the oversite as a snub.

They stopped when they reached a mustard yellow mailbox with a slightly bent red flag. A white-sided cottage with a matching, mustard-colored front door sat at the end of the gravel laneway. Withered raspberry canes had taken over most of the front garden, and both sides of the small porch had dried out clematis vines clinging to the railings.

Every fence board on the Westcott property received a fresh coat of paint every other year. The white-picket fence surrounding Raspberry Cottage was no exception. The annual spring project kept most of the teenagers in town flush with summer cash.

A large pond behind the house harbored a rickety yellow boat, pulled up out of the water, capsized on the sloping lawn. In the side yard, a giant oak, with an elaborate tree house perched between its three main branches, held a wooden swing dangling from a sturdy limb. Rayna soon found herself lured into the yard.

"We have to stop," she said, laughing. "Do you mind?"

"Lead the way." They rode into the side yard and tied the

restless horses to a nearby picnic table. "Aragon could drag this old chunk of wood all the way back to the farm if he takes a mind to."

Rayna backed into the seat, grabbing the ropes high above her head. She tugged on them a few times to check their strength before jumping up onto the seat, allowing the swing to glide forward. Within minutes, she'd lulled herself into a trance. Gliding peacefully, her eyes closed as the wind caught her hair.

Her mother leaned against the trunk of the tree, playing with a crimson oak leaf she'd picked off a low branch.

"Ahh … this is so relaxing."

Her mother gave her a chance to enjoy the swing for a moment before breaking the spell. "We couldn't keep you and Cole off this swing when you were little."

Rayna was slow to respond. "I remember. I loved this swing." She noticed new, shiny nails shoring up the laddered slats leading to the tree fort. *Interesting.*

"Over the years, your father hung at least a half a dozen different swings by the house. Rope, wood, tire, even fancy store-bought, but you and your brother always managed to work your way back over to this one."

Rayna twisted the ropes, causing the swing to twirl, left then right. "That would be frustrating."

"We always knew where to find you. And with the Jacksons a holler away, we were never too worried."

Rayna opened her eyes and stared at the little house. "Were you and Daddy surprised when Beaker moved out of Raspberry Cottage?"

"Not at all. Don't forget, he lived here for nine years." She smiled, surely replaying a distant memory. "You know, when he left, he paid cash for the house he is in now." She shook her head. "He wasn't a teenager anymore. It was time."

"True." The swing twirled ever so slowly.

She tilted her head, listening carefully as Rayna poured out her thoughts.

"There comes a time when we just need a change." The swing continued to creak as it slowly twirled. "Then we make decisions that aren't necessarily the right ones … or good ones."

Her mother let her enjoy the magic for a moment longer before commenting, "Are we still talking about Beaker?"

She looked up, trying to decipher her mother's comment, but short of a puzzled glance she kept her thoughts to herself.

Rayna jumped off the swing, eyeing Trent and Charlotte Jackson's house as they remounted and rode out of the yard. Rayna gave a sigh of relief to see the empty driveway, and next door at the new bungalow Harland's truck was gone as well. Without much direction, King carried Rayna past the property, allowing her the freedom to study the place for signs of life.

Floral sheets flapped on a clothesline in the side yard of the gray-sided Cape Cod. Handmade planter boxes, plucked clean, sat at the top of the porch stairs, and a matching wooden swing wavered empty on the veranda. Surely Trent's handiwork. The curtains were tied back at the middle, producing a soft swag. It seemed like a style that Charlotte would be fond of, or maybe she wanted the light to get in. Details Rayna would never know.

Her eyes locked on the front door in disbelief, where a vibrant, rust-colored wreath with a puffy, cream lace bow hung prominently from a strip of burlap. A searing stab went through her stomach, like the blade of a serrated knife, and her hand instinctively covered the imaginary wound. *Here, too, everything is exactly as it should be.*

Her mother watched her survey the property and gave her a look that cautioned her to move forward, and Rayna knew she wasn't referring to the ride. Rayna turned to face the road and never looked back, suddenly anxious to put the emotional day behind her.

Chapter 8

It rained for the next two days. Rayna had little to do except ramble around the house, trying to entertain herself. She finished reading a cozy mystery, helped in the kitchen, and in the evenings, she would visit the barn. But when she woke to the third day of rain, she decided to brave the storm and take the thirty-minute trip into Starling for a little retail therapy.

With torrents of water pouring over the windshield, she wondered if she'd survive the treacherous drive to the quaint little town. The wind strengthened and pressed against the side of the truck, and the steady surge fell harder with each mile. For the better part of the way, she wished she'd listened to her mother, who'd insisted it was too dangerous to venture into the storm. Rayna clenched the steering wheel, trying to get as close to the glass as possible, and never eased off until safely parked in town.

Just looking out the window made her shiver. She decided to wait in the warm truck for a break in the weather. The wipers clacked from side to side in a soothing rhythm while she admired the autumn window displays and planned her exit strategy. The street was fairly deserted, except for a few unfortunate people who had no alternative but to brave the downpour.

Rayna loved shopping in Starling. The shops boasted unique collections from some of the finest artisans in the country, from high-end clothing to handmade jewelry, and it was the sole reason she didn't hesitate to brave the monsoon.

While she directed the vents to blow warm air toward her

feet, Rayna spotted a bright red umbrella as it popped open through a crack in the door of the medical center building. Between the waves of water sloshing across the windshield, she watched it bob around in the wind. She was surprised to see Charlotte and her father-in-law lay claim to the wayward cover, mashing under it together as they made a beeline for her red hatchback. Charlotte tried to rush him along, but Harland continued to move cautiously, having no part of it. When an unexpected gust took hold of the umbrella, pointing it randomly in every direction, she collapsed the weapon before they reached the car.

Rayna watched as Charlotte opened his door then zipped around to the driver's side. At the exact second she reached for the door handle, a renegade car barreled through a puddle beside her, sending murky water in her direction, dousing her from the knees down. She braced long enough to take the second hit, then flapped the umbrella several times before flinging it into the back seat. Charlotte gathered her long dark hair into a ponytail at the nape of her neck and shook the wet, stringy ends before tossing them forward over her shoulder. She dove into the car and yanked the door shut behind her, leaving the hem of her emerald skirt trailing out beyond the bottom of the door.

She couldn't help but wonder if the doctor's visit had anything to do with Harland punishing himself with liquor after he lost his farm. Certain that many of his health issues were self-inflicted, she hated that Charlotte and Trent had to deal with a sick parent. Rayna's mother and father had escaped many of the health problems other families had been forced to cope with, and Rayna was aware having money had helped. Being well-off was more than a privilege.

Yesterday her mother had performed like a twenty-year-old on Aragon, and her father could still outwork most of his young farmhands. Since Cole's accident, it hadn't always been easy to feel blessed, but Rayna knew they truly were.

With her sopping wet skirt still hanging below the door,

Charlotte pulled her car into the street, then did a double take as she passed by the Westcott truck. Rayna kept her head low and her eyes fixed on her purse sitting on the passenger seat. It wasn't until Charlotte's car disappeared that Rayna made a mad dash for the closest shop.

Best Dressed occupied the end unit in a row of twelve designer shops that spanned the entire block. Once inside, there were openings cut between the various retailers, creating a center passageway that allowed shoppers the luxury of accessing all the stores, from one end of the building to the other. The boutiques were on slightly different levels, two stairs up or down, and offered continuous, uninterrupted shopping. Because each storefront replicated the old-world theme, it was aptly dubbed The Victorian Mall and designed with just such a soggy day in mind. Rayna smiled and rubbed her hands together, grateful she'd braved the weather.

In Tweed and Cashmere, she tried on an ill-fitting jacket before finding an ivory sweater that looked amazing and would match most of her wardrobe. She bought flowers for her mother in From the Stem Up, stopped for lunch at The Harvest Table, and attempted to slink past Parchment Press without being noticed.

"Hello, Rayna. Larissa told me you were home for an unexpected visit."

Myra Wagner Stiles. Gold-digging phony! "I am indeed." Rayna made no attempt to appease the old biddy and proceeded on to the next shop, her favorite, Strait Laced, a classic fashion and accessory shop.

"Rayna!" A petite woman with a mahogany pixie cut, dropped her packages to the floor and threw her arms around Rayna's shoulders.

"Sage! I wasn't expecting you until tomorrow."

"I got here early."

"Where are the kids, the family, are they here with you?" Rayna looked around, hoping to see them appear from a nearby aisle.

"They're with my parents. They weren't about to part with the grandkids. Mark had an important case he had to work on, so he stayed in the city. Big court date next week. He's been taking on a lot of extra work. He's obsessed with making partner at the firm, so ..." She waved her hands and rolled her eyes. "Life is crazy right now."

"Too bad he couldn't be here with you. We're still riding tomorrow, I hope. It's supposed to clear by this evening."

"Of course. Dust off my helmet." She touched Rayna's arm. "Did you see Beaker in The Harvest Table?"

"No, I didn't. And I had lunch there a half hour ago." Rayna smiled, secretly pleased to learn he was in town.

"He's with a classy-looking woman, quite attractive with big br— Blonde hair." She laughed.

Rayna's face stiffened as she wondered who he was with. "In the two hours since I left the house it's gone back and forth between teaming rain and an annoying drizzle." She tried to hide her disappointment.

"I know, it's dismal."

Rayna looked between the mannequins in the store window, assessing the storm and wondering what the odds were of escaping town before she had the misfortune of bumping into Beaker and his friend. "Call me in the morning, Sage. We can work around your schedule with the kids."

"Thanks, Rayna. You're so thoughtful."

They laughed as they passed packages back and forth, trying to sort out their parcels before continuing with their shopping. Sage still had to buy a new leash from It's a Ruff Ruff Life, and Rayna decided to browse what she called the 'accessories you buy to fill a void' section, in Strait Laced.

Soon after, weighed down with packages, Rayna returned home before dinner. She tossed the assortment of bags onto the bed and took a few moments to look them over, as she'd so often done in front of the same mirror so many times before.

It was a typical girl's room, complete with a porcelain-doll lamp wearing a vacant stare and a pink fascinator that doubled as the shade. The walls still wore the burgundy floral wallpaper she'd gazed at as a young girl, dreaming for hours, the faded marks were quick to remind her of youthful posters that had lost their appeal. A pile of pillows covered the bed, all sewn from fabric cut from her favorite old clothes. Dresses she'd outgrown, and once considered too special to part with, hung in the closet, waiting to be discarded. She'd often felt guilty for not passing them on to Charlotte with the others.

Not much had changed through the years. If she wanted, she could close her eyes and see the room exactly as it had been when she'd slept there nightly as a carefree girl. During difficult times she'd wither and hide under the pink duvet, and even now there were days she continued to do just that.

She twirled in front of a long dressing mirror, holding the cream sweater against her breasts and a card of earrings close to the side of her face. She viewed her reflection from several angles before smiling. Rayna stopped for a moment, eyeing the pictures tucked into the edge of the oval frame. They were randomly placed between ribbons and event tickets and offered an unofficial tour through her history, highlighting most of the main events.

A black-and-white photo caught her attention and she removed it for a closer look. It was a picture of her sitting beside Beaker on the top rail of a cedar fence. A surveyor had been on the farm, staking out a new property line, and in flash of good fortune they'd ended up in one of his shots.

It had been taken in a quiet corner of the property they called Lone Pine. A spot Beaker often called his hideout. She'd always thought he related to the single pine tree soaring above the tranquil paddy. It was the only place he let his true feelings out, and the first year she'd found him there often, sullen.

The photo had an artistic quality. Captured from behind, she loved the silhouette they cast and the way the sunset seemed to frame them. Sitting side by side, they were leaning toward each other ever so slightly and he was adjusting his new cowboy hat. She remembered his exact words: 'I'm never going to take this off.' He'd told her how lucky he felt to have landed on Westcott Farm. At the time, Rayna was a mere fourteen and childlike, and yet to learn why.

"Rayna, are you home?" her mother called.

She wedged the picture back into its rightful place. "I'm putting stuff away. I'll be right there." She grabbed the empty bags and made her way downstairs.

"Can you make a quick run to the hangar with Beaker later?"

"Sure. What do you need from there?"

"I need a few measurements. I wrote it all here in the notebook." Her mother tipped the book toward her, pointing at various pictures. Can you measure the actual, usable floor area and the width of the three walls? And we need to know the size of the Lancaster if we are going to leave it tucked in the corner, coming out at a diagonal. We'll have to see how much space it will need before we decide."

"Mom, it's going to look amazing."

"I'll call Beaker and tell him you'll be ready right after dinner."

Rayna huffed. "How do I ever manage to survive in the city all by myself?"

"I'm aware how capable you are, but he knows how to use the laser measuring tool—and where to find it. And you always say it takes you a little bit of time to get comfortable driving around in the dark after relying on cabs for months." Gloating, she walked by Rayna with a baking sheet loaded with warm peanut butter cookies. "And for dinner I've made sun-dried tomato chicken, seasoned carrots, and double-baked potatoes."

"Okay, that's it! I'm never leaving."

"I hope that's a promise, because it certainly is the plan." Her mother smiled as she used a spatula to remove the cookies from the baking sheet, offering Rayna the first and eating the second.

Rayna chomped on the cookie, worried that Beaker would resent having to drop whatever he was doing to run her around.

Chapter 9

Rayna and her mother were standing in the sidelight of the front door when Beaker's truck appeared through the drizzle. She watched as he tinkered with the radio and tweaked the rearview mirror as he waited for her to emerge onto the porch, oblivious to the fact they were scrutinizing his every move. He moistened a napkin by shamelessly dragging it along the outside of the wet truck, then wiped it along the dusty dash. Finding it impossible to look away, her mother put her hand over her mouth to hide her grin. Totally entertained and unabashed, Rayna delivered one wicked giggle after another. They watched him bend forward a few times, then straighten up again.

"He must be picking stuff up off the floor." Her mother said as she struggled to keep her reaction to a guilty smirk.

"Throwing stuff under the seat would be my guess." Rayna burst into another fit of laughter. She fanned her face and blew a soft flow of air through her pursed lips until she managed to pull herself together. She stepped onto the porch, composed, but inside she was still reeling from their misconduct.

He gave her his usual devious grin as he leaned sideways and shoved the truck door open. "Hey, Brat. I already stopped to pick up the laser tool."

"Thanks, Beaker. Sorry my mother pulled you away from whatever you were working on. She loves to treat me like I'm a teenager still."

"No problem."

"I can't wait to see the Lancaster."

"They've been able to taxi it for months now. On the

weekend you can see them moving it around the runway. A few locals usually stroll over to watch. They'll be flying it within the year."

Unable to hide her shock and excitement, she blurted out, "What? Are you sure, Beaker?"

"That's what I heard." Beaker drove along the circle and headed for the back road. "They have an engine specialist tuning it up."

She imagined how thrilled Cole would've been to know that his vision had made it to this point. That's what she hated the most. He was missing it all. Determined to experience everything for him, Rayna knew the trip to the hangar was no exception. Even though it terrified her to imagine flying, she tried to live and breathe his dream the way she knew her brother would. Saddened, she quietly turned to face the window.

"Hey, I washed my truck for ya."

She continued to stare into the darkness.

In silence, he adjusted his seat, clicked the fog lights on, and moved the side mirrors a negligible amount. He gave the dash a cursive glance and wiped the plastic covers on the front of the gauges. He waited, giving her the space she needed, then after a decent amount of time, broke the silence. "Are ya in there?"

She fought the tug at the corners of her mouth, but Rayna knew the tears would fall whether she tried to stop them or not. "Sorry, Beaker, my mind drifted off a little." Staring straight ahead, her eyes welled, and a single, bold tear pushed its way onto her bottom lash before spilling onto her cheek.

He fished around for a napkin and handed it to her. "Hey … don't cry. Everything's going to be okay, you'll see."

She sopped up the tear and dabbed her eyes, the starchy napkin scraping like sandpaper against her delicate skin. She unraveled it, studying the creases. "Beaker … did you get this from under the seat?"

"It was clean."

"Seriously!" She laughed as she rolled it into a tight ball and tossed it at him. He gave it a backhand, knocking it out of the air before it hit him.

"I just threw it there, right before you got into the truck."

"Wonderful, thank you." She shook her head in disbelief. "Anyway, I'm fine now." She recalled the worried look on his face as he'd handed her the napkin. "You *are* a softy, Beaker. Some chick's going to snap you up one day. Good-looking guy … with a big heart." She turned toward the passenger window and watched the drizzle flow across the glass. *Yup, a nice young woman is going to realize what a catch you are.* An uneasiness moved through her. *Damn! I hope she's nice.*

Rayna tried to push her concerns aside while Beaker tapped the steering wheel in time with the heavy base notes coming from the rear speakers. He sat quietly, wearing a devilish grin and no doubt reading her mind.

Again, she found herself wondering why he'd never married. There must have been someone special at one time. Why hadn't she known about it? Beaker had all the qualities most women were looking for; he had a great sense of humor and was thoughtful and sensitive when the occasion called for it□

Screech!

Beaker stiffened. His body leaned back as he stomped hard on the brake pedal. The force careened them forward toward the dash and he stretched his arm across her chest, pressing her back into the seat. With pinpoint accuracy, he cut the wheel hard and forced the truck to swerve, narrowly missing a frightened deer that had wandered up out of the ditch and darted onto the dark road ahead of them. She glanced at him sideways, his left hand locked solid on the wheel at twelve o'clock and his right arm protecting her from harm.

"You okay?" He looked at her with horror.

"I'm fine." She took a deep breath, studying him with a hooded stare, suddenly realizing how manly he was.

He looked out over his shoulder, speeding up as they pulled ahead. "Man, I didn't see that coming." With a puzzled expression, he looked back at her a couple of times.

They remained quiet for the remainder of the ride. A spell had been cast that neither wanted to dismiss.

The wipers sent streams of water across the windshield. Rayna stared at a single drop of rain clinging to the glass, growing as it fought to hang on, and she let him think she was unaware of his occasional glances. *Yes, he definitely is good-looking.*

Chapter 10

Before the truck had even driven onto airport property, Rayna had already scanned the parking lot for Trent's army green Jeep. Thankfully, it was nowhere to be seen.

Beaker parked the truck, and they rushed through the rain until they reached the hangar. Constructed from slate-colored corrugated metal, it spanned the width of a city block and Lancaster Charter Co. was prominently displayed on a large black sign above. As they rounded the building, they could see the mammoth sliding doors pushed wide open, with a few sections stacked in front of each other on both sides of the opening. And there, in full view, was the refurbished Avro Lancaster Bomber.

The foreboding aircraft sat squarely in the middle of the concrete slab, peering out from under the giant steel canopy. At two stories high, it had an imposing presence and struck a majestic pose—as if it had been waiting for her. The body of the massive black machine mimicked a railroad boxcar in size, with a formidable wingspan that equaled double its length.

They stepped over the five-inch deep, steel channels that cut into the concrete as they studied the bomber. There were four imposing propellers mounted across the wings, and three glass-enclosed gun turrets projected ominously from strategic points. The underside of the fuselage was almost entirely bay doors, notorious for housing some of the largest bombs that ever fell during the Second World War. They stood before the massive machine in silent reverence.

They crossed the smooth, gray cement floor, the halogen

lights reflecting off the glaze creating a theater-esque setting. No wonder her mother had chosen to have the Winter Ball at such an unusual location. She, too, could see the possibilities.

They stood next to the bomber. *Silent.* It was difficult to look at such a powerful machine and reconcile the horror with the heroism, it's capabilities for devastation and destruction with its life-saving history. She reminded herself, as deadly and as terrifying as it was, along with the allied bombers, the Lancaster honorably claimed some of the glory for helping to bring the lengthy and miserable Second World War to a merciful end. On many occasions she'd tell herself, for that reason alone, she could justify its glorification. But she refused to think about the bombs it had once dropped, or the damage they'd done.

"It's hard to imagine the noise of a night sky filled with these intimidating monsters." Rayna shivered. "How do you fall asleep knowing you have a son, a brother, or a fiancé tucked inside one of those gun turrets?" She looked at Beaker, trying not to think about such a nightmare.

"Or tuck your kids into bed during a blackout, with these roaring overhead?" Beaker's hands were clasped at the back of his head in disbelief. "How would you look into those innocent little eyes and explain a world that scary?" He sighed at the thought.

Rayna marveled at his tenderness but was unable to erase the grim images.

"How did this huge bird even end up here?"

"A local historian, British guy, purchased it following the war. Obsessed with the Lanc, he had it flown here from Canada with visions of creating a heritage warplane-type of museum. But it never materialized. The B-17 on the back tarmac is the only other aircraft to make it here. It was supposed to be the next restoration on their list."

"Lucky KB420, nice call sign." Beaker's fist bounced off a rock-hard tire. "Man, if this bird could talk."

"Actually, it can … sort of. We researched the history on it, and apparently, it flew fifteen successful missions and made it back to tell the tale. Bombers were often lost on the first flight, or only saw a few battles before meeting their … demise, should we say. Until the restoration project started twelve years ago, it's pretty much sat here, deteriorating from the moment it landed, since the war ended."

"What a waste." Beaker climbed up on a small scaffold that surrounded an engine to get a closer look. He peered between the extensive blades, and with a modest amount of force he moved the propeller just a hair.

"As kids, we had a riot playing in this relic. I still remember climbing in through the back and pulling ourselves along the inside of the cabin, all the way up to the cockpit." In her mind, she could still see the view from the pilot's seat. Nothing but blue sky. "Flying this around after school became a daily ritual." A faint smile floated up from somewhere deep inside.

Almost as an afterthought, she noticed Trent's white charter plane. In comparison to the Lancaster, it all but disappeared into the background. She couldn't help but stare at the surreal image, a twin-engine six-seater tucked under the bomber's massive black wing, toy-like.

"I can't believe it." She wrapped her unbuttoned coat close to her body and walked under the bomber, every step tentative "The last time I stopped by here, you couldn't see the floor for aircraft parts."

"Trent's flying charters through the day, and back here until all hours working on it. The guy must be exhausted." He looked at Rayna, as if expecting a reaction.

She hid the small rush of air that caught in her chest at the mention of Trent's name. "The Lancaster will remain inside. We'll decorate around it."

"That's going to take a ton of creativity, but I'm sure Larissa has a plan."

The dismal weather had dampened most of the activity at the airport. The gas boys were rushing around the tarmac with wet overalls stuck to their backs, tying down the single plane that had caught a break in the weather and dared to venture out. When the crew finished securing it, they checked the locks on the new hangar where the more expensive planes were stored. Within minutes the ground crew made their way across the taxi strip to where Rayna and Beaker were standing. The young guys were probably tired, and about to put the run to them. She quickly handed the measuring device to Beaker.

"Okay, Brat, what else do you need?"

She wrote down the numbers in the notebook as he called them, and within minutes they had all the measurements.

"Thanks, Beaker."

"No problem." He took the notebook from her hand and tucked it under his arm.

She gave him an innocent smile. "Are you going to carry my books?"

"I'd do anything for ya," he said with a sly grin.

Beaker's eyes pierced deep into hers. Lacking a witty response, she remained quiet. She hated when he played with her. She suddenly found herself wondering if Beaker was a good cook, and if he had a woman stashed away somewhere for cold nights or slept in the nude. She shook her head, pushing the images from her mind.

"Sorry, folks, are you almost done? We need to lock up for the night."

"We're leaving. Have a good night, guys," Beaker said as they stepped over the tracks and onto the tarmac.

They watched as the gas boys straddled the deep grooves and used their body weight to pull the enormous doors across the cement floor. Metal on metal, they rolled like thunder as they ground their way along the channel, each heavy panel catching the next section until they met in the center with a loud shudder, that reverberated through them all. Rayna and Beaker were now standing on the outside, facing the closed doors.

She put her palms face up—not a drop. "Hopefully, that's

the end of the rain." They took their time walking back to the truck in the fresh evening air. She was having such a nice time she almost dreaded the thought of going home.

"Larissa must have a heck of an imagination if she thinks she can turn that place into a ballroom." He opened the passenger door.

"There'll be tons of soft, draping chiffon, flowers, and a million tiny white lights. Honestly, the hangar will be unrecognizable."

"Except for the bomber."

"Oh yes, except for that." She tapped her pursed lips. "Hmm."

It was a different world, growing up with an airport in your backyard. She'd become accustomed to an unusual sense of awareness: a heightened appreciation for a clear sky; a preoccupation with inclement weather; and a tolerance, no, an affinity, for the sound of engines taking off at all hours. Thanks to Cole, she could often identify most of them. 'That's a twin-engine low wing,' he'd say. 'That one's a four-seater. Trent and I are going to get that old Lanc flying again and start our own charter company.'

Since Cole's death, she'd often regretted living next to the airport. She climbed into Beaker's truck, wishing they'd grown-up next to a golf course or a ski hill.

Chapter 11

Following two days of rain, even drizzle would've been an improvement, but the sunshine came as an unexpected gift. Rayna tipped her face toward the warm sunshine as she meandered down the laneway to the stable, wondering if autumn would surprise them with one last sweater day.

She watched Beaker saunter around the field, pointing and giving instructions to various farmhands and stopping to joke with a few before disappearing into the barn. They loved Beaker's attention. It seemed to energize them, leaving a smile on their face and an extra lift in their step. But when she arrived at the stable, he was nowhere to be seen. Sage stood in front of a display cabinet with a black suede riding helmet tucked under her arm.

"Look at how young your mom looks in these pictures. And there." She pointed. "With your dad. What a striking couple." Sage leaned in for a closer look. "I love these. Such prestige, so much history."

It had become a ritual. Rayna gave her a moment to enjoy the pictures. "Sage, I'm so glad you're here."

"Wouldn't want to be anywhere else."

They shared a hug and were on the trail within minutes.

"With the weather, this is only the second time I've had King out this week." Rayna pulled her fingers through his flowing mane and adjusted the reins.

"It's going to be a sweet ride. I'm not sure if Empty Pockets even remembers who I am." She leaned forward and caressed the horse's neck.

"That's not Empty Pockets. You're riding Hellfire." Rayna forced herself to remain serious.

"What?" Sage straightened up in the saddle, hyperalert.

"He was going to kick his stall gate off if we didn't let him out. We had no choice. Someone had to ride him."

"Well, he hasn't thrown me off yet … so I guess I'm okay." She nervously looked at Rayna for reassurance.

"Don't get comfortable. That doesn't mean anything." Rayna could keep from smiling, but when she saw the concerned look on Sage's face, she started laughing and dashed ahead. She made a *kiss-kiss* sound with her tongue and called out, "Come on, Empty Pockets, let's go boy!"

"That wasn't funny." Sage followed quickly behind. "I knew Harvey wouldn't do that to me. By the way, man, he's looking rough. He's bent over like a rainbow."

Rayna bristled at the thoughtless comment. "His back is curved from osteoporosis, and it's very painful, Sage." She shook her head as she continued riding along. "My father tries to give him pretend jobs, but he just keeps digging in, struggling to work as hard as everyone else. You have no idea how much he suffers."

"Yeah, it looks excruciating. I'm sorry. You know how much I love Harvey."

"I do." She forced a smile. "I guess there's a lesson in there somewhere."

"Yeah … drink your milk."

"True." Rayna nodded as she dashed them onward for a playful sprint. Moments later they settled into a lazy walk and followed the hollowed-out path through the field, taking the gentle pace they'd maintain for the remainder of the ride.

Sage took a deep breath and dropped her shoulders as she exhaled. "It's been a long time since we were able to ride. I miss this."

"Thanksgiving last year. I don't get back home as often as I should anymore. Time has a way of marching by without me noticing."

"You need to notice."

Rayna finally returned her gaze with a hint of a smile.

"I hope you're not getting charmed by the sparkling excitement of the city. I won't see you at all, soon."

"Not a chance. I kind of keep to myself. All the excitement starts to feel like chaos after a while. Honestly, I don't fit in there. I'm not a city girl. They can tell."

"Now I'm worried. That doesn't sound like you."

"Oh gosh, I didn't even ask about Mark and the kids, or how Kristen's dance recital went?"

"They're fine. Really well. And nice try." Sage pulled lightly on the reins, bringing Empty Pockets to a quick halt. "What's going on with you?"

Rayna continued another thirty feet, riding along on her own before waiting for Sage to catch up.

"Is it work?" Sage asked in a soft voice.

"Honestly, it's my entire world."

Sage never tried to fill the void with pointless chatter. She hung back waiting for Rayna to let it go, which she did.

She twisted King's reins as she spoke. "I'm having a few issues at the paper … Mom and I were at the cemetery … Yesterday I bumped into Charlotte downtown … Last night Beaker and I were at the hangar …" She couldn't mention the cold case, or the flash drive—Sage would've really thought she'd lost it.

"Rayna, talk to me."

"For starters … I hate what I'm doing at the newspaper. It's too gritty. I'm finding I have an exceptionally low tolerance for being around dangerous people and in creepy situations. It's depressing—and scary, I might add." She moved King forward and Empty Pockets followed.

"I knew you were having issues at work, but I assumed you'd put in for a transfer and that would be the end of that."

"It's not that simple. The truth is … I'm not a particularly good investigative journalist."

"Don't say that."

"I'm not saying that, the newspaper is. In so many words." She looked away. "They said my last few stories were underwhelming and written as if the facts were intentionally being withheld." *Little do they know how right they are.* And now, she'd just finished canceling another story that'd been ready for print all because it unnerved her. They'd be ready to fire her, for sure.

"All I know is … I couldn't do your job. I'd continually be looking over my shoulder and I'd lose too much sleep walking around, checking things that went bump in the night." She waited for Rayna to comment, but she remained quiet. "Fashion can be scary, too, but in a totally different way. Wait until you see the gruesome shade of plum that is going to be all the rage in the spring. Now that's scary."

Rayna gave in to a sudden burst of laughter. "Depressing and scary, because I look horrible in plum."

"Leave there, Rayna. Find a position you love."

"Everyone makes it sound so easy. If I leave now, I'm not going to get the kind of reference I'd need to open any new doors. I'm not even sure what else is left to fail at."

"Stop that. I refuse to listen to you beat on yourself. When we were in school, from Westmount Public to Talsburg High, you won every creative writing award—except for the one that I managed to scoop when you were home sick with an ear infection. You're having a lapse in faith."

"Maybe."

They rode along in silence for the next few hundred feet.

"Rayna, I have a hunch you're going to win that writing contest you entered. I know how much effort you're willing to put in when you're invested."

"Well, from your mouth to God's ears …"

"Are you sure they still pick up the mail from that old postal box at Fallencrest Station?"

"Of course they do. Why wouldn't they?"

"I don't know … cutbacks."

"Cutbacks?" Rayna laughed, but for the next twenty minutes she worried Sage might be right. Worse yet, she questioned why she'd been counting on winning some random contest to overhaul her career … and her life.

A couple of hours into the ride they passed by Trent and Charlotte's, but there was still no Jeep. It was a toss-up who'd broach the subject, but the silence confirmed they both knew what was coming. Sage gave in first.

"Did you see Trent at the airport last night?"

"No."

Rayna knew she wanted to discuss it, but she didn't know exactly what she wanted to say until she heard herself blurt it right out. "I dreaded the thought that I might have to see him, then I felt disappointed when he wasn't there. Strange. I know people want to read a lot into it, but we'd cared enough to remain close friends, and now we're not even supposed to talk to each other, or remember that we were even a couple. How do you cut away years, almost your entire life, as if it never happened?"

"You can't, Rayna, and people don't expect you to."

"Sure they do. It's not like I can pick up the phone and call him, or knock on his door." Her voice softened. "Anyway, he has a child now. I just want him to be happy."

"With her? Really? You're kinder than I am." Unable to control her frustration, Sage rattled on. "I don't get it. Charlotte was crazy about Cole. She dogged after him for years."

Rayna couldn't resist adding her two cents. "Even though he barely gave her the time of day."

"I know. Tell me about it. Then, without the slightest thought about your feelings, Callous in Wonderland marries Trent—and right after the accident. It still makes no sense."

Rayna sighed. "There were times I felt bad for her. Cole was way too sweet to blow her off and continually gave her the wrong idea. She read too much into any gesture he offered that seemed even remotely nice. He kept her from moving forward, from falling for another guy. I tried to explain it to him once, but he couldn't maintain a healthy boundary with Charlotte."

"Don't you feel sorry for her. She had the looks, and no one was more aware of it than Charlotte. She could've easily landed anyone she wanted. She was certainly crafty enough." Sage bit her lip. "Do you remember the dress she wore to the Christmas party?"

"Huh. The winterberry red halter?" Rayna shook her head.

"You have to admit it. She looked amazing."

"Ya, and she was obviously dressed to close a deal. She captivated the entire room." *Trent too, obviously.* She thought about it a little longer while Sage rattled on in the background. Could Sage be right? Had she missed all the signs?

"I'm sure Trent married her for revenge. He wanted to hurt you. Neither one of them were the type to be alone for long, anyway. Some people are better as a set."

"A set?" Rayna laughed.

"You know what I mean. *I'm hungry.* I'm talking like I have marbles in my mouth, and it's starting to sound like they're in my head, too. I'm done."

"Let's get you a snack."

They cut through the field, the quickest route back to the stable.

Rayna paused before commenting, "So, you think Trent wanted revenge, or to hurt me, but … not necessarily."

"You think there was more to it?"

"Trent and I were never the same after that horse deal imploded the relationship between our families."

"I can see that. He's very protective of his father."

"Yeah. We couldn't move past it."

"I'm sure he held it against you as much as he did Denver."

"Sage, I always said we mutually agreed to break up, and it's the truth. But I told Trent, once, that I didn't want to get married or settle down. I never misled him. I knew what I wanted … a year in London, a career in New York, a tour through Europe. He always knew the drill. My plans were never going to include the family he wanted, and he needed to rethink a life with me. In the end, Trent saw his future here. *With her.*" She hesitated. "Anyway, considering Cole's accident, I realized there was no way I could be with a pilot. And I would've felt horrible if I made him give up flying. It's his passion. He would've resented me for it, and it wouldn't have taken long."

"You're right. He lives to fly."

"But it hurt to walk away and watch him move on." *Why did it have to be with her?*

"I'm shocked you never told me this, I thought we shared everything."

"It's hard to admit to anyone, let alone your best friend, who's Mother Earth, that you're not the marrying kind. What does that say about me? Selfish, right."

"Trent wasn't the one, Rayna, or you would have happily fit him into your world. Even if it meant making changes and having to sacrifice."

She reached across to Sage and lightly touched the back of her hand. "I'm so glad you never found a new best friend over the years."

"Listen, my meltdown is coming up. You'll be there for it, right?"

"Wouldn't miss it."

"At the risk of spoiling our ride, have you gone out with that lawyer yet?"

The one subject Rayna wanted to discuss even less than Trent and Charlotte was Chase Darklend. His randomly bumping into her had been no accident. Thanks to her investigative skills paying off, she counted herself lucky to have realized it.

"Hmm." Rayna smiled as if hiding some juicy detail, and she

succeeded in persuading Sage to abandon her line of questioning.

She pushed King into a hard gallop, and a surprised Sage rode close behind. Rayna knew she couldn't run away from her thoughts, but that fact didn't stop her from trying.

They'd had a great ride, but with all they shared one thought loomed heavy on her heart. When Rayna had confessed never wanting to marry, Sage hadn't accepted a single word.

Chapter 12

Thanksgiving had come and gone, and so too had the fantasy of an unexpected sweater day. Most mornings a damp wind whipped through the fields, discouraging all but the bravest riders. It was still possible to enjoy the trails if she left after lunch, when the sun shone the warmest. But she was pretty much over it. Lately, her interest had shifted from riding to just spending time in the barn.

The moon hung low on the horizon by the time Rayna arrived at the stable for her nightly walk-through. The barn swallows were completing their final ballad for the day, the lapse between chirps equal to the pause between notes in an aria that, like the afternoon sun, would soon come to a full rest. The lights were dim above the stalls, but the breezeway remained brightly lit for the bustling evening rituals. Farmhands were busy with their routine of shifting horses from field to stall, grooming the stallions of the well-to-do and filling water troughs and feed bins.

The extensive care lavished on the almost priceless animals was a constant reminder that many of the horses were valued in the million-dollar range, with sire fees alone running into the hundreds of thousands. It was a serious business, not a single detail left to chance. Overnight staff remained behind to guard the stable and tend to the whims of the four-legged residents, and they left when the morning light ushered in the next shift of farmhands—and not before. Rayna walked along, staying out of the way.

The top half of the Dutch door on the feed room was

pressed open against the wall, while the bottom half was closed. She leaned against it, pushing her way in as she eyed her willow gathering basket hanging high above. Using a long pole with a hook on the end, Rayna plucked it off the wall, loading one end of the basket with slices of Crispin apples, and the other with green-topped carrots, layering them four rows deep. She searched a large wooden workbench for a ceramic shaker resembling a swallow and sprinkled a light dusting of peppermint powder on the treats.

The horses were oblivious to the tufts of freshly laid straw, but nostrils flared when the scent of peppermint escaped the basket she now carried through the breezeway. Rayna lazily made her way from one stall to the next, stroking manes and offering fragrant treats to the appreciative occupants, grateful for a place to escape her mother's intense watchfulness.

"Hey, Brat, did ya sneak out your bedroom window?" Beaker lifted the heavy basket from her arm and walked along beside her.

She tossed him a rebellious grin while her cheeks burned. "Working late?"

"No … sitting in the lounge, relaxing. Harvey was flaked out in the chair, talking in his sleep. I had to get the heck out of there."

"What was he saying?"

"Heck … I don't know. The same crap we ignore when he's awake."

"Guys are so mean."

"It's all in good fun. You only tease the people you like."

"So I've been told." She admired his new white shirt, deciding that she liked it. "You heading home now?"

"No. I'm meeting Denver."

"Ah yes, the new horse deal. That's going to be a profitable venture. Chasing First brought in a fair bit of hardware before retiring. He's a good bet to sire a few champions."

Beaker tried to hide his surprise. "That's right, the new horse deal. I didn't know you were keeping up on that."

"It's been generating most of the dinner table conversation since I arrived home. It takes a fair bit of effort to ignore it." Rayna paused, trying to find the right words. "I'm still traumatized from the last big deal. Disastrous. It ruined Harland."

"It shocked the entire industry to learn Harland's horse had picked up a fatal equine virus. No more than luck of the draw that Denver won Sheer Nobility. They traveled in the same trailer, they should've both suffered the same fate. Thank heavens your father had Higher Calling bedded down in the grooming quarters that night, or the entire team of horses might have gotten sick."

"True."

He paused. "Harland had too much on the line. He couldn't absorb the loss."

"That Christmas tree farm had been in his family for three generations. Now he's renting it from a stranger. Can you imagine how demeaning that would be?"

Beaker handed her a carrot. "Yeah. It would be tough."

Rayna passed it over the gate to a wily horse who pulled it through her fingers. "No one could move past the fallout. The strain was even noticeable between Trent and Cole."

As much as they'd all tried to put it in the past. No question, Trent treated her quite differently after, despite his protests. Rayna sensed the Jacksons were unable to forgive or forget her family any time soon, either. They checked the latches on the stalls as they passed.

"So, Rayna … you're down here every evening, walking around with a deep stare and a long face, doing what, trying to fatten the horses?" He separated the carrots and apples. "Or are you … trying to figure something out."

Rayna looked past Beaker, turning her attention to the back service entrance. The wooden door was rattling, and the wind was whistling through the jamb, making a few of the horses anxious and startling the others. A farmhand appeared to assess the situation, pulling on the door a couple of times to make sure it had closed tight before securing the bolt.

Beaker waited until she settled back into the task at hand. "I've done a lot of thinking here myself. Made a lot of plans here." With a peaceful expression he looked around, appreciating the beauty.

"You have?"

"Being in the barn helps me filter out the unimportant stuff."

She untangled a carrot from the basket. "I can see that."

He plucked the carrot from her hand and dropped it into the feed bin of an empty stall. Keeping his eyes fixed on the floor, he turned toward her and gently tapped the toe of his boot lightly against hers a few times as he spoke. "One thing I've always known … if I couldn't find the answers here, I knew I was asking myself the wrong questions."

They never made eye contact, but she could feel him staring at her, waiting for a response. Light-headed, a rush of air filled her chest.

"Such wisdom," she said with barely a whisper, conscious of each light tap.

A thump, followed by a slamming bang, quickly changed the tone. The loud shudder sent them hurrying on to the next stall, where a frustrated horse had taken a second back kick at the boards in anticipation of treats. They laughed as they loosened the greens, both offering carrots that were quickly devoured.

"You'll be wanting to go back to the city soon, I imagine?"

"Not really." She counted the remaining stalls and assessed the treats left in the basket.

"When are ya heading out?"

"I'm booked to leave tomorrow night." She already regretted not booking the early train. Leaving after dark depressed her.

He nodded but didn't comment right away. "You don't want to go back to the city at all, do you?" He watched her for a reaction. Rayna smiled but didn't give him one. "There's no harm in changing your plans. It's okay to go in one direction, then decide it isn't for you."

"Is this your inner shrink, Beaker?" She gave him a tight smile.

"I'm just saying, it can't be easy being a Westcott. Living up to all that history and heritage. I can't imagine the baggage that goes with all that … crap."

"You're right. It's even more difficult for a Westcott to admit defeat."

"Oh, I'm quite familiar with that philosophy." He paused, giving her a chance to elaborate before continuing. "It must be tough to have such a successful and well-respected father, and a mother who's an equestrian legend. You have some big hooves to fill."

"They never went from career to career, either." She rolled her eyes in frustration. "They decided what they wanted to do, excelled at it, and stuck with it."

"You're forgetting they chose something they loved. That's what made them successful. You need to have a passion for what you do."

Rayna stopped walking. "That seems to be the advice of the week. Mom, Sage …" Moonlight slipped through a skylight, illuminating his white shirt. "And now you."

"Maybe you should listen."

"Maybe I should." Their eyes met briefly before Rayna moved to the next stall and Beaker followed, listening. "You know, it's funny, but I grew up feeling … this sounds horrible, but … so privileged, respected, and□"

"Spoiled?" Beaker smirked.

"Okay, spoiled even." She tipped her nose into the air and raised her eyebrows. "Back to my point. Then you strike out on your own and realize, it's your parents who are respected and successful, not you. And when you're not part of the Westcott machine, a lot of that privilege disappears. It's a shock when reality sets in and you face the realization that … you're nothing. And like everyone else, you're starting from scratch."

"I'd hardly call owning an apartment in New York City, 'scratch.'" He pushed the tip of his nose in the air. "Like I said … spoiled." He hesitated before adding, in a serious tone, "I always thought you were on this other level." He gestured above his head.

"Really?" Puzzled, she added, "That's surprising. You never seemed to be impressed with the Westcotts, not the way most people are."

"I'm not, especially now that I've gotten to know you guys." He tugged on a strand of hair that'd fallen in front of her shoulder.

"Be serious." She rolled her eyes. "It's easy for you, Beaker. You don't have anything to prove. You're not expected to earn a prestigious piece of", she motioned air quotes, "hardware."

"I don't let people put those kinds of demands on me." He adjusted the basket. "And I'm quite happy."

"Yeah, but you don't have goals getting in your way either."

"I have goals." He stared at her long and hard until she looked away. "But they're not tied into what other people expect of me."

The thought that he might not be content with things exactly as they were had never crossed her mind. He'd always been such a mystery. *What would he long for?* "What are your goals, Beaker? What do you dream about?"

"Since you're asking, I'd like to sell the house I'm in and buy a place with a bit of land. Where I can spread out. I had lunch with my financial adviser yesterday, and she's made a few solid investments that are set to pay off. Now I'm looking for the perfect property." He smiled as he stared off into the distance.

His financial planner! The blonde? Oddly, Rayna felt relieved. "What else do you see in your future, Beaker?"

He pulled a carrot from the basket and brushed the green sprouts across her cheek. "If I told you more, I'd embarrass ya."

He tickled her face with the sprigs.

"Beaker!" Annoyed, she swiped at the carrot greens, feeling like a four-year-old.

The entrance door slid open, and Denver's heavy footfalls closed in on them within seconds. "Your mother just put on a pot of tea."

"Sounds tempting. Thanks, Daddy."

Rayna found herself alone holding the basket as the men headed off to the office, the wicker handle still warm from when he'd passed it to her. Lost in thought, she stood for a moment, tapping the toe of her boot lightly on the ground behind her. When she became aware of it she looked down, watching the subconscious behavior with curiosity. She shook her head and continued making the rounds until every horse had been showered with attention and given a bedtime snack. She hung up her basket and turned down the radio that droned nonstop in the tack room.

As she made her way back to the house, she ran the conversation over and over in her mind. Beaker made sense, and with every replay she felt like she was shedding lead weights as she crossed the field. By the time she reached the front porch, there was an unmistakable lightness in her step, yet also the added burden of figuring out just where those next steps were meant to take her.

Chapter 13

Thanks to her concierge service, Rayna's mail arrived by courier before her feet had even touched the cold hardwood floor the next morning. A day later, it would have been shipped back to her apartment in the city. She could hear her mother's voice at the front door, offering the driver a cold bottle of water as she accepted the package.

Rayna threw on a floral housecoat and dashed down the stairs, the satin fabric floating behind her as she tried to tie it shut. She spotted the stack on the side table and went straight to work rifling through it, searching for the one piece of mail she hoped would be in there.

A few letters were intermingled with a couple of silver-edged, white invitations, and there were two magazines, *Equestrian Royal* and the winter edition of *Shawl*, from Sage's fashion house. After shuffling a large lawyer's envelope to the bottom of the pile, she gasped when she spotted the letter. *That's it!* With little concern for etiquette, she skipped the letter opener and tore the side of the manila envelope. She slid the bundle out and read the cover page clipped to a quarter-inch thick manuscript.

Thank you for entering our New Writer Mentorship Contest. We regret to inform you that your manuscript was not our first choice. Thank you for your submission, and for giving us the official authorization to use your name in any publications related to our contest.

Rayna lowered herself onto the bottom step as she read the remainder of the letter. She learned it had been a difficult decision, but in the end, her synopsis had failed to arouse interest or make it past twelfth place.

"It might as well have been last," she mumbled with a frown.

"Rayna! What is it? Why are you upset?"

Her stomach ached at the thought of sharing the details of yet another failure, so she tucked the letter back into the envelope. "Is the coffee on?" She headed for the kitchen.

"It is." Her mother followed her.

Rayna eyed the lemon-cranberry scones on the counter. Her mother's baking had pre-warmed the kitchen and she felt comforted, wrapped in the toasty room. Her mother poured the java while Rayna poured out the details.

"Back in June, a colleague convinced me to enter a writing contest. Entrants had to submit a two-page synopsis along with the first three chapters of a book they'd be willing to write if they were chosen. The winner would be mentored by a famous published author and have the support of an acclaimed editor to ensure the book's success. My coworker received a rejection slip a few months later, but I received a notice saying I'd placed in the top twenty-five."

"Fantastic!" Her mother smiled, twisting her hands. "And?"

"Their public relations department insisted on a disclosure form so they could share my name when the contest results were announced. I signed it on the train and mailed it at the station." She tipped her chin toward the ceiling and closed her eyes. "So … I just gave them permission to publish my name with the rest of the losers."

With care, her mother tried to console her. "It's still quite an accomplishment, Rayna."

"Being nineth doesn't come with a book deal."

Her mother wrapped both arms around her and spoke in a soft voice. "I want to tell you how proud I am more than I want to say I'm sorry, but I know it's not what you want to hear from me."

"I'm fine, really I am. I'm disappointed because it would've changed so much." *For one thing, I wouldn't have to go back to the city.*

I would've been packing for Paris. "I shouldn't have let myself get so invested in winning. It was a long shot, at best."

"Tell you what," her mother wiped her hands on her apron. "I am going to give you five minutes to lick your wounds." She walked toward the kitchen door and looked back at Rayna. "Keep it in perspective. No one has ever died from losing a contest. No one is sick here, Rayna. You're not in heart failure, although it might feel like it right now."

Rayna curled up in the window, her legs pulled in tight beside her. She gulped the coffee just fine but nibbled on the scone, having to swallow every piece twice to get it past the lump of pride stuck in her throat. The realization was quick to set in; with no back-up plan, Major Crime owned her now. With a deadpan stare, she looked out at the damp and dreary morning. The trees had lost the last of their colorful leaves since she'd arrived. Rayna appreciated her attention changing to the drab weather over her dismal future.

Ten minutes later, her mother marched back into the kitchen, picked up her notepad off the windowsill and flipped through it. With a look of concern, she stopped on the page Rayna had written the measurements.

"Did I make a mistake getting the numbers?" Rayna tried to put on a brave face, but the disappointment had drowned her spirit.

"No. It was my fault." She squinted at the writing and used her index finger to draw an invisible line under the words as she analyzed the numbers. "I missed asking for a couple of measurements the decorator is going to need. I'm excited to see what he designs based on the information I provide. I want to get this to him as soon as possible."

"I can go right after lunch. I don't have much to pack, and not much else to do before I leave tonight."

"I'll call Beaker, see if he is free around … one o'clock? If you're sure you don't mind."

"One works." She scanned the page. "Show me what you

missed."

Her mother made a list of the measurements she needed and handed Rayna the notebook. She paused, a serious expression on her face.

"What's up?" Rayna questioned, as she flipped through the pages.

"Your father and Beaker went to the farm auction this morning."

"Did he buy much?" Rayna scribbled a few notes.

"No. The auction is more of a social event for your father, a chance to visit with old friends." She walked toward Rayna. "But he had a troubling story to tell when he arrived home."

"Oh?" Rayna stopped writing and set the pen beside the notebook.

"He said Jordy Grainger showed up, and completely avoided your father. Denver tried to engage with him, but he never spoke. He refused to acknowledge your father *or* Beaker, and Jordy has always idolized both of them. Denver was quite bothered by it."

"Great, he's really going to be upset with me now."

"Your father or Jordy?"

"Take your pick." Rayna pressed her palms against the edge of the table.

"Young Jordy has so many challenges. Since his father died, he can barely function even on a good day."

"Mom … what do you remember about the fire on the Grainger farm?"

"Bits and pieces. We're talking fifteen or more years ago. The case presented a mystery even then."

"Daddy ever mention it?"

"No. But he thinks about it." She folded her arms across her chest, fending off a chill. "A devastating fire ripped through the entire barn in less than thirty minutes. Fortunately, most of the horses were in the pastures and hadn't been brought in for the night. They still lost a dozen prized animals."

"I couldn't imagine how devastating it would be to lose a stable full of horses. Daddy would never be able to get his head around it."

"I do remember your father saying Jordy changed after the fire."

"That makes sense. He would've been in his early teens at the time. Then to have a handler stomped to death in one of their stalls less than a month later … horrible."

"Thank heavens old man Grainger found the poor man, and not Jordy." Her mother shivered and rubbed her arms.

"Why were there not more questions about the death? If Buck had been the sheriff back then, there would've been a deeper investigation. It wouldn't have needed to be reopened as an unsolved cold case."

Her mother fussed with her apron. "Let's change the subject. This is giving me the creeps."

"Yeah, let's. Sorry, Mom." Rayna had always been frustrated with her inability to get answers over the years, and she was beginning to understand why. But Rayna was starting to get curious about the old Grainger place and hadn't ruled out a covert drive past, something she'd never share with her mother.

* * *

She spent most of the morning packing her bag and cleaning out a few drawers, trying to clear her mind, but she knew there'd be no such task that interesting. As hard as she tried, she couldn't stop second-guessing her Grainger story. She'd come home prepared to deal with her family's backlash; their reaction was already boiled into the soup. The guilt, on the other hand, left her with an unexpected aftertaste.

Combined with the contest rejection weighing heavily in the back of her mind, she needed a distraction, and without much thought she called the barn to have King bridled up, tossed on a few extra layers, and left the house.

With each breath, the frigid air crystallized in her chest before trailing off like puffs of smoke behind her. She'd have to ride hard to warm up, and fast if she'd any intention of getting back by lunch. She pushed up her sleeve, exposing a bare wrist. *Darn.* She wouldn't even know when it was lunch. She suddenly felt her spur-of-the-moment plan might not have been such a good idea.

Before long, she had King plucked from his stall and running the trails at a brisk gallop. Riding wasn't as easy as it looked. She held on with every muscle in her body, pushing herself to the limit. Her calculations had been correct; the swift pace was the perfect solution for combating the cold. Rayna switched to a light canter that soon evolved into her preferred gait, a peaceful walk.

There was a bundle of fresh purple flowers at the cemetery, visible from the path as she rode by. She wondered when her mother had made the trip, and why she'd gone alone. From the top of hill, she could see the Lancaster being taxied into the hangar.

With the cold dampness cutting ever deeper, she decided to guide King down the cemetery hill on foot. But, as she walked along beside him, without warning, he slipped a little near the top. They moved forward cautiously, but King's back legs skidded around and came up beside her. He took a few quick steps and neighed as he stumbled to adjust his stance.

"Easy, easy, big fella!" she cautioned in a soft voice. Stunned but composed, Rayna stayed out of King's way and watched from the side as he shook his mane and flung his head around in every direction. "Calm down, King! Easy. Easy, boy." Within seconds, his hooves were firmly planted on the ground, but she gave him a second more to smooth out before they continued to the bottom of the hill. When they reached the side of the road she stepped into the stirrup and remounted. The slip would be considered a minor incident by most riders, but it shook her confidence for the remainder of the ride.

By lunch, Rayna was riding past the Jacksons. Charlotte's car sat alone in the driveway, and the curtains were closed. She studied the place as she passed, trying to figure out who they were as a couple. She knew Charlotte and Trent in an entirely different context. Picturing them as husband and wife was so foreign to her, she couldn't help but look for signs that it was indeed true.

Next door, an intricately carved sign displayed the tragic words *Pine Hill Estate* and was prominently hung over the laneway leading to the new bungalow. Harland had always wanted to feel important, to have the respect her father enjoyed. Simply looking at the sign played with her emotions.

She cut through the field, arriving back at King's stall just as the farmhands were taking their break. The gate was wide open, and she questioned whether she'd been in that much of a hurry. King walked in without any nudging and gulped endless amounts of water before feasting on fresh oats and beet greens.

"You forgot to post your itinerary!" Beaker ranted from the doorway, carrying a saddle. He adjusted his grip, hoisting the chunk of leather with such force she was sure it became airborne.

"I don't get a, 'Hey, Brat,' today?" She gave him a teasing smile.

"No." Beaker huffed, clearly in no mood for games.

She recoiled and dropped her arms to her sides, like a scolded child. Rayna had rarely seen him upset, and never with her.

"When you take a horse out, you let people know where you're going and when you'll be back." He huffed again before adding, "What are we supposed to think when there's nothing posted … and the stall gate is open?"

"Sorry, but in the spur-of-the-moment I forgot a few things." She watched him stomp into the tack room with the saddle and leave empty-handed. Rattled by his curt behavior, she called after him. "Where were you going with the saddle?"

Before disappearing from sight, she heard him mutter, "Where do ya think?"

What's the big deal? She'd missed writing in her itinerary, but it was only lunch time. Hardly enough to get upset about. She pushed it out of her mind and rewarded King with a lengthy brushing. He posed, statue-still with his wispy tail swishing behind him, bringing an instant smile to her face. This would be her last chance to spoil him before returning at Christmas. Just a month away, but it would seem like three.

The radio hummed louder than usual in the tack room as she put away her riding gear and hung King's saddle in its place.

"Folks, we're not going to escape that nasty weather," the radio announcer warned. "We're looking at a high probability of a flash freeze. Take extra care if you're brave enough to venture out. Better yet, stay inside if you can."

"Oh, damn!" She cursed herself. King was such a joy to ride, she often forgot he ranked high on Westcott Farms list of prized horses. Rayna stuck her head into the breezeway and looked around, wondering who all knew how reckless she'd been.

Chapter 14

As the temperature climbed, the risk of freezing rain and black ice lifted. With the trip to the hangar still on she planned to apologize to Beaker the minute she climbed into his truck, but she never got the chance. When she opened the truck door, Harvey was sitting behind the wheel.

"Rayna." He nodded, rolling his right shoulder and rubbing it with the opposite hand.

"Oh! Hi, Harvey. Where's Beaker? Hey … how is that shoulder of yours?" She tried to hide her surprise, acting as if she didn't expect an answer to the first question.

"Shoulder's a little grumpy. They say the cold and dank weather aggravates old injuries and broken bones and the like. I have to say I agree."

Rayna endured the painful trip to the hangar, listening to Harvey describe every malady he'd ever suffered in full detail—the cause and the cure. The ten-minute drive seemed endless. She was careful to nod on cue and inject enough uh-huhs to feign interest, but she really wanted to jump from the moving truck. It was a relief when the airport appeared ahead of them, and they pulled off the side road.

Harvey snaked through the lanes, looking for an empty parking space while she looked for Trent's Jeep, although she hated to admit it. Judging by the number of parked cars, she knew the entire team must have shown up to work on the Lancaster. Driving down the last lane she spied the Jeep sitting right next to Charlotte's hatchback.

Every pore on her body opened and blood shot to her face.

Within seconds her skin became clammy, and her knees weak. Anxious, and unable to leave the truck, she fumbled with her bag and the laser measuring tool for a moment while she composed herself.

This would be her first time coming face-to-face with Trent and Charlotte as a married couple. She'd passed them on the road, seen them from a distance, but she'd always been able to avoid this moment. Rayna didn't feel ready to see them together, but knew she never would be. She slid out onto the gravel.

With a bit of conniving, she encouraged Harvey to stay in the truck where he could avoid the dampness. It was a good deal for both. Clutching the notepad and measuring tool, she made her way to the hangar, a million thoughts competing for her attention, and one nagging question rising above the others. *Why is this so difficult?*

Arriving at the side door, she followed a narrow hallway that opened into the large hangar. Spotlights shone on specific areas of the Lancaster with the team scattered around them, the odd person working alone and the others in pairs. Right away, she wondered where Trent and Charlotte were. Starting to her left, in the furthest corner of the hangar, her eyes swept the room like the hands on a clock, covering every inch, until she'd surveyed the entire place. Taking in the last bit of floor space, she was shocked to see Charlotte and Trent practically standing right beside her, and she could tell by their confused expressions they'd seen her the moment she walked in. Worse yet, they'd watched her scan the entire area. She could only imagine what they were thinking: *What a psycho!* Any blood left in her legs soon disappeared.

"Charlotte, Trent, hi!" She readjusted her bag and notebook several times to avoid eye contact. As she walked the few feet between them, it suddenly occurred to her she'd absolutely no idea what to say. In any of the scenarios she dreamed up, she never factored in having to speak to them.

"Rayna." Charlotte tucked her dark chocolate waves behind

her ears and gave her a hug that was more like a bump.

Trent put his arm around the small of Rayna's back as he greeted her, then pulled it away almost as an afterthought. He playfully tossed a screwdriver a few inches into the air above his hand, catching it every time. "This is a surprise. I mean that in a good way."

They stood there staring at each other, unsure what to do or say. Charlotte tucked her hair behind her ears again, even though it had remained nicely secured from the first time.

"I need measurements for the Winter Ball. Actually, the decorator needs them, for draping fabric and stuff." Flustered, she waved her hands around and looked at Charlotte. "You know what I mean, right?"

Trent tilted his head to the side. "One of the gas boys told me you were already here one evening getting measurements."

"Yes. Yes I was. We were—Beaker and me. My mother needs a few more. We didn't get them all, apparently." *Rayna, get a grip!* "So, I'm here … again. You look really busy. I won't be too long, and I promise not to get in anyone's way."

"You won't at all." He stuffed the screwdriver in his back pocket. "Come." He waved for her to follow him to the bomber. "What do you think?" They stared up at the Lancaster. "Must have been a shock when you walked in the other night. Seeing it all back together."

"Impressive, Trent. You must be so proud, Charlotte."

The three walked closer to the bomber, standing under and around it as he pointed out and explained details of interest. He filled her in on the restoration and showed Rayna the contributions Cole had made to the project, parts he'd worked on or he'd planned to work on. They talked, and shared stories about, the changes the Lanc had undergone since they'd played in it as kids.

"We hope to be flying it, for real, within the year." He leaned against one of the large front tires. "The entire team is here on the weekends. And they mean business. Here at the crack of dawn."

"You must be excited. Cole would be thrilled."

Charlotte quietly broke away from Trent and Rayna and wove her way through the group, garnering interest in the prospects of a pot of hot coffee. It was torture to watch the men fawn over Charlotte as she crisscrossed the hangar, even though Rayna was accustomed to fading into the background the second Charlotte entered a room. She wished it didn't bother her so as she struggled with the negative emotions.

Rayna continued to listen to Trent's stories with one eye on Charlotte and one question on her mind. *Why her?* Rayna watched her smooth the back of her floral skirt, making it swirl around her legs as she walked. Charlotte bantered back and forth with the guys, but within minutes she'd disappeared behind the swinging canteen door.

"… in the end, it seemed like the best way to get the—" Trent leaned in closer. "Psst. Rayna?"

She looked around quickly. "What were you saying? Trent, I'm sorry, I …"

"I'm familiar with your drifting." He smirked. "Never mind."

"Some things never change, I guess." Rayna stared at him.

"Some things," he said, turning away.

Interesting. They'd repeated the exact same words, but the nuance in his had made them seem almost hurtful. She didn't know what to make of it. She wondered if he was still angry with her. His cutting remark sure seemed to give that impression.

As the comfort of their old friendship set in, Rayna and Trent laughed as they shared more childhood memories. Subconsciously aware that recent history was strictly off-limits, they both seemed to silently agree on this rule. She smiled, shocked to hear the depth of her own laughter. Joy wasn't an emotion she experienced a lot of lately.

Charlotte reappeared carrying two cups of freshly brewed coffee, and carefully delivered them to the team before returning to the kitchen. At least a head shorter than Rayna, with a petite but curvy build, she floated across the hangar like a veil of smoke. It pained Rayna to admit it, but she'd forgotten how attractive Charlotte was, and how graceful. Coupled with the slight lilt in her voice, she was completely disarming. A fatal combination for most men.

Charlotte brought the last, steaming cups over to Rayna and Trent, smiling as she offered them. She had a model's smile and perfect skin—completely flawless. With Charlotte's return, so too did Rayna's discomfort. She excused herself to collect the last of the measurements, and as she walked away she rubbed her furrowed brow until it relaxed.

Rayna struggled with the laser level. It kept displaying a weird code or giving a bizarre reading, and a few times she wrote the numbers down wrong, but eventually it came together. Double-checking the final entries, she stood back against the wall, trying to visualize the Winter Ball. She could see the white draping chiffon with a hint of sparkle, thousands of tiny white lights and candle-lit tables encircling a black plexiglass dance floor. She tried to envision how they'd backlight the Lancaster for a dramatic effect.

She watched Charlotte and Trent talking as they wandered around the hangar. He steered her around a wet spot on the concrete and she helped him clean it, handing him rags and putting them in a garbage bag. A striking couple, they looked like models stepping away from a photo shoot with their dark hair and extreme good looks that matched perfectly. She'd probably never had a split end in her life, or experienced the ravages of humidity. They were both smiling, and totally engrossed in their conversation. Rayna hadn't even left and already she felt invisible, or worse yet, like she'd never been there at all.

Within minutes, Rayna slipped out the side door without saying goodbye. *Enough torture for one day.* Her wish was to be tucked away in a quiet stall with King so she could process the chance encounter. Instead, she'd be trapped in the truck listening to Harvey's medical history or learning the price of soya beans and soda pop. She walked as slowly as she could, trying to make the short distance take as long as possible.

Rayna realized she was heading in the wrong direction and twirled in a circle, looking for the truck, until Harvey flashed the headlights and tapped the horn to get her attention. She made a sharp turn and started walking toward him, glancing over her shoulder to see if anyone had noticed. Rayna did a double take when she looked back at the rectangular window in the hangar door, where a dark figure stood, watching her walk away. They'd quickly stepped out of view when she spun around.

"Interesting." It did little more than arouse her curiosity, but she no longer felt invisible.

Chapter 15

For the better part of the night Charlotte wrestled with the cotton quilt, and her emotions. She watched Trent, soundly drawing deep breaths beside her. He was the perfect bed partner. She could scarcely tell the difference whether he was beside her or not□most of the time. What did he dream about … awake and asleep? His stillness gave her no clues. *What's going on in that gorgeous head of yours?*

Avoiding Rayna the few times a year when she came home for a visit had never amounted to more than a mild annoyance for Charlotte, but this time she wasn't as certain. There was something about the way the corners of Rayna's mouth turned up without producing a real smile, and the look of surprise on her face when she'd caught herself laughing that concerned Charlotte. Rayna's demeanor reeked of trouble. Charlotte sensed that all the rain they were experiencing would be a drop in the sink compared to the storm about to move in on them.

She extracted herself from the knotted sheets and headed downstairs in her flannel nightgown. To avoid squeaks and groans from the antique staircase, Charlotte maneuvered each tread with precision, stepping to the far left or right, as her fawn-colored pug watched her from the landing. The closer she got, the faster Shivers wagged his tail.

Unlike me, you're thrilled I can't sleep, aren't you? When she reached the last step, she stared into his perpetually sad, little face and spoke in a silky whisper. "Are you my good boy? Eh, you good boy?" His tail wagged. "Want to snuggle? Do you want to snuggle with Mommy?" He followed her into the kitchen, panting as he watched her slice cucumbers and drop them into a glass water bottle. She picked a fluffy piece of popcorn from a baggy and held it between them. He circled her legs, faster and faster, wagging his tail, waiting for the magic words.

"Pop-pop?"

He sat in front of her, ready to be offered the treat. She pinched the small kernel between her thumb and index finger and smiled as he nibbled. Careful not to nip her fingers, it took several seconds before the popcorn disappeared. She returned to the family room with her cucumber water, Shivers trailing along behind her.

With her arms folded tightly across her chest, she crossed the chilly room. She studied the wood pile, selecting two good-sized logs and tossing them into the cast-iron stove. Flames exploded around the bark, sending a faint whiff of smoke drifting from the firebox as the door shut. She watched as the fire crackled and seasoned wood slipped deeper into the burning red embers, a simple pleasure that never failed to mystify and entertain her.

She curled up on the sofa and drew her legs in tight. Shivers sat on the floor in front of her, waiting.

"Do you …?" His head tipped sideways as he looked up at her. "Do you want …?" His head tipped to the other side and back again as he waited, listening for the magic phrase. "Do you want to snuggle?"

She tapped the sofa once, and he jumped onto the cushion. He walked around, trying to find the exact spot that appealed to him, which usually involved lying on her feet or against the side of her leg. Within seconds he dropped beside her, propped his head on her lap, and looked at her with his big, sad eyes and let out a deep sigh.

"You thought I'd never sit. Didn't ya? My little monkey face."

Charlotte grabbed a quilted sewing bag that sat beside the end of the sofa. She fished around for a ball of pink yarn and a steel crochet hook, still attached to a small swatch of knotted wool. She carefully assessed the project, strategically dipping the hook into the woven square. Charlotte twisted and looped the soft skein, mulling over Rayna's visit to the hangar. Why hadn't Larissa just called and asked her to get the measurements? Rayna had always gone out of her way to avoid them. *Why would she go to the airport knowing Trent and I were there?*

She mulled over the details without finding any answers, surprised when she realized a couple of hours had passed. She snipped the woolen strand, smiling as she laid an open palm on the silky fibers. Charlotte squeezed the billowy mesh of threads, then set the tiny pink square on the coffee table. She stared at it for a second, thinking, before returning it to the knitting bag. She took the ball of yarn and twisted a single strand around the hook in several directions. When the piece grew to the size of a postage stamp, she pierced the square with the hook, pinning it to the ball of yarn, then tossed it back into the bag as well.

With no distractions, she thought again about Rayna. Charlotte had always liked her, envied her even. On the rare occasion she was able to get past the fact that Trent was still in love with Rayna, Charlotte actually missed her. But those moments were rare. Anyway, Charlotte already had everyone she needed.

She remembered all the experiences they'd shared throughout their lives, and what good friends the Westcotts had been. They'd practically dressed her. Whatever Rayna outgrew went to Charlotte. The kids at school often teased her, 'I hope you like Rayna's navy coat, because you'll be wearing it next year, Charlotte.' She was always so grateful for Larissa and Denver's support, so she'd never let it bother her. It was sad the way things had turned out. With no way of knowing how long Rayna would be in town, she wondered about the likelihood of running into her again.

There was plenty of wood in the stove when she opened the door, so she gave the logs a couple of stabs with the poker. The rush of air invigorated the flames and sent sparks shooting about. With her thoughts and worries temporarily silenced, she carried Shivers to his bed and tucked a plush bunny between his front paws before heading for the stairs. A faint snore slipped from his drowsy face, causing her to miss a step on the old staircase. She covered her mouth to muffle her surprise.

Charlotte crept into the dimly lit nursery and leaned against the wall opposite a small junior bed. The cot sat close to the floor and seemed shorter than standard, but even then it looked far too large for the sleeping toddler. She gathered the blanket that'd slid halfway onto the floor and tucked it around the tiny figure. She thought about the day she'd bought the whimsical bedspread. Quinn loved the fire trucks and police cars, and went right for them. Her heart swelled as she laid her palm on his warm forehead and slipped her fingers through the wisps of sandy hair.

"Mommy loves you," she whispered as she kissed his soft cheek. She then crossed the hall and quietly slipped between the sheets.

Trent lifted his head off the pillow. "Everything okay?"

Charlotte tossed the bottom corner of the quilt to cover his feet, then tugged it up to warm his bare shoulders. "Everything's fine. Go back to sleep." She lowered herself onto her pillow, hoping she was right. Within seconds, she expelled her last troubled breath of the day.

Chapter 16

The scent of roast beef and onion drifted into Rayna's bedroom, where she busied herself by tidying up the room. The aroma made her instantly homesick, and she hadn't even left yet. As she walked down the stairs, she realized it was the first day she'd felt anxious from the minute she opened her eyes. Rayna hated the prospect of leaving, and her bags waiting at the bottom was a depressing reminder she had a life somewhere else.

Rayna could almost taste the roasted onions when she walked into the kitchen, and she basked in the warmth as she moved into the heart of the room. They enjoyed the best dinner she could ever remember having but ate in near silence, everyone dreading the goodbyes to come.

After dinner, she poured one last Earl Grey in her favorite mug and nestled into the window seat. There was always hot coffee in the morning and a pot of tea starting midafternoon, a predictable comfort she always missed when she was back in the city. She loved the freedom of living on her own and had absolutely no use for an entire pot of tea—or coffee, for that matter—but as she sipped the comforting brew, she wondered why it bothered her so.

The sun had dropped from the sky, and the grounds resembled a movie set. Every tree and fence post stood in silhouette, backlit with a flood of violet and rose. Flickering in the distance, lampposts provided a guiding light to the stables and tiny lanterns in the garden offered a dreamy place for her gaze to fall while a million thoughts rolled through her mind. *Why did I book a night train?*

Rayna knew Beaker would forget they'd had a tiff by the time she returned for Christmas, but she wished she hadn't upset him. Or at the very least apologized. Rayna's father had kissed her cheek on his way to the stables, which meant one less goodbye. She waited for her mother to speak first.

"Your father moved your bags beside the door. I guess you're ready to go."

"Lately, I'm never ready to go." She scanned the grounds one more time, painting a mental picture soothing enough to last until Christmas. "I remember a time when I couldn't get back to the city fast enough. Funny how life can change us."

Her mother slipped a twisted lock of hair from Rayna's trusting fingers. "You're tying yourself in knots." She waited patiently, but Rayna didn't respond. "I can tell you're troubled. It's not healthy to keep pushing things down. You need to make a decision, Rayna."

To make decisions you need options, and Rayna couldn't see any. She presented a reassuring smile and hugged her mother. She had a sudden joyless image of driving to Fallencrest Station with Harvey, and momentarily contemplated saying goodbye to her parents on the station platform. She dreaded the dismal drive but decided it would be the more tolerable option. In that instant, she vowed never to book another late train back to the city.

Ever.

* * *

When the truck pulled into the circle Rayna walked across the front porch, watching for the interior light to come on when the door opened. But it didn't. As usual, Harvey wasn't going to be much help. She adjusted her bags before descending the steep set of stairs and, out of nowhere, other trips home came to mind. Beaker would have dashed from the truck to meet her halfway, grabbed her bags, and practically walked in front of her in case she lost her footing.

She reached over the side of the truck and set the small carry-on in the box. The passenger door popped slightly open as she pulled on the handle, and it flew open toward her.

"Beaker!" she gushed as the door whooshed open.

"Sorry, I didn't see you come out of the house." He was staring like a hawk at something far beyond the driver's-side window. "Can you see that?"

"See what?" Rayna asked as she stared into the darkness.

He remained quiet but pointed, gesturing far off in the field.

His silence made the hair on her scalp prickle. "Beaker, you're scaring me."

He made a lame attempt at a reassuring smile. "I thought I saw a fox or something."

She sat still as a statue, the seatbelt stretched around her but holding the buckle in the air in front. "You're not fooling anyone, with your pasted-on smile."

He pried the buckle from her fingers and clipped her seatbelt into place. "If we sit here any longer, we'll miss your train."

Beaker drove along the laneway at a normal pace but slowed to a noticeable crawl when he reached the stable. He obviously thought he could discreetly scan the area as they passed by, and she decided she'd let him think he was getting away with it. But then he stopped the truck and stepped outside—taking extra care not to let the door click shut behind him. He walked around by the stable, at one point standing still, listening. She looked away for a second, and when she turned back he'd disappeared into the blackness.

Moonlight flickered through the branches, casting shadows across the hood of the truck. She cowered at the thought of something—worse than the darkness—creeping in through the unlatched door. She wanted Beaker to get back in the truck, but she resisted calling him. Her jaw tightened and her teeth clicked together while she waited for him.

A few minutes passed and the door opened. Beaker

hesitated, taking one last look around before getting back behind the wheel. "A fox. I'm sure of it."

What had been in the shadows that alarmed him so? Rayna shivered with terror and could only imagine the look that must have been plastered across her face. He tried to lighten the mood, joking about how the horses were going to miss their evening snacks when she left. But her ears were ringing, she couldn't hear a sound. And by the way he looked in her eyes, she could tell he knew it.

Her mind raced, suddenly reminded of the chilling stories she'd covered at the newspaper and how she'd cowered in her apartment after. Many nights she'd lain in bed just as Sage had described it. Alert to every tap or rustle, shivering, her jaw tight and her teeth chattering uncontrollably. It hadn't seemed possible until it happened to her.

"You look like you're miles away."

Rayna was miles away, three hundred to be exact, walking around her apartment in the middle of the night, checking the locks and looking in closets.

She suddenly realized the danger wasn't lurking in the field—it was in her mind.

Chapter 17

Rayna's heart pounded against her chest, as a wave of fear awakened every fight-or-flight response ever allotted a human body. With the back of her hand, she wiped the beads of sweat from her clammy cheeks. *Breathe, Rayna, breathe!*

Beaker tried to make small talk but finally gave in to her silence and clicked the radio on. He tapped his fingers on the steering wheel while the truck inched along the driveway, but when they reached the road he sped away in the direction of station.

The entire experience was a reminder of the life she had waiting for her in the city. A stark dose of reality at the exact moment she needed it.

"I'm not getting on the train."

He switched the radio off. "Did I miss something?"

"Can you take me home, Beaker?"

"What's going on with you?"

"I'm done, Beaker."

"Done?" His head jerked to the side as he searched her face for an explanation.

"I'm not going back."

"Ever?" The silence hovering between them, prompting him to pull onto the gravel shoulder and shut off the truck. With the patience he was known for, he waited for her to respond.

The calm resolve in Rayna's voice surprised even her. "I don't know about ever, but I'm not going back tonight."

Beaker turned to look at her. "You're blowing this way out of proportion. There was nothing in the field except a curious little animal lost in the dark, probably more scared than you were."

"It's not that." She hesitated. "I can't leave right now." With her elbow resting on the console between the seats she pressed on her temple, trying to use her hand to shield her face. "Don't ask, because I can't explain it."

Beaker's concern was palpable, but he didn't question her. He glanced through the back window before steering the truck into a tight three-point turn and heading back to the farm. He seemed to know exactly what she needed and turned the music up slightly, tapping his fingers on the steering wheel while a tortured blues guitar lamented in the background.

She turned to face him, resting her cheek against the back of the seat. She spoke softly as their eyes met. "Thanks, Beaker."

He winked. There was a hint of a smile in his eyes, but his serious expression told her whatever he saw when he looked at her left him alarmed as well.

"This is going to make your parents happy," he said with a sideways glance when they reached the Westcott laneway.

The image was more frightening than what she'd just been through. In their eyes, she was perpetually eighteen years old. She pictured them trying to protect and control her, and she bristled at the thought. Even though, on this night, with her world upside down, she longed to feel safe and taken care of.

"Hey, Brat, what do I always tell ya?"

"The sky will still be there tomorrow."

Staring at the road, he nodded.

Grateful for the calming effect he had over her, a smile tugged at the corners of her lips. In the most troubling times, he could always persuade her to keep the faith. He had a way of inventing believable rationales for why things were going to work out the way she wanted them to—the way they were supposed to, he'd say. More than that, he had a way of convincing her that, even in the worst-case scenario, her strength would pull her through. She'd always trusted him, and always been glad she had. Even on the rare occasions he'd been wrong.

Chapter 18

Just as Beaker had always promised, the sky was, indeed, still there the next morning, and the morning after. But it took Rayna five days to don a brave face and book a seat on an early train back to the city. Luckily, everyone believed her delay in leaving had to do with flu-like symptoms. She wasn't about to let her mother monitor her every move, and she'd definitely try if Rayna had told her the truth.

Twenty minutes from her office building Rayna stepped into a taxi, running her proposal through her head. People make accommodation requests all the time, and there were several departments she could easily qualify for. With her strategy committed to memory, she didn't expect her plan would be challenged.

As they drove closer to the familiar tower she leaned forward. "Can you stop here, please? I'd like to walk the last couple blocks."

The driver stomped on the brake, leaving a line of traffic waiting behind them. With a smile, Rayna dropped a few bills over the front seat and stepped out onto the curb.

Rush hour never ended in the city, and with her senses unusually heightened everything bothered her. The noise pained her eardrums, and the whirling traffic whipped her hair and thoughts into a frenzy. She waited her turn to enter the crosswalk while the exhaust from yellow taxis infused her hair with soot, and a potpourri of expensive perfumes mingled together to singe her nostrils.

People moved along the crowded sidewalk as if they were a

solid unit, twisting her clothing from side to side simply due to their proximity. There were more bodies than walkway, and every one of them was on a mission, rushing in and out of buildings and hailing cabs.

And, for some reason, every tenth guy reminded her of Darklend or Grainger, or any number of creeps she'd lost sleep over. Within minutes she walked into the lobby of the newspaper, relieved to be free of the crowd outside.

* * *

"So that's it, that's all you're going to offer me?" Rayna asked in disbelief.

"I'm afraid so. We distribute journalists where they'll be the most beneficial. You're a strong writer, which puts you in high demand. Covering social gatherings, on who attended the biggest fundraiser of the decade, is not the best allocation of your skills. We need you to contribute in a more significant way."

"It would only be for six months." She pulled on her scarf while she lied to him, and herself.

"Major Crime is the only thing I can offer you."

"I would be very grateful for a fresh assignment." *Is he even listening?* She persisted. "Life section, or maybe Entertainment?"

He had a stiff air that matched his absurdly sculpted hair. "I wish I could help you, Rayna." He faced his computer and started tapping on the keys.

She shuffled her feet, shifting her weight from side to side. "How much time do I have to make a decision?"

"Take the day."

"That's it?"

"We need to backfill it sooner rather than later."

She watched as he frantically shuffled papers from one side of his desk to other. A gold pen stood upright in a tiny holder beside a miniature clock that ticked annoyingly on the corner of his desk. The entire scene felt surreal. *Who has a ticking clock on their friggin' desk?*

"Rayna?" He looked at his watch. "Is there another issue we need to discuss?"

"No." Heat radiated from under her coat as the clock ticked away. "You haven't left me with any options at all."

"I'm sorry you see it that way."

Not once did he look at her or stop typing. Rayna walked toward the plateglass wall separating his suite from the open-concept office. She watched as conspicuous stares and prying glances were redirected to fake concern and the reading of upside-down documents. It would become classic water cooler gossip, sure to last for days. She eyed the elevator on the far wall and tried to calculate how long it would take her to get there as opposed to how long the walk would actually feel.

"You don't have to make a decision now," he said in a thankless tone.

"I have made a decision." She took one last look at the elevator and drew a mental map of the quickest route out.

"Excellent." He rummaged around for a pen, sliding loose papers left and right.

She walked to his office doorway.

"Well?"

His lifeless expression foreshadowed how miserable she would have felt the second she signed a new contract, and the ticking clock reminded her she didn't have another minute of life to waste.

"Take care."

With a puzzled look, he watched her leave the office.

"Rayna!?"

He fumbled out from behind the imposing walnut desk and stood with both palms facing up, like he was waiting for an answer to fall out of the ceiling tiles. He slammed his hands onto his hips as she turned and walked away.

Their eyes met as she faced forward in the elevator. *Idiot!*

The doors slid shut, and the elevator dropped with such

speed she thought she was about to pass out. She reassured herself that it was the sudden decent that had caused her heart to flutter, and nothing more. But her anxiety heightened the instant the doors slid open—the revolving turnstile leading to the street was jammed. Black suits and nude heels were backed up to the gilded elevators. She struggled to breath in the overcrowded lobby, waiting for her chance to escape through the emergency exit. Minutes later, the impatient group lurched forward, and to her relief she spilled onto the bustling street.

Rayna found her designated spot on the crowded sidewalk, and staring at the concrete, she followed it all the way to her apartment on the other side of town. In desperation she glanced at the only open space she knew to be available, a tiny dot of uninspiring sky ever-present amid the imposing towers. In a flash of brilliance between watershed moments, the clarity was ethereal. *This is not the life I want to live.*

Chapter 19

Rayna's apartment was located in a modest area on the west side of the city, the twenty-three-story building considered iconic by most. Dressed in a navy uniform, the concierge tipped his cap and opened the impressive glass doors when she appeared under the canvas awning.

"Have a nice evening, Ms. Westcott."

"Thank you, George." Rayna pushed the elevator button, but the second he moved out of sight she stole away into the stairwell.

Rayna warily stepped into her unit and stood, frozen, with her head turned to the side, listening. Using the light from the hallway, she swiped a wall switch, triggering a lamp on the living room end table to glow warmly. She double-locked the door and tossed her keys onto the mirrored console.

Without reservation, Rayna systematically checked each room. A small row of closets connected the hall to the bedroom, and she opened each door along the route to survey every nook. She pushed back the shower curtain, looked in the large armoire beside the vanity, and double-checked the window locks. Having saved one last humiliation until the end, she walked into the generous master suite, knelt on all fours, and lifted the bed skirt to confirm what she already knew. No one was hiding under the bed.

With her ritual complete, Rayna crossed the living room, her sullen face staring back at her from the glass doors as she moved toward them. She peered out onto the street where, three stories below, a menagerie of lights reflected off the wet pavement and loving couples emerged from under the navy awning that stretched from the building to the sidewalk—a parade of yellow taxis appeared, synchronized to their arrival. It all looked so perfect from the promise of her Juliette balcony.

She stared at the twinkling lights as she tried to figure out how her dreams had gone awry. For at least a year, a distinct gloom had been hanging over her, and if she wanted to be honest with herself, she first noticed it a few weeks after she'd arrived at the paper. At some point it had morphed into a gnawing fear, spreading inside her like poison, and it made her the sickest late at night. While most people were laughing and watching talk shows, Rayna wandered around, investigating a noise or a questionable light that'd flashed across her bedroom wall. More times than she wanted to admit, she'd gotten out of bed to check that the doors were locked. Even as she stood there, looking down at the street, Rayna couldn't resist reaching out and twisting the bolt on the glass door.

Fear had crept into every aspect of her life, escalated, and become debilitating. There were days she hated leaving her apartment. She couldn't cope in a crowd, or shop in a mall, and if she was lost or disoriented, she'd panic. Just minutes before, she'd sensed she was being forewarned not to get into the elevator. And she'd heeded the cautionary omen.

But the worse symptom, by far, was that she'd started to avoid doing anything that caused her unease. Rayna was a prisoner within her own life as her world became smaller and smaller. She was always in search of a safe place, but no such space existed outside of Westcott Farm, and now even that was questionable. She'd no choice but to go home and spill the embarrassing details. At first light, she'd book the train and worry about what everyone thought tomorrow.

Admitting the collapse of her big-city plans would be painful. She could already imagine the look of disappointment on her father's face.

It wasn't like she hadn't tried to make things work. She was desperate to be a good investigative journalist, like her peers at the paper who were brave beyond words. But most of the time she only managed to bluff her way along, suppressing her natural tendencies, and she had a low threshold for dealing with dangerous situations and seedy characters.

Staring at her reflection in the window, it became shamefully clear that she was a fraud and a coward, and now, by running home—a failure.

The next afternoon, with keys in hand and a winter coat folded over her arm, Rayna opened the door of her apartment and switched off the light, leaving nothing on but the waning red beacon of the soon-to-be-abandoned cell phone.

Chapter 20

The first few days after she returned home were the worst. Keeping busy had never been a problem for Rayna in the past. Now she looked for tasks to fill the hours while she worried about losing her mind.

Even the brief spurts of planning the Winter Ball with her mother, and the details she managed on her own could only occupy a fraction of time. But when she became reluctant to leave the farm, Rayna knew she was in trouble. On the fifth day, Dr. Parlton's secretary told her to come into the office at 3:00 p.m.—and not a second later.

* * *

"So, you think I'm having anxiety attacks?" Rayna's legs dangled over the side of the examination table.

"I'm certain of it. I'm going to run tests to be sure, but they'll come back negative." Dr. Parlton tucked a tiny penlight into the breast pocket of his white lab coat, and the sleeves stretched tight across his forearms as he wheeled his way over to the corner of the small examination room. "Judging by what you've told me, the symptoms and the duration, it fits all the criteria." Pictures of his hang-gliding days hung on the wall over a wheelchair-accessible computer station where he was entering notes, and a small printer beside the hydraulic bed spit out a requisition for blood work. "You have to pay attention to what your body is trying to tell you. If you let your stress level get out of control, it tends to come back and visit you in another form."

The sheet of white tissue rustled beneath her. "Is it going to happen again?"

He rolled up in front of her. "There's something you're not dealing with, and your body is trying to tell you the issue needs to get resolved. You were able to function in spite of it for a while, but your body can no longer compensate. It's reached its breaking point, so to speak. You need to determine what it is that you're avoiding, what you're not dealing with, and face it head-on." He went back to the computer station before adding, "If you need professional help to sort through this, Rayna, I can arrange counseling."

The statement, coupled with the sympathetic look on his face, made her heart race. "Should I be worried?"

"See, there you go. Stop worrying!" He smiled and tapped the back of her arm. "Go home, relax, and try to have a little fun. Talk to your friends, maybe they can help you work through this."

"So, you think I should put some thought into where the stress is coming from, make a few changes, and this will all just go away?"

"The mind is complicated. It's our job to listen to what our body is trying to tell us."

He went into a lengthy discussion about anxiety being a tool the body uses to make you pay attention to threatening situations, and he offered suggestions on dealing with stress and coping with anxiety attacks.

"Do most people get through this on their own?" Again, except for the crackling tissue, *silence.*

He removed his stethoscope and set it on the bed beside her. "Come back and see me in two weeks. If anything shows up in your blood work, I'll let you know, but I'm confident nothing will." He made a note on the computer. "I don't want to prescribe medication. There's no silver bullet that'll make this easy. You have to do the work."

"Thank you, doctor." She made her way to the receptionist's

desk to book a follow-up.

"Doctor Parlton's office." The receptionist held up her index finger while she listened to the lengthy dialogue coming from the other end of the phone. "I have an appointment available Friday at 10:00 a.m. sharp. Can you come in then?" She tapped the eraser end of her pencil on the desk. "Okay, dear. Don't forget to bring in a urine sample, the first one of the day. We'll see you at ten, Charlotte."

Charlotte!? Rayna's interest was piqued. How many Charlottes were there likely to be in the community? And Rayna could think of only one reason for an early morning urine sample. Over the years Sage had collected two, to be exact.

"Here you go, dear." The receptionist smiled as she handed her an appointment card. "The doctor will see you in two weeks."

She tucked the card in her purse and left the office, relieved. And judging by the grim expressions in the waiting room, she felt fortunate to be leaving with, what seemed, such a benign diagnosis.

* * *

Rayna tried to follow doctor's orders, but with so much to deal with, as hard as she tried, she couldn't relax. There wasn't any one thing she could point to and say, 'It all started when *this* happened.' It had been building, and she had no doubt it was related to her unnerving profession. She couldn't help but wonder how this would change her. Would she ever feel like the old Rayna?

When she'd left Westcott Farm to become a serious journalist the world had looked so harmless. Now, there'd been stories she'd been a part of, and things she'd seen, that she wanted nothing more than to forget.

She remembered a colleague who'd been in a threatening situation. 'Hazard of the job', her coworker had said, and who never seemed to get too concerned. 'People who really want to hurt you don't tell you. They just do it.'

Rayna had developed a theory. If she treated everyone respectfully, if she didn't let her pursuit of a story seem like a personal attack, she'd be seen as a professional reporter just doing her job. And it had worked well, until lately. She tried to remember why she loved writing, why it had been so alluring. Rayna suddenly felt like the little stick figure, running with a lantern on the cover of her book, only this time she was running in search of a light.

But on the last day of her second lost week, she called Sage for a girls' night. Rayna's heart swelled when Sage suggested a sleepover.

Chapter 21

By early evening, Sage had appeared on the Westcott doorstep with a sympathetic smile and a backpack.

"I'm glad you invited me. I hate to think you've been stewing over this and didn't even call me."

Rayna lifted the heavy bag. "Yikes, what've you got in here?" She set it at the entrance to the family room. Sage burrowed into it and grabbed her pajamas before they dashed up to the bedroom to change.

"Honestly, it's been horrible. I can't seem to pull myself together and move forward. I just ramble around this house."

"I had a neighbor with a similar condition. She's CEO at a Fortune 500 company in California. I guess it resolved. It will for you, too, Rayna."

"You're my rock, Sage." They made their way downstairs. "Mark okay with our plans?"

Sage huffed. "If he'd voiced even one complaint … let me tell ya, he would've wished he personally dropped me off at your house. He wouldn't have gotten one wink of sleep all night. Besides, he's so happy I could've stayed for a week," she gushed. "Mark made partner!"

"Amazing! I'm so happy for you."

Sage rubbed her hands together and spoke in a singsong voice. "I see a bigger house on the horizon."

"Oh, I love your house. It has such character."

"I love the way people always say how much character your house has when it's obvious it has zero else going for it."

"That's not true at all." When they got to the bottom of the stairs Rayna pointed to the family room. "Let's sit in there. And your place is adorable, by the way."

"Are you kidding me? Our squatty house is the equivalent of Raspberry Cottage compared to this place."

"You can't compare anything to Westcott Farm."

Sage grabbed her bag from the hall and stopped in the open doorway. "Wow! Someone knows how to build a fire."

Raging flames filled the firebox and a warm glow emanated from the stone hearth, welcoming them into the room. They shared the designer pillows and knitted throw blankets before nestling into two creamy white sofas separated by a round, glass table.

The first item to appear from Sage's backpack was a family-sized bag of barbecue potato chips, followed by a bottle of pinot noir. Giddy at the prospects, the women wasted no time uncorking the bottle and munching on the salty snack.

"It feels like old times." Rayna smiled as she filled their glasses.

"Indeed, it does. You, me, and junk food." She bit into a potato chip. "Except for the wine. Your parents would never have allowed booze."

"What would we never have allowed?" Rayna's mother peeked in the doorway and shook her head when she noticed the wine. "Hello, Sage."

"Mom, hi." Sage tossed the pillow she'd been hugging and sprung off the sofa to greet her. "I'm corrupting your daughter."

"I see that."

"Look at you." Sage stood back, eyeing Larissa. "The other day in the barn I was looking at pictures, and I said to Rayna, 'Your parents are like freaks of nature, they never age.'"

"What a nice compliment." They hugged and stood with their arms linked together. "My second daughter." She drew Sage closer. "We were so happy to hear you were coming for a sleepover. How are your little ones?"

"Great! And, thankfully, still young enough that most of

life's disappointments can be remedied with a trip to the ice cream parlor."

"They are children for such a brief time, but they are always your babies." Larissa smiled at Rayna, who rolled her eyes and embarrassingly tried to imply that she grasped the full depth of the insightful, but maternal, comment.

"Who built the amazing fire?"

"Denver knew you girls would probably be using the room tonight, so he put it on before he went to the barn. You shouldn't need to add any wood." She moved the screen tightly against the stones and glanced at the pictures on the mantel, adjusting one or two before disappearing upstairs.

"So, tell me, what's going on with you? I want to know every detail." Sage played with a tube of lip balm she'd plucked from her bag.

"Where to start?" Rayna unloaded her disappointment with the paper, and the shocking news of her anxiety attacks. She revealed the details of her life in the city, and how her fear and anxiety had made life there unbearable for months.

"You should've told me."

"So much for trying to keep secrets. Unfortunately, everyone's going to be aware of them soon." She stared at the burgundy liquid as she swirled the wine around in her glass. "You know them all now."

Sage moved her glass onto a coaster and wiped the condensation off the table with her palm. "Not all of them."

Rayna stared into her wine.

"I'm sensing negative vibes surrounding that lawyer." Sage adjusted the knitted blanket to cover her legs. "There are a few details you're not telling me." She waited, but Rayna remained quiet. "He was a bad guy, wasn't he?"

"Chase Darklend … yes, he was a bad guy." She walked to the fireplace and nudged a burning log with a brass poker. The flames burst around it, sending sparks popping in all directions as it sank deeper into the flickering coals.

"I stumbled onto a story last year, and as I started to get close to whatever they were hiding, it felt different. Things got weird." She stirred the coals with the poker before returning the tool to the rack. "I don't even want to risk spoiling our evening with the creepy details."

"It won't … so tell me."

Rayna crumpled into a small ball on the sofa. "Darklend started showing up at my coffee shop in the morning, then my personal gym. He said he had a friend in my office building when I bumped into him in the lobby as I was leaving work. I brushed it off at first, not the least bit concerned." She rubbed her arms, hoping the friction would flatten the tiny goose bumps covering them.

"One night I took in a show with the girls, and we went for a few cocktails afterward. We called a taxi quite late, and my stop was the last on the route. I'm sitting there alone, and all of sudden the driver pulls over. A mechanical problem, he insisted. But it didn't seem right. He left the driver's-side door open and raised the hood. The streets were deserted. I sat there, waiting, ready to dial 911."

"Oh my God. You must have been terrified."

"A set of headlights hit the rearview mirror, and a car rolled in behind us. Through the back window, I could see the outline of a man in a dark trench coat emerge from the driver's side of the car. I froze, petrified, watching this figure close in on us.

"I couldn't see much with the headlights beaming behind him, and with the steam from the taxi exhaust. It was surreal, this dark figure walking through waves of smoky exhaust, backlit by headlights. A cloud of heavy cologne drifted into the taxi as he passed the open door on his way to the front of the cab. He asked the driver if he needed any help. When he leaned into the open door the smell of bourbon made my eyes water, but not before I got a good look at him. It was Darklend! In that moment it all came together. I later learned he worked for one of the guys I was investigating, clearly sent to keep an eye on me and see how much I knew."

"So, all along, bumping into him was no accident?"

"No."

"That's frightening! I could tell this story didn't make sense." Sage drew her feet off the floor and tucked them under her. "What did you say, what happened?"

"Even the taxi driver looked terrified, and he started babbling. 'It's all good, all under control. A fuse or a loose connection causing my dash lights to flicker. Happens all the time.' He dove back into the cab and pulled away like he had seen a ghost. I never had a chance to say a word. We left Darklend standing there on the street."

She hastened Rayna for a response. "So, what did you do? Did you call the police?"

"No, and I've never told anyone." She sipped her wine. "When I went home … I swear my teeth were chattering, and I couldn't make them stop." She circled the rim of her glass with her finger. "I spent most of the night peeking around the curtains and looking at the elevators through the peephole in my apartment door. I decided right then, for my sanity□and safety—I needed to kill the story. The next day, I did just that."

"Can you do that?"

"Apparently." Rayna sat her empty glass on the coffee table. "I told my editor I dropped it because I couldn't trust my sources. No one in the office had a clue what I was even working on, and it was nowhere ready to print, so it made the story easy to bury. I found out the other day that you can cancel them at the last minute as well, when they're on their way to print. Mind you, my boss had a fit. Probably why they never offered me one of the positions I wanted. Punishment."

"That story is so creepy. Did he ever bother you again?"

"I bumped into Darklend one last time. I could tell he wondered how much I knew. I thanked him for stopping to help when the cab broke down. 'What a coincidence,' I said, laughing and acting as if I had no suspicions. I made it clear I had no interest in him, and that I had a sweetheart back home in Kansas. Haven't seen him since, and it's been three months."

"Oh my God. Sorry I keep repeating myself, but I have few other words. I'm shaking."

Rayna refilled their glasses and topped up the chip bowl. "I've worked with investigative journalists with *real grit.* Tough, no-nonsense reporters, with integrity and morals. They were the whole package. I've never had the guts for it, and I've felt like a fraud ever since I let those guys intimidate me."

"I think this would have affected most people—and they would have responded the same way, too. I'd bet on it."

"I can't describe it, but they managed to take my power away. I have this overwhelming sense of vulnerability. And it's strange because, before I started working at the paper, I saw the best in people and the world seemed so bright. Now, every stranger is suspicious, every situation is suspect. It's like I'm stuck inside a nightmare. I can't explain it, but … you know that eerie feeling you get when you wake up from a bad dream and it still feels real? Your heart is pounding, and the terror just hangs over you, even though you realize you were only dreaming and there's nothing to actually be afraid of. Does that make sense?"

"Yes. That's horrible. I never knew how you were able to tolerate working there in the first place, or why you ever wanted to. You're being hard on yourself. Most of us are not meant to be in such a shadowy world. Not everyone is built for it and you, my friend, are one of those people." She continued, in a soft voice. "And it's what I love the most about you."

Rayna smiled and fussed with her blanket. "Unfortunately, I never dealt with my issues properly and that's why I'm having all this anxiety. My body started to give me strong hints, and when I didn't face them … I had a full-blown anxiety attack when a little fox decided to take a shortcut across our field on his way home. It sounds ridiculous, but honestly, Sage, I thought I was having a heart attack, dying, right there in Beaker's truck."

"Well, you didn't, and you're not going to." She squeezed

her pillow against her chest. "Do you want to change the subject?"

"Yes."

"Good. Let's move it along."

"Yeah, let's. The other stuff is all in the past." Rayna watched her shiver and worried she'd ruined their sleepover. The fire crackled as they tried to move past the gloomy turn the evening had taken.

"Kansas?" Sage blurted.

"I didn't want to tell him where I lived." Rayna hid her face with the blanket. "It seemed believable when it popped into my head."

"I'm fairly certain he knew you were making that up."

"True."

"And, if you were having a heart attack … I'm sure Beaker would've been quite happy to revive you with a little mouth-to-mouth. Man, he's hot."

"Sage! You think every guy is hot. Anyway … he doesn't look at me like that, and I wouldn't want him to."

"Ohh … okay." She gave Rayna a skeptical grim.

"Enough!" Rayna shook her head, miffed.

Sage walked to the mantel. "I love looking at your family pictures. Wow, the prestige of belonging to one of the most recognized horse establishments in the country. Denver is the most respected person ever to walk, and as a father he'd crawl across glass to keep you safe and happy. Larissa, too. She's adored by everyone, and for good reason. Embrace the positive, Rayna. You've really had a dream life."

"A dream life if you don't count losing a twin brother in your twenties." She sighed. "Sorry, I shouldn't have …"

"Nonsense, I'm the one who should be sorry." She chose Rayna's favorite picture of Cole and walked back to the sofa with it. She sat beside Rayna where they both stared at the snapshot. "I often recall how Larissa held your family together. She insisted on keeping his memory alive, celebrating him, while you navigated the whole bereavement process. I've seen families lose a loved one and not even be able to mention the person's name without the entire room falling apart. They quit having family functions because it would be too painful with their loved one not there. After a while they put away all their personal things, all the reminders. They become debilitated and can't move past it. They're in a permanent state of grief." She looked at Rayna. "Your family never got *stuck* like that."

"I credit my mother's strength. She still tends the garden at the cemetery at least once a week, like it happened yesterday." She spoke in a low, somber tone. "Whether it's a sweltering summer day or the middle of an ice storm in winter, Cole's site is never without fresh purple flowers."

"I think the color purple is symbolic of grief and bereavement."

"I'm starting to realize that."

A smile emerged as Sage looked at the picture she'd chosen from the mantel, and the longer she stared at it, the bigger her smile grew. "Cole was so much fun."

"I know. It's tough not to miss him." Rayna took a deep breath.

"Do you remember when we were camping in your backyard? We were almost asleep when we heard this ghastly moaning sound right outside of the tent□"

"Yes! And we looked everywhere. Nothing! We were scared silly and ended up sleeping in my room."

"The next day, your brother showed us a long garden hose. He'd tucked one end underneath the floor of the tent□"

"And he'd been hiding beside the house moaning in the other end, and it sounded like a bear crawling around outside our tent." Rayna buried her face in the pillow, laughing.

Sage returned the picture to its rightful place. "We couldn't even get mad at him."

"Not even a little bit." Rayna was quiet for a moment, thinking.

"You're going to laugh when I say this, but I think your brother had a soft spot for Charlotte."

"You're funny. Sympathy, maybe."

"No, really, I always sensed it. I think he knew he had to give her just enough attention to keep her interested."

"Interested? For what? This is news." Rayna shook her head.

"It's natural to be a little more guarded around your family. Especially you, his sister. But … I saw a few tender looks between them, a moment here and there over the years."

Rayna listened while her mind downloaded a hundred different scenarios.

"The night of the Christmas party it occurred to me, for the first time, I could see them ending up together at some point. That maybe he wasn't just being nice to spare her feelings. I could see a spark there."

"You saw nothing more than the reflection of a bright red dress, and so did he." Rayna tried to laugh it off. She refused to entertain the thought any longer, at least not until she had a chance to process it. *Had she gotten her hooks into Cole, too?* As hard as she tried to shut off the thoughts, they kept coming. Cole's death suddenly seemed even more tragic when she considered events from Charlotte's perspective. *Could Sage be right?* Had Charlotte been close to getting what she'd always wanted, but it wasn't meant to be?

"It's obvious you don't agree." Sage snapped the lid on and off the tube of lip balm as she spoke.

"Maybe you don't recall, but she left the party with Trent. And Cole left with Samantha Granderville … after chatting her up for less than twenty minutes."

"Your family couldn't have been happy to witness them leaving together, remembering how Cole struggled when he and Samantha called it off."

"Exactly. He signed up for a three-year stint on account of her. They were like sulfur and kerosene. You knew there was going to be an explosion, you just didn't know when. You're right, we didn't like the thought of their relationship reigniting."

"I don't think anyone doubted they were headed for the altar at one time, including Charlotte. I thought she was going to have a nervous breakdown over their relationship." Sage opened her eyes wide and looked at Rayna.

"I hear ya."

"Rayna, did you know Samantha joined the police force? She works undercover on the Ho Squad in Starling."

"The *what* squad!?" Rayna asked, horrified, before she took away Sage's glass of wine. "You, my friend, are cut off!" She could barely contain herself. "Ho Squad." They tumbled around the sofas, laughing. "Shh. We're going to wake my parents," Rayna whispered.

"All I know is she arrests men for taking advantage of vulnerable women. The street-walker crew, whatever." Sage waved her hand in the air.

"That's horrible." Somehow, Sage never failed to shock her. "The respectful term is the Vice Squad. Okay, can we change the subject, again, please?"

"Sure. But getting back to Charlotte …" Sage spoke in a serious tone. "Listen, Rayna, I'm not sure if you're ready to hear the details or not, but I have inside information on how Trent *popped the question*."

Rayna shrugged, her thoughts racing. "I might be."

Sage left her sofa and sat beside Rayna. "Well, rumor is, they were at the airport one evening, sitting on the wing of the Lancaster, enjoying a moonlit sky and a glass of champagne. He leaned close to Charlotte, put his hand under her chin, tilted her face toward his and said … 'Oh my God! You're what!?'"

"You're too much!" She tossed her pillow at Sage's head.

"Enough about her." Sage looked at Rayna.

"Yes … please!"

"Sorry to hear the news about the contest. I know how much you wanted to win."

"Thanks. It wasn't in the cards I guess."

"What are you going to do, now that the paper has cast you free?"

"I have no idea."

"Well … I do." Sage glowed with enthusiasm. "You're looking at this all wrong. You're a free agent. What an opportunity. You can do whatever you want now. Your future is a blank page."

Rayna agreed, and for the first time even she was starting to see the advantages. "I have no idea what I'm going to do … or want to do. Going back to the magazine might be an option."

"It would be amazing for me, but you were miserable there. You could go to a different magazine. Equestrian Royal retains their best writers with amazing perks … trips, theater tickets, an annual bonus."

"Definitely an option. At least you're aware of the kind of articles you're expected to write. Magazines have that predictable format." As soon as the words left Rayna's lips, she added, "Yuk! How uninspiring."

"Boring, actually." Sage raised her eyebrows. "I have an idea, Rayna, but it's going to sound a little crazy and outside the box." She took the lid off the tube and smeared the scented balm on her lips. "You … should … finish your book!"

"What!? You're right. That's way beyond the craziest of boxes."

"Why? Tell me." She listened but Rayna had no response. "You have a degree in literature, experience, and from day one, your master plan always involved writing a book. Not only that, but you, my friend, can afford to sit back in the lap of luxury and take the time needed to compose a jaw-dropping novel."

Rayna offered no argument and listened intently. "Go on."

"You don't need an award-winning writer to work with you. How many writers start off with the advantages you have? When the time is right you can hire an editor." She tossed the tube into her purse and traced her lips with her ring finger. "Tell me, honestly … what've you got to lose?"

And in that moment, between the wine and the friendship, minus a shred of hesitation, Rayna answered. "Absolutely nothing!"

Chapter 22

On the outside Raspberry Cottage resembled everything else the Westcott's owned, every inch well-loved and cared for.

The cobblestone walkway lay hidden under a carpet of fall leaves, and Rayna soon gave up searching for it, opting to swish knee-deep through the mounds of crispy bits as she made her way to the mustard-colored front door. Any other time she would have headed straight for the tree swing, but not today. She slipped the key into the brass lock, and without the slightest creak, the heavy door swung open.

The late afternoon sun poured in behind her, laying a beam of light across the dusty hardwood floor. Her heart fluttered with excitement as she stepped into the tiny entrance. She held the screen open and leaned against the storm door, letting a gentle breeze remove the last residue of stale air. She gathered a handful of crumpled orange leaves that had snuck in with her and tossed them over the porch railing. Chilled to the bone, Rayna closed the door behind her.

She peeked around the alcove to the right. Her hollow spirit lifted at the sight of the pink-and-white, checkered tile floor. She could still picture footprints trailing through a skiff of flour from a baking session with Gramma Westcott.

With a hint of sadness, she remembered the tray of poinsettia cupcakes her gramma had so painstakingly decorated for a Christmas bazaar, and how grown-up she'd felt carrying them to the car before the box dropped on the driveway and the fancy cakes bounced across the gravel. 'Oh, come on now, Rayna,' her gramma had said, smiling. 'You've heard of the five-second rule. No one will even know. It'll be our little secret.'

Her gramma had blown bits of sand off the perfect petals made of ruby red frosting and set the fancy cakes back in the box. The next day, Rayna found her gramma's prized sweets stashed under the sink, the once-beautiful cakes topsy-turvy in the box with grit stuck in the icing. The memory still had the power to break her heart. She shook her head, trying to fling the painful images from her mind.

One by one, she opened the white cabinets, admiring the hodgepodge of dishes. Teacups adorned with purple lilacs sat on matching saucers, and an assortment of dinner plates, stacked largest to smallest, sported no less than six different China patterns. She smiled when she noticed the grouping of chemistry equipment lining an open shelf above the sink. There were eight clear glass measuring decanters, with most of the printed increments running up the side worn off, and as many shallow saucer-like dishes with matching lids. Eight cone-shaped flasks distinguished the lot, forming an interesting collection.

She remembered Beaker had found them at a yard sale, in a box labeled in all-caps: Petri Dishes & Measuring Beakers (Never Used). He thought it was a fancy name for expensive dishes and cooking utensils. It didn't pan out to be the amazing find he'd anticipated, but it was indeed a service for eight. A smile rose from deep inside, and with it, a serenity she'd long forgotten.

Rayna went back to the entranceway and slipped off her boots. A row of wire hangers tinkled on an open steel pole when she brushed into them. The living room was left of the front door, and the windows were covered in ivory lace backed by horizontal wooden louvers. An olive sofa faced the window, and above it a pastel quilt hung over a wooden dowel. Rayna carefully inspected the stitching, turning the fabric several times before straightening the edges. The room was circa 1950s, judging from the teak color palette.

The end tables had two levels. The lower step formed a

cubby, an assortment of books and magazines tucked into one and a candy dish in the other. A tall brass lamp with a white drum shade, wrapped in plastic, sat on the upper level of each. There was a wood stove sitting in the corner, attached to a large black pipe that jutted out through the wall.

Her eyes opened wide when she spotted the red oak desk and matching chair. She rushed to the bay window and pushed the curtains back, delighted to discover it offered a clear view in both directions. She shoved an empty plant stand out of the way. Carefully dragging the heavy desk, an inch at a time, across the dark hardwood, Rayna tucked it into the empty nook.

Two tiny bedrooms were tucked in the back, barely large enough to hold a chest of drawers and a double bed. Her gramma's room was still wallpapered with a pattern of yellow roses, with a tulip sconce poised to shine down on the white chenille bedspread, just as she remembered.

Perfect! She could see herself writing in front of the window and sipping tea in the dollhouse kitchen. She rolled the antique chair over and sat quietly at her new writing desk. When Rayna discovered it swiveled, she was in heaven.

The thought of her new adventure transmitted energy to every cell in her body, and she felt strangely effervescent. But instead of the unfamiliar sensation giving her the usual unease, she liked it.

A slow, moving ballad played in her head as she crossed the kitchen, humming. "Hmmm … mmm … hmmm … hmm." It was a simple thing she used to do all the time but hadn't done in years. She hummed louder and more joyfully, and she danced, her feet sliding across the hardwood and her arms over her head as she moved. Within minutes it felt natural, and her spirits soared as if she'd rediscovered an old friend. When she'd ran through the tune enough times in her head, suddenly self-conscious, she stopped abruptly and looked out the window. To her relief, the North Line was deserted.

With the sun setting, she took one last look at the pink-and-white tile floor and closed the lace curtains before leaving. She tried to picture Beaker cooking in the feminine kitchen and entertaining the guys with lace hanging everywhere. As a man, Beaker had always seemed so comfortable in his own skin, but as she stepped onto the porch it occurred to her: Raspberry Cottage must have tested his manhood, and more than once. No one was that secure.

Her mind drifted through a string of memories. She had an image of Beaker standing on the front porch, weeks shy of sixteen, drinking milk from what looked like a normal glass but on closer inspection she'd realized it was a chemistry beaker—and his friends had never let him forget it.

Rayna's smile evaporated as the memory played out. She could still see the fresh gash cutting through his left eyebrow, a parting gift from the last beating his father ever had the chance to lay on him. His mother had made a run for it, years earlier. Rayna pushed on her eyelids in a vain attempt to erase the image, but there was no escaping it. She'd been barely fifteen at the time, innocent and carefree. He'd looked so serious, with the life and responsibilities of a man, even then.

Chapter 23

Three days later, Rayna walked into a freshly cleaned Raspberry Cottage to find a bouquet of Christmas flowers waiting for her on the kitchen counter.

While she dreamed of being an author, Rayna gave the ends of the red and white roses a fresh clip and loosely arranged the branches of snowy pine. The scent was exhilarating and reminded her of the rush of taking that first deep breath after swimming under water. She pushed the fragrant blooms into the center of the table and looked around the cottage, wondering where to start.

A fruit platter and vegetable tray were the first items to go into the refrigerator, followed by enough milk and cheese to last a week. She stashed a bottle of Riesling in the crisper drawer to chill, and a merlot in the lower cupboard beside the sink, just in case. The next few hours were spent unpacking boxes and rearranging furniture.

She took a last look around, but there was only one carton to empty, and she dragged it across the floor and parked it in front of the desk. As soon as she opened the box, the overhead light hit the tiny red USB she'd taped to the inside of one of the flaps. *Darklend!*

Rayna had tried to forget about the device, but the images burned deep within its tiny case were seared into her mental hard drive. She ripped the flash drive off the lid and threw it into the long narrow drawer in the middle of the old desk. The lock clicked as the key rotated. She pulled on the handle to be sure.

Rayna crawled under the desk and screwed a hook into a soft

piece of wood, then threaded the key over the curved metal. Her mood lagged for a second, but with all the excitement she quickly put the device out of her mind.

The last item released from the box was her brushed chrome laptop, and she set it squarely in the middle of the desk. "There." She connected her printer, loaded the drawers with writing tools, and did a few other odd jobs. *Ready for duty.* After taking a short break, she sat in front of the desk and pulled on the locked drawer, wondering if she'd think about the device every time she sat to write.

She sipped mint tea in the swivel chair, staring at her reflection in the computer screen. "Well, are you going to make this easy on yourself, or will I have to torture every word out of you?" Rayna rested her head on the back of the chair and closed her eyes. Lolled by the gentle twirl and rhythmic squeak from the rickety chair, her thoughts floated like puffs of dandelion seeds in a spring breeze. She could see Gramma Westcott sitting on the front porch eating fresh raspberries right off the bushes, her face hidden by a wide brimmed hat that tied under her chin with a length of yellow chiffon.

"Hello!" Her mother called from the entranceway.

Rayna's eyes flew open, and she grappled to get her bearings. Had she fallen asleep? *Impossible!* She staggered to the door.

"Coming!"

"I brought you one of the cell phones from the house. You may need it." She laid it on the counter beside a set of pink, tin canisters. "How did you manage to leave yours in the city?"

Rayna shrugged, grateful not to have the connection to her past.

"Don't get too settled in here. You are coming back to the farm at night?"

"That's the plan. Daddy won't miss Old Blue, I hope?"

"Of course not, no one ever drives that jalopy. There are two other reliable trucks not being used, why wouldn't you take one of those?"

"I like to live right on the edge."

"And keep me awake at night, no doubt." Larissa stood to the side of the desk, pulled back the lace curtain, and studied the North Road. "It should be ideal for writing. Nice and quiet." She did the same on the right side but soon stiffened and moved closer to the glass. "The Jacksons are just getting home." The curtain slowly dropped as she straightened. Her concerned expression spoke for itself.

"Don't look at me like that. It's fine." Rayna huffed.

"They seem a little too close for comfort." She waved her hands in the air. "That's all I'm going to say about it."

"Good." She took a deep breath. "Are you staying? Can I make you a tea?"

"No. I wish I could. I'm meeting Myra for dinner at The Harvest Table."

"Myra?" Rayna winced at the thought.

"Yes, Myra. People are not meant to be perfect, Rayna." She wandered around the cottage and eventually hovered over the bouquet of flowers, inhaling deeply as she enjoyed the heady rush. "I love the scent of fresh-cut pine." She drew a second breath. "I'll be decorating the house this weekend. This makes me all the more excited to get started."

"Mom, where's the chemistry equipment that was on the open shelf?"

"They're in the bottom of one of the cabinets. Why are you looking for them? We moved them to make room for dishes."

"They are dishes." Rayna searched the bottom cupboards, opening one door after another. "I want them where I can see them." She grinned as she spied the glassware at the back of a cabinet. "Just looking at them makes me happy." Rayna held up a flask and it caught the sunlight. "There you are." She smiled, showing her mother.

"Yes, you're right. They do make you smile." She pulled Rayna in for a hug and rocked her back and forth.

"Thanks for the support, Mom. And the flowers. Thank

Daddy for me."

"Your father thinks you should apply to be a television journalist or launch your own newspaper here in town. The pencil factory has been vacant for a decade. It would be the perfect size. This town, as well as the neighboring communities, could benefit from a paper."

A television journalist? Rayna couldn't believe the pipe dreams spewing from her mother's mouth. *Oh God, the pressure.* "Launch a newspaper? It's just a tad unrealistic, isn't it? Let alone the fact that I wouldn't have the slightest clue how to go about it, and print media is a dying art."

"You used to believe in yourself. Where has that person gone?"

Frustrated, Rayna changed the subject. "Talk about believing. It's hard to believe the holiday season is almost here, isn't it?" She hooked her arm through her mother's, and with a smile, walked her to the front door.

"I get the hint." She picked up her purse. "And right after Christmas we'll be preparing for the Winter Ball." She slipped her gloves on. "Whatever you need, tell the guys. I'll see you back at the house later, right?"

"Right, Mom."

Rayna waved from the porch until the SUV passed the Jacksons. She turned to study her reflection in the glass of the storm door, pressing on the small lines between her eyebrows. Her hand brushed a withered raspberry cane clinging to the railing and she stripped it away, tossing it into the garden. She swept the trailings off the porch while she watched the Jacksons fawn-colored pug bark and dart back and forth on their front lawn with an orange toy clutched in his teeth.

"Shivers! Come here, Shivers." Charlotte removed a couple of bags from the car. "Come on, monkey face, we're going in the house." She walked toward their veranda while the rambunctious pug growled and pressed the toy against the back of her legs several times.

"Stop that! Silly dog."

When the orange toy failed to garner a reaction, he scampered about, grabbed a neon green toy, and pressed that one against the back of her legs.

"Shivers! No. Stop that." She adjusted the bags.

Grrr! He whimpered, dropping the toy and sprinting to the side of the house, only to reappear with a loop of rope. With renewed vigor, he circled Charlotte several times, waiting.

"Okay. Okay!" Charlotte laughed, setting her bags down on the ground. She shook one end of the rope and let Shivers pull on the other. He growled and tugged with all his might, waiting for the predictable outcome. "Good dog," she said as the rope flew from her hands. She ruffled the fur around behind his ears and pushed her face into his neck. Within minutes, they disappeared inside.

Like the sunlight, Rayna found herself fading as well. Taking a last look around, she closed the cottage and headed back home with a hollow feeling in the pit of her stomach. When she arrived at the farm the warm lanterns lured her to the barn, where she went happily, grateful for the distraction.

She walked through the deserted breezeway to the staff lounge, stopping in front of a large plateglass window that gave a full view of the cozy room. Harvey sat crumpled in a recliner reading a ragged paperback. A western-inspired pole lamp, with cow hide and leather lacing, reflected off the bald spot on the top of his head. A few farmhands were playing cards at an old pedestal table, and Beaker was stretched out on a brown leather couch with his eyes closed. His ankles were crossed and hanging out past the end of the sofa and his arms were folded behind his head, making his biceps bulge beneath his plaid shirt.

She raised her hand to tap on the door, then changed her mind. Harvey waved her in, but she returned a smile and headed to the feed room. She barely heard the footsteps inching close behind her.

"Hey, Brat." Beaker scooped her up from behind, her hair

bouncing and shining under the lights as he carried her.

"Beaker? Put me down!" She wormed and squirmed in his arms but laughed at the absurdity. He set her down all right, in the middle of the lounge with a half dozen farmhands looking as surprised as she was.

"What the heck, Beaker!" She smoothed her clothes. "Are you drinking?"

"Just coffee." Harvey joined in. "Have a cup with us."

Beaker walked to a kitchenette and chose a yellow mug dangling from a brass cup hook. "Cream? Sugar?"

"Coffee? Do you realize how late it is?"

"Don't think of it as a moral dilemma." Beaker shook his head. "You want some?"

"Sure." She dropped onto the couch.

Harvey put his face next to the window to get a better view into the breezeway. "No doc yet."

"Vet's on his way." Beaker set the mugs on the coffee table and sat beside her. "One of the mares is about to foal. Long night ahead of us."

"Are they expecting a difficult birth?"

"Could be." He watched her sip her coffee. "You look deep in thought."

"I'm wishing I never had the Grainger case reopened."

"You did your job. People will come around and see it that way."

"I hope you're right."

Harvey swatted a pesky fly against the wall as he piped up. "I think it's important to open up the can of worms, even though they may never figure out what happened this late in time. There isn't much evidence to be had. I guess that's why they call 'em cold cases."

"Ya, I guess," Rayna added. "Beaker, what do you think happened at the Grainger farm that night?"

"Don't you want to sweet-talk me before uncovering my deepest, darkest secrets?"

She ignored his teasing. "Most people agree the fire was likely accidental, but ..."

He stared into his cup. "The death ... maybe not."

Harvey flopped back into the recliner. "The stall gate must've closed behind the farmhand because Brimstone trampled that bugger with a vengeance. There's no way the horse knocked him out on the first stomp like folks would have you think."

"What makes you so sure?" She folded her arms across her chest, shivering, sorry she mentioned it.

Harvey clicked off the pole lamp. "There was blood on every wall. You could tell the young fella went in circles trying to get the hell out of there."

Rayna's spine tingled. "You don't believe it was an accident either, do you?"

"Does a pin ever land on its head?" Harvey set his book on the cushion beside him then walked to the window.

Beaker sipped his coffee before commenting. "Let's just say, there's no handler that stupid and no horse that mean."

Rayna tried to make sense of Beaker's remark but quickly changed the subject. "You make a good cup of coffee. Thanks, Beaker." She tipped her head toward him as she spoke and he turned to her just as she did, burying his face in the mass of chestnut curls.

His eyes lit up as he inhaled deeply "What *is* that?"

"What?" She gathered the locks in her hand and leaned away from him.

"Your hair, it smells like ... Christmas." He seemed to stare at every individual shaft.

"Pine."

"Sorry," he said with a confused look.

"I spent the afternoon arranging a bouquet of flowers. Every corner of the cottage has a hint of pine in the air. Me too, I guess."

"You smell ... amazing." A slow puff of air escaped his

pursed lips. "Pine boughs and strawberry shampoo."

Rayna blushed, unable to speak.

"Are you getting settled in okay? I heard the guys were there earlier this week cleaning the woodstove and stacking logs. I guess your mother helped direct the operation."

She rolled her eyes. *Nothing stays a secret in this town for long.* Beaker looked unimpressed. "I know I'm lucky to have their support."

"Yeah, you are." He stirred his coffee. "So, what're your plans? I heard you're going to be spending a bit of time there. Writing. Are you hanging around here long?"

"A month, maybe two."

"Why isn't that surprising." He leaned back against the sofa.

What does that even mean? She didn't respond.

Dr. Allister smiled when she pushed the staff lounge door open, and three farmhands jumped to their feet and squared their shoulders, each trying to look bigger and more manly than the others.

"I understand you have a mare about to foal," she said in a breathy voice. The vet was striking, and a tiny figure for a profession that challenging. Everything she'd carried in quickly got stripped away as the farmhands emptied her hands and lead her into the breezeway.

Beaker drank the last of his coffee and sauntered to the door. "There's more in the pot if you want it." He winked, then disappeared into the breezeway.

Abandoned in the lounge, his comment looped through her mind: 'Why isn't that surprising?' Not only was she left staring at an almost full cup of coffee she'd never wanted, she had no one to share it with and a brainteaser she didn't need right before bed.

Chapter 24

Rayna swiveled in her desk chair as she grappled with the challenge of the white screen, and her future. For most, setting out to write a book was a pipe dream, but for Rayna, the stakes were higher. She had to finish it, and it had to be good. Being a Westcott meant there were no other options.

Early on, she'd decided not to put too much emphasis on the first draft. She knew with time she could polish and finesse her manuscript to life, and that mantra seemed to eliminate most of the pressure, but she had no back-up plan and a mountain of expectations bearing down on her. She envisioned the look of disappointment on her father's face if her plan to reinvent her career failed.

Rayna walked around the desk and stood closer to the window. The Jacksons were taking advantage of the sunshine and getting the house ready for winter, Trent storing the lawn furniture in the shed, and Charlotte, dressed in warm earth tones, transforming an empty planter into a basketball hoop for Quinn. With Trent watching her, Charlotte floated across the yard in a mid-length skirt, her long, chocolate brown hair tumbling over a winter-white waistcoat.

Rayna had a tough time admitting it, but Charlotte had no shortage of the *come-hither* gene, that mysterious quality that makes a man push a door open for a woman, and wipe ketchup off the corner of her mouth. And Charlotte's presence had become a constant reminder of the elusive chromosome Rayna knew she was missing. *Enough!* She walked away from the window and washed a sink-load of dishes.

When she returned to the laptop, Rayna had a glass of orange juice and a fresh outlook. Determined, her fingers struck the keypad with haste and confidence. She typed colorful phrases and long passages of absolute garbage, only to be followed by the rhythmic *tap-tap-tap* of the backspace key. After several attempts to crack her writer's block, she decided a notepad may be a better way to capture her thoughts. And she knew where to get one.

Chomping on a cookie, Rayna jumped into the truck and drove to the farm for supplies. She borrowed a couple of writing pads from her father's office, and an expensive rollerball pen that she convinced herself would do most of the work for her—in pressing the words against the paper, anyway.

"Hi, sweetie." Her mother set a pair of scissors on a table when Rayna walked into the sewing den.

"Can I watch?"

Her mother leaned into the center of a pool table-sized workbench. "Sure, I would love the company." She spread a tissue pattern piece over a sheet of midnight blue satin.

Rayna walked past a large cabinet bursting with multicolored bolts of fabric standing on end, side by side. Cardboard pattern cutouts and plastic dressmaking tools hung from cup hooks on a side wall, and three headless dress forms mingled in the corner, silent. They'd given Rayna the willies as a young girl. She wasn't sure how she felt about them, even now.

She sprawled out on a blue-and-rose plaid sofa that backed onto a wall of windows.

Throughout the years, Rayna had spent many memorable hours watching her mother toil over dress patterns. Sewing was a necessity for some, but no more than a way to while away the days for her mother. Rayna never tired of her back-in-the-day stories, and she often shared them when she was in the middle of a sewing project.

"Writer's block?"

Rayna tucked a cushion under her head. "Writing true crime

is easier. The story's there. You just have to get it on paper."

Tiny pins rattled in a plastic case as her mother withdrew them one by one. "Certainly does *sound* easier. If that's what you're looking for." She stuck a pin into a section of the pattern, creating a crackling tissue-and-satin sandwich.

"You love sewing, don't you, Mom?"

"I do," she said, smoothing the fabric. "Sometimes I have a design in mind and I'm on the hunt for the perfect fabric. Other times, a bolt of fabric inspires me to create a new dress from an old pattern." She straightened for a moment. "Oh, there are times I get stuck too. In that way, our passion is more similar than different. But I welcome the challenge. I work through it." She snapped the plastic pin box shut. "When I've completed a sewing project, it's often the details I've struggled with that bring a garment to life. And those design elements are often part of the outfits I'm most proud of."

Rayna joined her mother at the cutting table and ran her palm along the slippery fabric, admiring the crisp cut along the edge. "Nice work."

"If you look at most of the clothes I've sewn, you'll see that I never color too far outside of the lines." She slipped her fingers from the scissors, letting them drop to the table. "I experiment a little, but I stick with what I know."

"All I know lately is self-loathing, self-doubt, and□"

"Self-pity?" Her mother glanced up, briefly, then pinned another section together.

"Okay, I hear you."

"Let those emotions work for you. Color inside those lines."

"You make it sound easy." Rayna flipped through sewing patterns stored in an old trunk doubling as a coffee table. The colored drawings on the front of the packages were faded, but the styles on the willowy models were all classics. "Wow! Old. Do you still use any of these?"

Her mother squinted, looking across the room at the packages before continuing to wind the scissors along the edge of the tissue, snipping away at the fabric. One last cut and a block of satin in the shape of half a skirt fell away from the main sheet, pins and all. "Sure, I still use them." She gave Rayna a wry glance as she added, "But only when I'm looking for ... easy."

Her mother had a knack for bringing issues into sharp relief. She made perfect sense. Better yet, she made all things seem possible. Rayna tucked the patterns back into the trunk and bolted for the door. "The dress is going to be beautiful. Don't hold dinner." She dashed off to her room.

Breathless by the time she opened her closet door, she grabbed a shoe box from the top shelf. She removed a bundle of papers, held together with a piece of jute, and set it on the bed.

She eyed the stack of notepaper in the bottom of the box. It was tied up like a Christmas package, with burgundy satin ribbon crisscrossing the paper and knotted at the front. A novel, by Rayna Lynn Westcott, was scrawled across the front page in her signature combo of calligraphy and personal style. In anticipation she held the pages against her chest, surprised by the weight of the bundle. Rayna wasted no time getting back to Raspberry Cottage with her treasure.

* * *

She'd tossed carrot sticks, cauliflower, and a slice of cheese onto a petri dish and nibbled away as she swiveled in the creaky chair. A faint whistle of icy air seeped into the cabin from around the bay windows. She scurried to the thermostat and cranked up the heat. Without hesitating, she raced to the stove and quickly tossed some kindling and a small log on top of a stack of discarded pages she'd been editing. A wooden match struck the side of the stove and burst into flames before lighting up the inside of the stove. With her legs under a throw blanket, she huddled on the sofa, shivering, staring at the vague but familiar stack of pages from her past, soon to be part of her future.

Sage had reviewed the first half of the book a few years

before, and Rayna had her to thank for getting it finished. One minute, Sage was hounding her to get it done, and in what seemed like the next, Rayna watched in disbelief as she'd printed the complete first draft. With the excitement of the Christmas holidays just days away, she'd decided to put it aside until the new year. But the crushing news changed her plans, and it had been tucked away in the box ever since.

Five hundred and thirty was scribbled in the bottom-right corner. At a minimum, that was one hundred and thirty pages too many. She rubbed the silky ribbons and fiddled with the knot. Editing had never been her forte, but challenges were. She gathered a pillow from the bedroom, and a handful of sharpened pencils. She laid on the sofa with her legs tossed over the backrest and settled in for a long night of reading.

Rayna started with a glass of merlot, then rotated between hot coffee and an assortment of herbal teas. She stopped to make a sandwich or a snack, but for the most part she concentrated on getting the last page read by morning. Rayna dozed off from time to time but continued flipping through the pages the minute her eyes opened.

Most of the story had been committed to memory, but a good portion of the minor details had escaped her recollection. There were sections she had no awareness of writing and experienced the horrible composition anew. In the end, no amount of wine made reading it tolerable.

As the sun peeked through the blinds, Rayna deemed the story workable, and as the first ray of sunlight settled across the pond, Rayna closed her eyes and let the last sheet fall to the floor.

Rayna only slept until lunch. A quick shower revived her energy levels, and she went right to the sofa and fastened Chapter One to the clipboard. After a brief read of the first paragraph, she freed a red pencil from her teeth and scratched at the sheet. She marked "X" on sections to be deleted and circled phrases to be polished. She underlined words to be replaced, and curvy lines with arrows indicated sections to be moved—and to where. Within minutes the first page resembled a map to a pirate's chest. She tore the sheet off the stack and placed it facedown on the sofa beside her, then subjected the next page to the same ruthless treatment.

With the help of a full pot of coffee, Rayna cut through the manuscript at lightning speed, and the pile of edited pages began to grow. But when she thought about the daunting task ahead, she felt instant exhaustion.

She'd often listened to people in her field profess, 'I'm working on a book' or 'I'm almost finished my first draft.' The words started to make sense. In all likelihood her book would join the ranks of unfinished manuscripts, and like millions of others, never see a cover. *What are the chances?* Her mood sank at the thought.

Like a child to a jellybean Rayna had always been drawn to a blank page, both crisp white paper and a digital display. With renewed determination, she snapped another chapter to the clipboard and forged ahead, accepting the fact that one day she may abandon her publishing dream. *But it won't be today.*

Chapter 25

When Charlotte detected the pattern of the Westcott truck, arriving every day at lunch and leaving late in the evening, she struggled to accept her new reality. At times she'd get up to check Quinn in the night, only to spot it pulling out of the driveway in the wee hours of the morning. When it first started to appear, it would be gone by supper time. You could set your watch by it. Although she hadn't yet caught sight of the not-so-mysterious occupant, her Aunt Myra had been more than eager to inform her of Rayna's presence on the North Line when Charlotte arrived at Parchment Press.

"Thanks for coming in. I should be back in time to close." Her Aunt Myra put on her hat and scarf.

Charlotte took Quinn by the hand and led him to a small play table beside the cash register. The toddler was quick to get busy, thrilled with the new collection of toys that seemed a little familiar.

Myra pointed at Quinn. "I'm surprised you didn't make arrangements for him."

"He'll be fine." She turned away from her aunt and kneeled beside the table, watching Quinn alternate between toy cars and building blocks in rapid succession. A bell chimed as her aunt left the shop and a customer entered. Charlotte heaved a sigh of relief as the door closed behind Myra.

An elderly woman shuffled up to the counter clutching a handful of envelopes. "Postage for five local pieces of mail, please."

Charlotte tore a strip of five stamps off a roll and placed

them on the letters before dropping them into a tray behind the counter. "They won't leave here until tomorrow morning."

"That'll be fine." The customer leaned over the play table. "Aren't you a busy boy. Did you make the big castle by yourself?"

Quinn nodded.

"As we get older, we find children even more entertaining."

"Not everyone would agree."

The customer seemed confused. "I'm sorry, what did you say?"

"Nothing." Charlotte smiled. "Can I help you with anything else?"

"No, thank you, dear." She looked at the greeting cards on her way out.

An hour later Myra charged through the door. Anxious to leave, Charlotte quickly filled her in on any details she needed to know as she straightened up the toys. She didn't mind helping to cover the shop, but her aunt was such a toxic person she had a way of making Charlotte regret it.

The bitter woman's lack of warmth toward Quinn was a reminder of Charlotte's own depressing memories of being raised by her aunt. She'd never forget the day child protective services told her that her mother had been killed in a head-on collision after taking off on the back of a motorcycle for a three-day joyride. From the moment they left her on Myra's doorstep, Charlotte never received a fraction more than necessary from the ice-cold woman, emotionally or physically. Painful memories Charlotte tried never to relive.

* * *

Rayna's truck was idling in the driveway when Charlotte arrived home from Parchment Press. A gold light radiating from the bay window fizzled just before Rayna appeared on the porch. Charlotte hurried inside and watched from behind the lace curtains. Rayna drove by without looking at the house, marking the first time Charlotte witnessed her leave. She wondered if Rayna was as aware of *her,* as *she* was of Rayna. It seemed impossible not to be.

Charlotte settled Quinn in front of a box of toys in his bedroom. Watching him play with the blocks always amused her. One minute they were a castle, and the next a car. She marveled at the imagination of a two-year-old.

"Hello!" Trent called from the front hall.

Charlotte looked at Quinn with animation. "Oh, boy! Guess who's home?"

"Papa!" He dropped the bricks and headed for the stairs.

"Wait for Mommy, Quinn." She slowed his pace as he barrelled down the stairs, always leading with his left foot, one step at a time.

"There's Daddy's boy!" Trent scooped him up from the fourth step and flipped him up onto his wide shoulders while Quinn squealed. "What did you do today?"

"Nuttin'."

"You did nuttin'?" Trent looked at Charlotte and grinned. "I don't believe you." He hesitated. "Did you play with your toys?"

"I did it."

"Did you play with Shivers and Mommy?"

Quinn smiled. "I did it."

Trent lifted Quinn off his shoulders and held him upside down for a second before setting him on the floor. "And did you play in the yard?"

Quinn squealed and Trent flipped him right-side up and set him firmly on the floor.

"Papa!" Quinn laughed.

"You didn't do nuttin' then, did you?" Trent poked Quinn's tummy before dragging himself into the kitchen and pulling a cold beer from the fridge. He yawned and rolled his neck before snapping the cap off.

"You're exhausted." Charlotte rubbed her hand along his

back.

"Yeah, I am, and I have a charter tomorrow morning at seven." He pressed his palm to his mouth as he yawned. "I still have two hours of work tonight if I want to get the radio assembled. The team will need it Saturday."

Charlotte grabbed a dish from the cupboard. "Go ahead, I'll bring your dinner to the shed."

"Are you sure? I haven't spent much time with you two this week at all."

"Yes. It's fine. Go." Charlotte stirred a pot of gravy. "We've already eaten."

Trent picked Quinn up and tossed him into the air, catching him easily and setting him in the middle of his toys. "Be a good boy for Mommy."

ATVs, sleds, and even an airplane—Trent had all the toys. And she gave him as much freedom as he needed, the very demon she struggled with the most. Determined to keep him happy Charlotte spoiled him, and she was always attentive–in every way.

With a large fork, she piled baked chicken and potatoes onto a plate and watched Trent from the kitchen window while she waited for the gravy to boil. He bent to pick up a toy Shivers dropped in the middle of the lawn and tossed it under a tree. He was Gorgeous, even from a distance. The way he carried himself, the square shoulders—it always surprised her when she noticed it. He hesitated as he opened the shed door. *What did you forget?* She smiled. Charlotte then watched in disbelief as he looked toward Rayna's house, checked his watch, and disappeared into the shop.

She backed away from the window, as if she'd been hit by lightning. She wandered around the kitchen, frustrated at how powerless she felt. Rayna had always been the sole person Charlotte couldn't manipulate. Worse yet, Rayna had the ability to shift the ground under Charlotte's feet, and she hated anyone having that amount of control over her. Charlotte had too much to lose, and Rayna wasn't easily duped.

Before Rayna got too comfortable on the North Line, she needed to be gently persuaded to return to the big city. Charlotte decided she'd see to it that she did.

Chapter 26

Rayna stretched out on the sofa in her dedicated writing pose, a cushion under her head and her legs tossed over the back. It had taken a few weeks, but she'd mastered the positioning of the clipboard and had become quite adept at writing upside down with a pencil—the sharper the better.

She preferred writing longhand on a legal pad, then transcribing her notes onto the laptop, but after mastering both, she moved easily between the two. It didn't take her long to realize that with a laptop she could create, but with a pencil ... she could imagine.

There were times she considered writing to be pure torture and running back to the city seemed like a good plan. But she always managed to stay dedicated to finishing her story. Each day started with a simple goal, to *write*! She often worried about the quality of her story and wondered if she had what it took to get it done, but without hesitation she reminded herself that a story was just a thread of sentences, and she could write sentences. And she believed, in her core, she had the power to string together as many as her story needed.

She considered it a rare event when a wave of creativity hit between sunup and sundown. Inspired to write at night, she preferred to work later and later as time went on. There were days she woke on the sofa at lunch time after a late writing session. Her schedule was so erratic it produced the welcome consequence that no one expected her anywhere at any given time, and the independence appealed to her. A luxury living in the city had offered, yet it was the only thing she missed.

One night, when Rayna finished typing the last of her notes, she leaned back in the padded seat, listening to soft piano ballads interrupt the melodic squeak from the comfy chair. She could see the light glowing from the steel Quonset hut in the Jacksons' side yard. She wondered what Trent was working on at such a late hour. A few minutes passed before the shed light went off, leaving the property in darkness.

Rayna looked at her watch and decided to call it a night. She shut the computer down, switched off the lights, and locked the door on her way out. The fresh air blew through her hair as she walked to the truck, in no hurry to climb inside. She backed out of her driveway, positioning herself to survey the Jackson house. Her skin prickled with embarrassment when she spotted Trent sitting on the porch swing as she passed.

What's he doing outside this late? It's freezing!

Rayna remembered many an evening pulling in and out of his driveway at all hours, but now Charlotte waited for him inside.

Rayna's life had changed, and it made her appreciate the simple pleasures, like the sight of the stables as she approached the farm. She eyed the dimly lit buildings, mildly regretting her decision to stay so late at Raspberry Cottage. She enjoyed kibitzing with the guys in the evening. It was a welcome distraction from the pressure of finishing her novel and rethinking her choices in life.

When she arrived home, she went straight to the kitchen and poked around in the cupboards for a snack. "Oh! Raisin tea biscuits." She rolled one into a paper towel, poured a tall glass of milk to go with it, and headed for her room.

Most nights she didn't notice the light from the clock radio spilling into the hall from Cole's room—but on others, she did. The volume was set low when she turned the music on. While Rayna laid on the bed, watching the tiny planes twirl, she noticed the canister that held the house plans was nowhere to be seen. She wondered if her parents had finally opened it, curious to see the home their son had dreamed of building.

While Rayna walked around the room looking for the cylinder she stepped on a round object, which ricocheted out from under the toe of her slipper and flew across the room like a pinball. Startled, she set down her biscuit, clicked on the desk lamp, and looked around.

On her hands and knees, she put her cheek against the cool hardwood for a better look, the elusive item nowhere to be seen. She scanned the floor and looked under the bed, and all but gave up when something else came into view. A small, white box was sitting under the dresser, against the wall, tucked off to the side.

Rayna flattened her hand and slid it under the decorative arch at the base of the chest of drawers. She struggled to pull the box out through the opening, the back of her hand scraping the wooden edge until it cleared the tight space. Minutes seemed to pass by before she took the lid off exposing a black velvet case, and she dumped it onto her palm. Her fingers twitched and moved as though they belonged to someone else. Moments later, her breath caught in her chest when the spring popped the lid open, revealing a brilliant diamond ring tucked inside.

Sparkling regally against a black satin backdrop, a square-cut solitaire floated above a tiny gold band. It was a striking piece of ice, clear, luminous, and large by anyone's standard. She plucked the mysterious ring from the case and slid it onto her baby finger, the only one it fit. She blinked to the beat of her racing heart, and she tipped her hand toward the bedside lamp to enhance the shimmer.

Feeling like she'd been caught snooping through someone's pocket, she glanced behind her at the bedroom door. With Cole gone it didn't feel wrong, but technically it remained his room, his box … his pocket. As stunning as it was, the question remained. Why did Cole have an engagement ring? Hidden!

Rayna slid the box back under the dresser, but when she did, her arm grazed a tiny round object and she fumbled trying to grasp it. An acorn. She remembered spilling the jar and looked around to make sure there weren't any others lying about. After checking everywhere, she shut the radio off and left for Raspberry Cottage in a haze.

The next night, sitting in front of the laptop, Rayna couldn't stop thinking about the ring or concentrate on her story. The same questions swirled through her mind in an endless loop; was anyone else aware the ring existed? She wondered if she could figure out the answer without asking her parents outright. And, more important, she wondered if they didn't know—should they?

She couldn't understand why she felt so guilty. Had she breached Cole's privacy? She hadn't gone snooping or looking to see what she could find. It had just appeared to her. More puzzling was what it meant.

Cole had often said, 'I'll never bring home a girlfriend, only a future wife,' and he'd held to it. Secretive, she could never pry more out of him than he wanted her to know. Rayna hated that. Secrets were a burden. She always thought it was more work and stress to keep them than to come clean. To avoid them at all costs was her number-one rule.

Rayna forced herself to write, well aware the results would be worthy of the trash heap. The alternative was churning the mystery over relentlessly in her head. But, once she started writing, it surprised her how fast she pushed the event from her mind.

Before she knew it, the oven timer chimed 8:00 p.m. and her frozen pizza had filled the cottage with the scent of warmed oregano. A second glass of merlot helped to wash down her third slice and tamp down her imagination as well.

Ka-bang!

A loud thud stopped her in mid-stride as she crossed the kitchen. The cottage lights flickered, then disappeared completely.

Chapter 27

"Noooo!" Rayna rushed to the window to find the road cloaked in blackness. "Oh great! A power failure."

She worried how much of her writing she might've lost but remembered hitting the save button. She hadn't noticed a flashlight or candles when she'd been poking around. *Too dark to look for any now.* Rayna wandered around in the dark for another ten minutes, disappointed. She had no choice but to return to the main house.

Under her breath, she slipped out a couple of swear words, threw her coat on, then groped around, looking for the keys. She stopped to grab another slice of pizza, stubbing her toe on the leg of the sofa as she stumbled her way to the door, trying not to get sauce on her coat. Halfway to the driveway she remembered the second glass of wine. She couldn't leave; she couldn't drive. The worst swear word she could think of flew out of her mouth. She went back inside and set the pizza on the coffee table, balled her coat up, and hurled it across the room.

Moonlight streaked in through the half open blinds, making the center of the living room the brightest place in the house. But with no electricity, she had few ways to entertain herself until the effects of the wine wore off. She needed a plan if she was going to be stuck, in the dark.

She was starting to settle in when a flicker of light on the front lawn caught her attention. She moved to the window to investigate. A faint tapping came from the front door, and Rayna tripped across the room on her way to answer it.

"Trent!" She crossed her arms as the frigid air seeped in

through the holes in her open-knit sweater.

"Thought you might need one of these." Carrying two lanterns, he dangled one from the tip of his index finger and offered it to her.

She shivered. "Maybe I don't have to leave after all." Rayna rubbed her hands together with premature optimism and gratefully accepted the lantern.

He looked doubtful. "A transformer likely blew. It could be off for the rest of the night." He spun a small lever around at the base of the lantern. "This is how you keep it going, but you'll be cranking it every ten minutes."

She thought for a second. "You're right. I should still leave."

"That's probably a good idea." He pointed to his shed. "I was working away when the power went off. I noticed your lights were on earlier, but sometimes you're already gone by now. I thought I'd come check in case you were here later than usual. I'm glad I did."

He knows my routine. Was he even aware of how obvious his comments were? "Thank you for thinking of me, Trent." Her words seemed to hang there alone for a few seconds.

He backed down the stairs. "Did you want me to hang around until you're ready to leave?"

"Sure, if you think there's a lunatic hiding in the cord of wood, betting against all odds there'd be a power failure tonight."

"Everyone's different. Just an offer." He gestured to his house and grinned. "I don't think I've ever met a person more afraid of the dark than Charlotte."

Rayna winced at the random mention of her name.

"One night, I went to bed early. When I heard Charlotte coming up the stairs, I crawled under the bed." He grinned. "I knew she'd leave the lights off while she got changed. Anyway, while she fumbled around in the dark"—he reached out and snatched the air— "I grabbed her ankle." He laughed. "She lost it. I almost had to sleep on the couch she was so mad."

Ouch! A twinge of jealousy cut through Rayna. He'd played the same sort of tricks on her at one time, and now Charlotte was the lucky recipient of his playful antics. She wished he hadn't shared the private moment.

"Well, if you're okay." He walked toward the driveway. "Night, Rayna."

"Thanks again, Trent."

His lantern light glowed along the road, turned into his driveway, and moved up onto the porch. Then it was gone. Rayna sat in the wistful glow of her lantern, wondering *what if* he wasn't going home *to her*. When the effects of the wine wore off and she couldn't stand her own thoughts any longer, she left for the farm.

As she drove into the Westcott laneway, Beaker flashed his truck lights and playfully cut her off. They pulled close to one another and rolled their windows down.

"Hey, Brat." His eyes sparkled as he handed her a flashlight through the window. "I guess I'm too late."

Rayna tucked Trent's lantern close beside her, where he couldn't see it. "Were you on your way to the cottage?"

"Yeah. Coming to check on ya."

"Thank you, Beaker. I appreciate the gesture." What made him think of her? Surely, he had enough to do with the hydro off.

"I should get back. When the juice gets flowing again, every light in the place will be on. Your mom will be relieved to have you home safe and sound."

He pivoted behind her truck and followed her along the laneway, pulling off toward the stable while she continued on and parked in front of the porch.

Except for the house and the main barn, which both had back-up generators, the farm waited in darkness. Surrounding the front porch, a group of solar lights shone brightly, but the ambiance of the grounds was lost to the blackout.

Her mother met her at the door. "What've you got there?"

She slipped her finger into the ring at the top of the lantern and spun it around to get a better look.

"Isn't it sweet?" Rayna pushed the two ends of the chamber together. The tube in the middle collapsed and it turned into a flashlight. "If I pull the two ends apart, it exposes the glass tube again and it becomes a lantern. It's perfect when you want the light to shine all around the room as opposed to a single spot."

"What a handy little gadget. I don't remember seeing that anywhere at the cottage. Where did you find it?"

Rayna walked past her mother as she spoke. "Trent brought it over to me when the power failed."

"Oh." She followed Rayna into the kitchen. "How thoughtful of him."

"Yes, it was." Rayna stood by the kitchen window, twisting and smoothing a lock of hair as she stared at Beaker's truck parked in front of the main barn.

"I sent Beaker to see if you were okay. Did he make it there before you left?"

Rayna spun around to face her. "You *sent* Beaker?"

"Don't look so annoyed. Yes, you are quite capable of defending yourself, but I clearly remembered not seeing any emergency lighting in the cottage. You would've needed a flashlight if Trent hadn't come along."

Rayna stood by the kitchen window and stared into the blackness, able to hide her disappointment from her mother but not from herself. It made perfect sense that Beaker wouldn't have shown up on his own. What was she thinking?

Her mother slipped the strand of hair from between Rayna's fingers and unraveled the tiny knot with a look of concern. "How did Trent know you were there?"

"The truck in the yard, I guess." The kitchen became quiet, and within minutes Rayna headed for the stairs. "See you in the morning."

For the amount of time it took her to climb the stairs, she wondered why it bothered her that Beaker had only checked on her because he'd been asked to. And why had Trent felt the need to rescue her? She found it strange he knew she'd normally have been gone at that hour. With a tinge of frustration, she tried to push them from her mind.

Rayna chided herself for making such a big deal over Trent's visit. A neighborly courtesy, it meant nothing to Trent, or to her, for that matter. Yet, somehow, that little lantern had managed to spark a flicker of interest and illuminated more than just Raspberry Cottage.

* * *

The lantern sat on Rayna's kitchen table for the next week before she mustered the nerve to return it. If she were secretly hoping Trent would come by to collect it, he didn't. She knocked on the Jacksons screen door and Charlotte pulled the curtain aside, peeking out as the door opened.

"Rayna." She smoothed her hair and tucked it behind her ears, her shock evident.

She handed Charlotte the lantern. "I forgot I had this."

Charlotte looked puzzled as she took the lantern.

"It's the lantern Trent brought me." Charlotte's face remained blank. Rayna could tell that Charlotte had no idea Trent had made a trip over with the light. "When the power failed the other night." Rayna waited for a response. "I couldn't have managed without it."

"Of course. You're welcome." With a pasted-on smile, Charlotte pointed at Shivers. "Stay! Sit nice. Good boy."

"I'll let you get the door shut." Rayna pointed to Shivers. "He might bolt on you." She headed toward the stairs. "Tell Trent I said thank you." But when she looked over her shoulder to give Charlotte a quick wave, the door was shut.

She walked to the cottage, mulling over the trouble she'd likely caused for Trent. Rayna had the distinct feeling that, not only had there been a power failure, there'd been a communication failure, too.

Chapter 28

Tapping away at the keyboard, Rayna barely noticed the holiday season as it came and went. Strings of lights had appeared while her favorite carols blanketed the air waves, and before she knew it Christmas trees were springing up in every living room window. But, as swiftly as it arrived, it was gone.

She did notice the snow. It fell lightly at first, a few flakes here and there, then winter moved in hard on the countryside. Occasionally a blizzard would make a mess of the roads, creating hours of extra writing time, while planning the Winter Ball would wreak havoc on her timetable, subtracting just as many.

Lately, middle-of-the-night retreats to the homestead had become predictable events, but it was nice to have the glistening white snow caps lending unexpected light to the nighttime shadows. Walking across the driveway, Rayna fished through her purse for her keys as heavy flakes fell straight to the ground, in slow motion. From inside the cab of the truck it gave the strangest illusion, like the flecks of snow were suspended in the air and she was rising up through them. Not wanting the magic to end, Rayna begrudged having to pull away.

She turned the key several times, but her attempts were met with sputtering and choking sounds. The headlights faded and flickered each time Rayna tried to start the engine. In disbelief, she rotated the key one last time and held it as the motor ground to a whimper.

True to form, Rayna refused to give in until the key twisted left, then right, without producing a sound and the last ray of light flickered from the dash. *Great!* In frustration, she pulled the key from the ignition and threw herself against the back of the seat. White flakes stuck to the windows, burying the hood as she weighed her options.

A bright light flashed in the rearview mirror. She squinted as the beam became brighter and more intense. Rayna leaned toward the mirror before turning around to investigate. With her spine tingling, she stared at the headlights slowly coasting down the driveway behind her. It was late, and the prospects were alarming. Rayna's memories dragged her back to her nightmare in the taxi□and Darklend.

Within seconds the vehicle door slammed. Her breath caught in her throat as the mysterious figure moved in on her through the growing whiteout, the crunch of footsteps growing louder as they trudged along beside the truck. In one swift move, she hit the power locks and slid away from the driver's-side window. There were two quick clicks as someone pulled the handle against the locked door. Every sense heightened, Rayna was suddenly aware of the smell of gasoline, the cold seat, and the sound of her own beating heart pulsing in her ears. The imposing figure leaned down to look inside the cab.

"Rayna?"

What!? "Trent!" She threw her palm to her chest. "Oh gosh!" She took a deep breath and rolled the driver's-side window down. "You scared me half to death."

He pointed with his thumb. "I was leaving the shed. I could hear the engine trying to start." He smiled with amusement.

Rayna sat quietly, trying to pull herself back from a not-too-distant memory.

He cocked his head to the side. "Are you okay?"

"I'm fine." She forced her lips into a tight smile.

Before she could move, he reached through the window, brushing past her knee as he pulled the hood release under the dash. She could smell the new leather from his black flight jacket. Covered in zippers, it donned no less than three gold-embossed flying insignia, and a silver pin with eagle wings gleamed on the lapel.

He gestured toward the cottage. "Wait inside where it's warm."

"I'm fine." She wrestled with her anxiety. *Stay calm, Rayna. You don't want to look like an idiot.*

He removed a penlight from a tiny pocket on his sleeve then disappeared under the hood. The spotlight flickered in the darkness, illuminating various flecks of snow. She soon found herself melting into the seat, enjoying the unexpected light show.

"Is it flooded?"

"That's your best guess?" He laughed. "I hope you're using a little more imagination to write your book."

"How did you know I was writing a book?"

Trent stepped to the side of the truck and shot her a look of dismay. "It's hard to keep a secret in a small town." He went back to work under the hood.

"True."

He rocked the truck as he banged around then reappeared with a skiff of white snow melting into his dark hair. He motioned for her to slide over, and she moved to the middle of the seat. He jumped in behind the wheel, right next to her. After a couple long groans, the engine started. They faced each other, silent, the heady scent of leather inviting her to be reckless.

"A frayed wire," he said with an air of satisfaction. "It'll get you home safe, but have it looked at tomorrow."

When he stepped onto the driveway, she worked her way back behind the wheel. "Thanks, Trent."

"No problem. I'm glad I heard the truck sputtering. Worst-case scenario, you would've had to spend two nights in a row here."

Surprised he knew she'd slept there the prior evening, she stared at him for a moment as she wondered what else he might be aware of.

He looked at her, puzzled. "What?"

"Trent …" How could she ask him about Cole's life? And

she certainly couldn't mention the ring. She shivered. "Was Cole seeing anyone around the time of the accident?" She trembled, more from relief than the frigid air.

"Whoa!" His eyes widened. "That was random." He looked toward his house and began to fidget with the zippers on his jacket. "Samantha Granderville. They were definitely getting serious again." He waited. "Where's all this coming from?"

"I've been wondering about things lately—no special reason." She searched his face to see if she'd given away any details. "There are a few things I'd like to ask you." She squeezed the steering wheel. "But … it seems we're not allowed to talk." She forced a smile. "It makes people more comfortable when we pretend not to know each other."

His face softened as he pulled his gloves from his pocket. "Ask me whatever, but another time." He touched her cheek with his gloves. "You're shivering. You better get home with this rig." He tapped the driver's-side door, then followed his tracks back to his Jeep.

Rayna clicked on the wipers and scanned the cottage as she backed up behind him. A single black glove was lying on top of the, freshly fallen snow, and she hopped out to retrieve it. Trent's taillights were turning into his yard by the time she climbed back into the truck and sped after him. She skidded along the roadway and stopped across the end of his drive. Rayna stepped from the truck, laughing as she waved the glove in the air.

"Thanks, I was about to check the floor." He moved toward the truck, meeting her halfway, and she handed him the glove.

"This stuff is slick." Sliding around, she waved goodnight on her way back to the truck.

Poof!

Rayna froze when a snowball exploded on the back of her cloth jacket. She stuck her hands into the snow and spun around to return fire, but it was too late. Already reloaded, Trent wore a grin that promised retribution.

Her joy ended abruptly when she caught sight of Charlotte's silhouette in the upstairs window. She was wearing a long, white nightgown, like a ghost. The exact moment Rayna spotted her Charlotte stepped forward, almost in defiance. *Strange.* Rayna's departure seemed all the more urgent. She dropped the snowball and climbed back into Blue.

He threw a second shot, which burst against the driver's-side door. "Careful driving home," he shouted as she backed onto the road.

As innocent as it looked, Rayna still felt like she'd been caught doing something despicable. *What must Charlotte be thinking?* She tried to justify it in her head, certain Trent would be forced to explain it when he got in the house. Charlotte had always been insecure; on the jealous side would be more accurate. Rayna cringed at the thought.

A steady stream of flakes barreled into the windshield. She squinted to see past the hood of the truck and follow the road. To make matters worse, she couldn't remember ever leaving the cottage feeling so tired. Emotionally drained and anxious to get home, Rayna had an awful feeling her misadventure with Trent and Charlotte would guarantee her at least one sleepless night.

Chapter 29

Before Trent reached the top stair, Charlotte rushed back under the covers. She grabbed a paperback off the nightstand and pretended she was reading when he crept into the room.

"I thought you'd be asleep."

She smiled. "Liar. You knew I'd be awake." She tossed the book onto the bed beside her. "How was your flight?"

"Long." He slipped his shirt over his head. "I'm beat."

"I wish you didn't have to fly when the weather is so unpredictable."

"And I wish you wouldn't worry about me. I didn't start flying yesterday. He yawned as he tossed his clothes across the bench at the foot of the bed. "I've been home for a while. The parts came in for the radio. I spent the last hour in the shed putting it back together."

Charlotte waited for him to mention Rayna, but within minutes he'd fallen asleep. She pulled the blankets over his shoulders and switched off the lamp. White pellets swirled and tapped at the bedroom window while a series of questions swirled around in her head.

The next morning, Trent had his back to Charlotte while he played with Quinn and tussled with Shivers on the living room floor.

"I hope you and Rayna enjoyed your snowball fight."

Trent stiffened. He handed Quinn a metal car and got up from the floor. He waited until he stood directly in front of her before answering.

"Leaving the shed I could hear her truck groaning. It

wouldn't start." He tucked his hands into his front pockets. "I drove over because I thought she needed a boost, but it was a frayed wire. I dropped my glove in her driveway. She left at the same time, saw the glove, and—"

"Why didn't you tell me?"

He paused. "It didn't seem like a big deal. Hardly worth mentioning."

"And the lantern? Not worth mentioning either?" She stomped into the kitchen.

Trent followed her. He leaned back against the counter, with his hands resting on the edge and his ankles crossed. "You get ticked when her name is mentioned. It didn't seem important. I didn't want to ruin your night."

"Maybe you didn't want to ruin *your* night." She shook her head in protest. "No. If you didn't want to upset me, you wouldn't have made two trips to her house in less than a month and not told me about either." She paced between the table and sink, dropping dishes into a bath of sudsy water as she ranted.

"Rayna dropped off the lantern a few days later, and she could tell by the look on my face I knew nothing about it." She huffed as she continued to load the sink. "Humiliating!"

He smiled as he prepared his usual charm offensive, and when Charlotte moved within arm's length Trent pulled her in.

"No!" She tugged away in protest.

"Listen to me. If you were here alone and the lights went out, wouldn't you appreciate it if a neighbor brought you a lantern? I'd want someone to help you and Quinn. That's all there was to it."

She searched his face for the truth. "If I hadn't seen it with my own eyes, I still wouldn't have a clue. It makes me second-guess us … and it hurts. Watching the two of you horsing around in the driveway made me wonder what else I might have missed." She huffed.

He squeezed Charlotte's hand. "The house was left to her. She could very well move in permanently and there's not much we could do about it. But, from now on … if I have any contact with her, I'll tell you right away." He leaned back from her, waiting for approval before nuzzling his face into her neck.

She sighed in frustration, slowly giving in to his powers of persuasion. *Why did it have to be her?*

"We okay?"

Charlotte nodded. But inside, she wondered.

Chapter 30

Once her mother received news of Rayna being stranded in the driveway, she'd insisted on installing exterior lights at the front and back of the cottage. They were on motion sensors, and if it happened to be windy the blowing branches would trigger the lights. The guys had made a dozen trips to the cottage to adjust the sensitivity level, but they kept her awake on and off for a week.

Early winter passed as Rayna whiled away the time tucked inside Raspberry Cottage, writing. Her novel was an all-consuming task. There were days Rayna worried she lacked the resilience needed to see it through. Then, one morning, gauging her progress, she realized she'd transitioned into a full-time writer. Her schedule had followed the same unremarkable path. At first, she'd leave the cottage later and later, but soon started falling asleep on the sofa. Eventually, she climbed into Gramma Westcott's lumpy bed if she was too tired to drive home, or when she'd indulged in a second glass of merlot. But this would be the first evening she'd planned on spending the night.

The printer spewed page after page, and she grabbed the first sheet and read it on the way to the kitchen. She made a cup of tea with one hand without spilling a drop, then set the paper on the counter while she buttered two slices of rye toast and piled them with tomato slices. With a satisfied smile, she stood in front of the counter, enjoying the sandwich, letting the crumbs fall into the sink while she finished reading the page.

Standing between the side of the desk and the window, sipping chai tea, she noticed the Jacksons shed light beaming across the lawn, and again she found herself wondering what Trent worked on until all hours. He seemed to be spending more and more time in the shed. Arriving home from the airport at 6:00 p.m., he'd be in there working an hour later. Charlotte had always been so needy; she couldn't possibly be happy in the role of shop widow. Their presence seemed to loom large in Rayna's life. She didn't understand it, or like it.

With that thought, Trent's silhouette appeared in the shed window. She hastily stepped back from the glass, but he was already aware of her presence. Facing each other, with nothing between them except the North Line, his hand slowly came up to greet her.

"Oh boy!" Reluctantly, she raised her hand in return. *This is awkward.*

It was her own fault. She sat in the window half the night with the curtains open, and she was guilty of watching them on occasion. She blamed it on boredom, but often wondered if she was just plain jealous. *Stop making something out of nothing!*

She stared at his outline, hating herself. With a tinge of shame, she clicked off the desk lamp. Within seconds, the shed went dark.

Fighting a bout of nostalgia, Rayna flipped through the remaining pages from the printer tray and added them to one of the growing stacks on the corner of the desk. She clicked the rest of the lights off on her way to the teeny back bedroom.

The double bed seemed tiny, its sagging springs becoming more evident each day. She thrashed around, pulling the chenille spread up under her chin and shivering as the cold blankets touched her bare skin. A hard wind whistled as it blew in around the windows, reminding her to hang heavier drapes. She was beginning to understand why her ancestors wore flannel pajamas and bed socks as she flipped from one side to the other, trying to get warm. As her top shoulder cooled she rolled onto it, burying her chilly side into the warm spot she'd created. She maintained the cycle half the night until she finally accepted that she'd have to get out of bed if she wanted to get any sleep at all.

The cottage sat directly on a slab of cement, which explained the stone-cold floors. She dipped her ice-cold feet straight into her slippers and made a mad dash to the thermostat. She put on a sweatshirt and socks before diving back under the covers in search of the warm spot. As she lay there, she debated how many extra blankets to gather from the house, agonized over story details, and thought about the ring.

She was determined to avoid distractions. Her story was already giving her a few challenges, and the fast-approaching Winter Ball threatened to rob her of the precious time she needed to finish. Her mind raced as she prepared to set her writing aside for the busy week ahead. Solving the mystery of the ring would have to wait.

How long could it sit there undetected? Did she have an obligation to tell her parents their son may have been considering marriage when their world had literally come crashing down? Samantha Granderville didn't strike her as the quiet, dutiful daughter-in-law her parents had dreamed of. They wouldn't have been impressed. *Charlotte would have been devastated.*

Rayna had little doubt no one else was aware the ring existed. For all she knew, the ring could've been bought years ago for Samantha, prior to Cole joining the service. She found it disappointing to accept how little she knew about her brother's life. Would it be unreasonable to contact Samantha? *Trent knows more than he's saying.* Rayna needed answers, and to do that she had to get Trent alone.

Chapter 31

Balancing Quinn on her hip, Charlotte trudged through the six inches of snow that had fallen during the night. She had one eye on the slippery driveway and the other on Raspberry Cottage, where movers were unloading a new box spring and mattress. Rayna had been spending most of her time at the cottage. It came as no surprise, but it was still worrisome.

"Ride to Papa," Quinn repeated, his red boots kicking the back of the front seat as Charlotte strapped him into his car seat.

"Yes, we're going to see Papa." She pulled his mittens over his teeny white wrists. "Mommy has to clean the snow off the car. You keep these on."

Charlotte jumped into the driver's side and started the car. She opened the vents and cranked the heat on full, making a silly face to amuse Quinn before grabbing the scraper and closing the door. Several inches of the white stuff covered the car from front to back. Packing snow, the stuff kids prayed for when they wanted to build a snowman and the kind most people dreaded when they had to shovel it.

She scraped every window but struggled to move the heavy load off the hood and roof. Charlotte brushed the headlights, then walked around to the rear of the car and cleaned the taillights. She pushed the last pile off the hood of the car and decided to let gravity do the rest. She leaned against the trunk to catch her breath. The fresh, cool air was exhilarating.

She climbed into the car and dropped the scraper over the headrest. "Do you want to see the airplanes?"

"Da big one!" Quinn threw both arms in the air, clapping.

She tried to throw her hands up, but the shoveling had turned her arms into wet dish rags. She looked over the seat and smiled. "Yes, the big one."

She backed onto the road, where she had a clear view of Rayna sitting on the front porch railing, laughing with the delivery drivers as Charlotte drove past. Both women stole a glance while pretending to ignore the other. Rayna looked so happy and carefree, Charlotte wondered what her life was really like—and how long she planned to stay on the North Line.

"Happy day!" Quinn squealed. "Happy day, Mommy?"

Seeing the new furniture going into the cottage made her sick with worry, but for Quinn's sake she tried to play along. "Yes, Quinn … it's a happy day."

Chapter 32

Rayna had Raspberry Cottage within sight when she spotted Harland's flatbed nose-deep in the ditch, with snow piled two feet high against the front grill. She sped up, then hit the brakes to slow down. The pavement didn't seem slippery, but if he'd driven off the road, odds were good she could find herself in there with him.

He had managed to crack a hydro pole, but it was otherwise intact, the wooden standard sunk into the crumpled metal of the passenger's-side door. Harland was banging on the steering wheel as she lowered herself into the gully, a trickle of blood running from his lips. A case of smashed beer bottles sat on the passenger floor, and he started to lift the broken bottles out one at time, looking for anything salvageable. Shards of glass pierced his hands as he dug through the box.

"Go away!" he yelled, in a hateful tone, through the closed windows.

"Harland, I'm going to get help."

She motioned for him to wind the window down, but he paid no attention and tamped on the gas pedal, rocking dangerously toward her. She climbed up onto the pavement, his swearing still audible from twenty feet away. Rayna scanned the Jackson driveway. Empty.

"Go away! I don't need anyone's help, especially not from a damn Westcott!"

"It's going to be fine, Harland. We'll get you out."

Rayna made a mad dash for the cottage and slammed against the door before the knob had fully turned, causing the door to explode open. She grabbed the cell phone off the kitchen counter and scrolled through the numbers.

"Daddy," she gasped, "Harland's gone off the road a few hundred feet west of the cottage. I think he's okay, but there's blood trickling from the corner of his mouth … and plenty of swear words. He's more mad than anything."

"Don't go near him. I'll be right there."

Within minutes, her father rolled up with Beaker. Harland was as miserable as humanly possible, a madman stomping on the gas petal, and it escalated when her father showed up.

"Damn it. Go away. I told ya!"

Beaker leaned his head toward the, now open, passenger window then walked to where they were standing. "Denver, the inside of the cab reeks of alcohol. He's drunk."

The group moved off beyond earshot of Harland.

"Lucky he was drinking." Denver shook his head in frustration. "He likely bounced around the inside of the cab. If he'd seen what was coming, he probably would've braced himself and really gotten hurt."

"Go home! I don't need your help, I said!"

"We should call Buck." Her father scrolled through his phone contacts and prepared to dial.

"No!" Rayna put her hand over the phone.

He looked at the truck buried in the snow and pointed to the broken hydro pole. "Sweetheart, we need to report this."

"No! We can't. It's Harland, Daddy."

He put his arm around her. "The pole is snapped, and it isn't going to fix itself. It might not be safe to leave it."

"Daddy, don't you see? Look at him! He doesn't need any more trouble. Haven't you hurt Harland enough?"

Her father's eyes narrowed, and he turned away from her without saying a word. He assessed the truck while Harland continued to rev the engine, trying to break free.

Rayna barely registered the words she'd blurted in frustration. "Let's just tow him home. No one will be the wiser.

We can notify the township after."

"It's your call, Denver." Beaker tucked his hands into his front coat pockets and waited for a decision.

Her father inspected the poll, scanning the hydro lines.

She could tell by his silence she was winning the argument. "Trent and Charlotte can convince him later to get checked. We can only do so much." She looked at Beaker for support.

Denver walked to the rear bumper, jutting out from ditch. He looked at Beaker and jerked his head in the direction of his Suburban. "Grab the chain."

The flatbed bounced as they hauled it up and onto the road. Harland gave a spiteful nod of appreciation, slinking away with his front bumper dragging on the road and a trail of green fluid following him. They watched until he safely drove into the Christmas tree farm.

Denver folded his arms across his chest. "I make a point of never going by his farm. It's painful to watch." He shook his head.

"I know, it's a dump." Rayna added.

"It's not the mess," her father added. "Harland's not managing the farm. The entire east lot is vacant for as far as the eye can see. Nothing but stumps."

"What does that mean?" Rayna asked, confused.

Beaker sighed before answering. "He's selling off the mature Christmas trees and not replanting."

"And?" She raised her palms, confused.

Beaker looked at Denver before continuing. "It's a little short-sighted. When they're gone … he'll be broke. That'll give him even more reason to drink."

Denver picked up the chain. "That's *why* he's drinking."

"Sorry, Daddy. I feel so bad for him. He's broken." Rayna's heart sunk when her father huffed and turned his back on her.

Beaker pulled out his phone. "I got it." He dialed a number, his eyes shifting between Rayna and her father while he waited for the township to answer. "Yeah, there's a busted hydro pole on the North Line, a half mile west of Hudson Road. Someone's gone off the road here." He gave a shifty smile and winked at Rayna. "They've already hauled their vehicle away. The tracks are pretty fresh."

"Thank you." Rayna mouthed the words.

Beaker smiled, and his eyes widened as he pointed to the trail of green antifreeze leading right into the Jacksons driveway.

She was grateful for Beaker. He had a way of keeping the mood light, and he could handle her father in a way no one else could.

Beaker closed the back of the Suburban. "We should get out of here. It won't take the township long to show up."

Her father was clearly shaken, his face bathed in regret as he spoke under his breath. "You're right."

Rayna wondered if he was referring to her comment, or Beaker's. But later, when Rayna visited the barn, her father hastily made his way to his office without as much as smile. Rayna was left abandoned in the breezeway, regretting her words.

Chapter 33

As predicted, the last week of February blew frigid cold, and with the Winter Ball upon them, the appointments started early Monday. Rayna and her mother left for the hangar after breakfast, arriving on schedule to meet with the decorator.

"There's Eldon."

Her mother pointed. He was easy to spot in a charcoal suit and plum shirt, no tie. The front fabric of his jacket flashed around while he shouted instructions.

"Larissa, we do have work ahead of us." He slid his foot sideways across the shiny cement floor. "How did you get this floor so shiny?"

"It's beautiful, isn't it?" She beamed with pride. "I had them give it a second coat of glaze. I want the hangar to be perfect."

"And it will be." Carrying a cell phone that chirped non-stop, Eldon motioned for them to follow him. "Come see."

Rayna grabbed her mother's hand and squeezed it. "Watch your step."

Eldon pointed to a network of extension cords slithering between the containers. With professional ease, he guided them through the maze of boxes and trunks piled sky-high in the center of the building.

The contents of each case were identified with heavy black marker. One stack read place setting/dishes, and another simply read linen. There were boxes marked fairy lights, and others with orange tape around them stamped fragile. Long bolts of white chiffon were sticking out of the taller boxes, the shimmering fabric visible under the clear protective wrap. Round folding tables were tilted against the wall, and rows of stacked chairs ensured they stayed there.

Only one recognizable object remained in the hangar, the Lancaster Bomber. Set in the corner at one end of the building, no less than three men were crawling on it, polishing chrome and cleaning glass gun turrets. With the restoration almost complete, unless you were a mechanic, you'd never guess the impressive machine wasn't air-worthy.

Trent stole the occasional glance from the cockpit as she moved around the hangar. He flashed his hand as she walked closer to the bomber, and she gave a playful salute before disappearing under one of the massive wings.

Eldon reviewed every last detail with them, and when they'd finalized the placement of the last chandelier they headed to the farm for a late lunch. Most of the week would be consumed with details related to the fundraiser, and Rayna needed every minute she could get to concentrate on her writing. When Charlotte offered to help her mother tie up any loose ends after the event, it came as a welcome relief for Rayna.

Back at the homestead, Rayna brushed past her mother when she glimpsed the cardboard cylinder on the kitchen table. "Have you and Daddy finally looked at these?"

"Yes. The other day." Her mother clasped her hands behind her back and peered over Rayna's shoulder as the contents slid from the barrel and onto the table.

Rayna fought the large sheets, smoothing them flat as they tried to roll back on themselves. "This is going to be interesting." She grabbed a nearby fruit bowl and set it on the corner to keep the plans from curling. The blueprints were intricate, but to her surprise, uncomplicated. She marveled at the floor plans, as layers of detail were added in with each subsequent sheet.

The house was post-and-beam construction, and the design utilized the largest timbers around the front, making it look even more impressive. A high arch directed the attention to a palatial window above the double-door entranceway. Exposed timbers framed the inside of the building, and the open-concept design featured a grand loft overlooking a center great room. Along the back, a floor-to-ceiling stone fireplace would be flanked by walls of glass to enhance the view.

The blue drawings confirmed Cole's dream home would never make it farther than the kitchen table. Rayna had a sudden image of Cole hosting family Scrabble night in the great room. And quibbling over tiles and who's turn it was to make coffee; never his, of course.

"Strange. I feel like I've been in this house." Rayna flipped the pages.

"He described it so often throughout the years." Her mother bit the inside of her lip. "Do you remember the model home he made?"

"Clothes pegs and popsicle sticks. Oh, I remember." Rayna rolled her eyes. "I had to listen to him explain mortise and tenon joints no less than ten times."

Her mother pointed to the blueprints. "So, you understand how the beams are able to hold this building up?"

"No! Not at all. I only pretended to listen."

"Rayna," her mother chided, with mild disappointment.

"Oh, Mom." She smirked. "He kind of went on and on explaining it." With her heart aching, she continued to skim the plans. "Now I'd walk barefoot for a mile on flaming hot tarmac to listen to him explain mortise and tenon joints, for the hundredth time. Even then it wouldn't be enough."

Her mother walked to the window. "Your father did a few calculations." She inhaled deeply. "The house would've sat at the top of the knoll on the east paddy." She pointed to the far corner of the property. "Because Lone Pine is higher, you probably would have seen the smoke rising from the chimney …" She looked at the floor before looking back toward the knoll. She carefully stepped to the left. "If you stood … *right here*."

Rayna spun the blueprints into a tight roll and faced the window. They stood quietly, processing her mother's depiction. Unable to bear it, seconds later she turned away.

"Your father told me the two of you had words when he went to help Harland."

"Mom, please don't worry. I'll talk to him." Rayna knew she had to apologize to her father. Even though no explanation existed that was capable of unwinding the hurt she'd caused.

"Your father knows about loss. And, unlike Harland, he didn't lose a prized horse or a piece of land□he lost a son." She took the blueprints from Rayna and fed them into the cardboard tube.

"Mom, trust me to handle this. Please."

Her mother smiled and sunk her fingers into Rayna's wild locks. "I like your hair." She smiled.

"You do?"

"Yes. Very much." She fluffed the loose curls. "You haven't worn it that way in a very long time." There was a sadness on her mother's face, as if she was counting the years that had passed.

"Don't worry, I'll talk to him. Soon—I promise." She twisted a curly strand of hair around her finger and coaxed it into a knot. "Did Daddy comment on the plans?"

Her mother closed her eyes and tightened her lips. "I can tell you his exact words. 'It would have been a beautiful home.'" She hesitated and took a deep breath, adding, "'Lone Pine is the nicest parcel of land on this property.'"

A growing lump formed in Rayna's throat. In silence, she stared at the corner of the property, trying to imagine a trail of smoke rising in the distance, wondering how she'd ever set things right with her father.

Chapter 34

The evening before the Winter Ball, the Westcotts descended on the airport for a final inspection. Like walking onto a movie set for a fairy-tale wedding, the decorations did not disappoint. Except for the Lancaster, the hangar was unrecognizable.

From floor to ceiling, the walls were draped with tiny fairy lights, trapped between two layers of sparkling white chiffon. Matching panels cascaded down as they stretched across the ceiling from corner to corner, gathered in the center by an impressive silver candelabra—grand in size and dripping with crystals. Modest pendants, by comparison, floated on invisible wire above each table and dotted the ceiling surrounding the main chandelier.

Two-foot high, glass Eiffel Tower-centerpieces prominently donned each table, with metallic twigs, white roses, and calla lilies shooting another three feet skyward from the top. The arrangements were wispy and dramatic, sitting in a shallow, glass tray of water, with a dozen floating candles circling the lavish display.

But the Lancaster Bomber was the crown jewel. Positioned crosswise in the corner on a sheet of jet-black plexiglass that would double as a dance floor. A fine string of lights twinkled where the sheet met the floor. The cockpit lights were on, so too were the dim red-and-green directional indicators and soft landing lights. A faint search beacon drifted slowly across the bomber, strictly for effect. Above the aircraft, a silkscreen mural depicting a night sky hung cornerwise, backlit for drama. Under the bomber's bay doors there were three standard-issue World

War II air force uniforms proudly displayed on mannequins. They represented an American pilot, Canadian navigator, and British gunner. The thought-provoking vignette was a reminder of their collective effort, as well as the loss and heroism of the times.

With the ball destined to be magical, they could go home and enjoy a well-deserved sleep, confident the arrangements were all in place. Eldon had brought her mother's vision to life, and they were one step closer to making Cole's dream a reality.

* * *

On the evening of the gala, a powerful search beacon streaked across the moonless sky, its sharp beam cutting the darkness and directing those aloft and afoot to the quaint Talsburg airport.

In the spirit of the event, many well-to-do guests flew in for the occasion and the tarmac became a showcase for slick, high-end aircraft. Other celebrities and government dignitaries arrived by limo, stepping onto a red carpet in front of the side door. Men in equally refined apparel greeted guests and relieved them of their coats, and a select few were escorted directly to their tables. Elite donors meandered around—the men in tuxedos, the women in fancy ballgowns draped with diamonds. A modest orchestra teased new life into forgotten favorites, their mellow tones creating an aura of grandeur.

It was the must-attend gala of the year. An event so aristocratic, you had to be born into extreme wealth or power to get an invite. But, for a select few, where the money wasn't quite as old, what their lack of noble breeding couldn't buy a hefty donation could.

"This is our table, here." Rayna set her silver clutch in front of her plate and Sage did the same.

Mark scanned the room, his jaw dropping each time he caught site of the bomber. "Holy crap! I've always dreamed of flying a massive plane."

"Keep dreaming, babe." Sage patted his shoulder. "This place looks spectacular. The tables are incredible." She pointed. "Oh. Here comes your mom."

"Sage, Mark, thank you for coming." Her mother leaned in and kissed them on the cheek.

Sage circled her, cooing. "Mom, you look amazing."

Her floor-length satin gown looked nothing like the cutouts Rayna had last viewed on the sewing table. Designed in a striking shade of midnight blue, with a velvet, empire waistband, it had a bateau neckline and flared at the bottom, with a hint of a sweep train.

"Thank you." She touched the diamond-and-sapphire choker, her white gloves reaching her elbow. "And you look beautiful. She eyed Sage's mulberry tuxedo. It matches the highlights in your hair." She looked at Mark. "Doesn't your wife look extra lovely?"

"She most certainly does." He put his arm around Sage with a proud look on his face, fidgeting with his tie and lapel, making sure he measured up. "I think we need a glass of liquid courage. Champagne anyone?" He looked around for the bar. "Excuse me, ladies."

Her mother wandered in amongst the guests, chatting and kissing cheeks.

Sage bubbled with excitement. "That teal green velvet looks so striking on you. Wow! You haven't worn that color in years and off the shoulder . . . ooh la la."

Rayna blushed. "Sage, you look sharp!"

"Why, thank you. I'm so thrilled that you invited us."

"You weren't invited. You're family. It's your duty to be here."

"You're the best friend ever." Sage pulled her in for a hug. "Oh, guess who just walked in?" Rayna tried to move but Sage hung on tight. "No, no," she fired off, "don't turn around! She's looking this way."

"Charlotte and Trent?" Rayna's breath hitched in her chest.

Sage rolled her eyes as she watched them over Rayna's shoulder. "Why am I even shocked?"

"Let me have it. What's she got on?" Rayna braced for the upsetting details.

Sage bit the inside of her cheek, casting Rayna a sympathetic look. "You're not going to like it."

"Tell me." She huffed in anticipation.

"A skin-tight, nude gown. And it shimmers with a hint of diamond dust. Wait until you see her. She's all curves."

"Of course," Rayna threw her hands in the air. "Heaven forbid the decorations sparkle more than she does."

Sage shook her head. "It looks like she's not wearing anything. I bet you're the only person in the room not looking at her right now."

Rayna tried to catch a peripheral glance, but Trent kept getting in between them. When she finally caught a peek, her disappointment was obvious. *Typical Charlotte.* "I swear, she always manages to make everything about her."

"I'm so upset for you?" Sage frowned.

Rayna stared at Charlotte. "Seriously … that's the best you got?" She winked at Sage and faked a smile before shifting her gaze to the floor as her shoulders dropped. "I don't understand why she gets to me."

"Rayna, it's not complicated. You still have feelings for Trent. Charlotte should have kept her distance. Given you and Trent the time and space to see if you were able to work things out. You didn't get the closure you needed. She made the decision *for* you."

Without question, seeing Charlotte had become a trigger for Rayna. It made her rethink a few of her choices, and her feelings for Trent, which were *not* easily deciphered. Yes, she missed him. Trent had been a major part of her entire world. Of course she'd felt the void when he'd clipped her from his life. But, deep inside, she knew her discontent had little to do with Charlotte.

Rayna tuned back in as Sage's pep talk continued.

"—and you look glamorous, Binderella over there looks like trash." She rolled her eyes. "Only Charlotte would wear a slutty wrapper to a fancy gala. She's a mother, for heaven's sake. Doesn't she care what people think?"

"No, she doesn't look trashy, and don't call her that."

"Sorry. But you're too nice."

Rayna placed her hand on her stomach as she sucked it in. "I couldn't squeeze into that dress, and I've never had a kid."

"I never could've pulled off that number, either." Sage frowned. "And you need a good reason to wear cling wrap."

"Yeah, like having curves in all the right places." Rayna shook her head.

"Here comes hubby, empty-handed."

"Our drinks are on the table, ladies."

Sage took his hand in hers. "Do you see anyone you recognize, babe?"

"No. Not a single person." He seemed surprised.

"Of course, you wouldn't. You spend your days with criminals. These people are way out of our league." Sage kissed his cheek. "Oh! I love this song." With a modest amount of coaxing, she dragged him onto the plexiglass.

Rayna watched as Trent swirled Charlotte around the dance floor, with his arm draped around her tiny waist, their movements effortless. She pictured them waltzing around in their kitchen. She'd heard of husbands and wives dancing at home while a pot roast simmered in the oven. They were an attractive pair. As Rayna looked around the room, she could tell they'd captured the attention of a few spectators. She hated herself for letting it bother her.

Rayna mingled with guests, constantly aware of the couple's presence. To her annoyance, Trent looked her way several times but never acknowledged her. *Charlotte's so insecure, he's probably been given some rules.* Rayna knew she was the bane of Charlotte, but oddly enough, at some point, Charlotte had become hers. She wondered how that had happened.

During the event she caught glimpses of her parents mingling with the guests, and she beamed with pride. They truly were Talsburg royalty. The deference and respect they were being shown was unmistakable. At one point or another during the gala, every single guest wandered by their table to pay homage. They were so gracious, aware of their position and stature in life, but they never let it define them.

After dinner, while some of the guests danced and socialized, others inspected the Lancaster. From her table, Rayna enjoyed studying their expressions as they changed from looks of amazement and curiosity to morbid unease. In the end, they roamed around the war bird, speechless, taking in the reality of it.

She was humming along to the music when she noticed Beaker leaning against the wall under one of the enormous wings, and she could tell he'd been watching her. He adjusted his tie, raising his glass to her in a toast. He was fastened into a black tux like every other male in the room, but strangely, he didn't blend in like the rest. The refined attire, and the fusion of shaggy hair and designer stubble, made him seem untamed in an odd sort of way. He was dressed to impress but didn't give a damn.

Sauntering through the guests he worked his way to her table, so focused it was as if she'd disappear if he lost sight of her. The coolest person she'd ever met, completely comfortable in his own skin, genuine and unaffected. She had to admit the allure of that level of confidence.

He flashed her a sly grin when he reached her table. "Rayna."

Her heart flipped. *Rayna?* She couldn't remember him ever calling her by her first name, and she'd never heard it sound so exotic.

"Why, Beaker, you're looking exceptionally reined-in this evening."

He tossed his head back. "Just the look I was going for."

With discretion, he scanned the length of her gown and loosely crossed ankles tucked in beside her chair. He squinted as their eyes locked. "You look lovelier than ever."

"Thank you." She blushed. "Sit for a minute." She tapped the seat of the chair next to her.

Beaker set his drink on the table and eased into the chair without breaking eye contact. Unnerved, she twisted to feign interest in the bodies strutting across the plexiglass, humming along. "Hmmm … hmm … hmmm… Do you dance, Beaker?"

"I don't dance." He stared into his glass.

"It's going to be a long night for you, then."

He surveyed the room. "So, tell me, anyone here catch your eye?"

"Well … the guy with the engineered body standing under the Lanc has my imagination swirling."

With keen interest, he looked in the general direction she'd gestured. "I hope you're not referring to the guy watching Charlotte prance around the dance floor in her invisible dress."

"Yes. That would be him." She shot Beaker a look of annoyance.

"Is it a real dress? I thought for a second she forgot to wear one." He dragged his hand down the rugged stubble that set him apart from the rest.

Rayna fell silent. *Not him, too.* Deflated, it was painful to accept that even Beaker found Charlotte desirable. She'd yet to discover a single male in Talsburg immune to her deception … and *beauty*.

Rayna squirmed in her seat as she simmered.

"I would have never taken you for someone who thinks she's second best." He shook his head, disappointed.

"I have no idea what you're referring to."

"You're such a brat. Why do you let her wind you up?"

Fuming inside, she looked away at the sound of the childish nickname. Would there ever be a time he wouldn't toy with her feelings? She stood to leave and reached for her clutch. His hand quickly circled her wrist and she pulled against his grip.

His eyes narrowed as he stared at her. "There's one detail ruining Charlotte's dress." He hesitated. "Charlotte." He let her wrist go and grabbed his drink. "It would look ten times better on you." He stood, pushing his chair in. "But, unfortunately, you'd have to smile." He walked away.

A flush of heat traveled across her body, leaving a faint glaze on her cheeks. With a sideways glance, she scanned the room, grateful no one seemed to be paying attention.

As she watched Beaker walk away, she felt a pang of regret.

Chapter 35

Sage and Mark spent most of the evening on the dance floor. She playfully gave Rayna the Queen's wave and Rayna curtsied as she passed them on her way to her parent's table. Her father was involved in a discussion with a few men standing off to the side, but she could tell that he didn't quite seem the same without Harland riding shotgun. She slipped into the empty chair beside her mother, and they shared their stories, reliving the night. She hadn't seen Beaker for an hour. She assumed he'd left.

They were busy watching the guests when her mother tapped her elbow, smiling. "Rayna." She motioned toward Beaker standing behind them.

"Could I have this dance?" He leaned in so close his lips touched her ear.

He spun Rayna's chair, and without missing a step, swept her onto the dance floor with movements so smooth they appeared choreographed. Her mother looked on favorably.

"Beaker." She smiled. "I thought you said you didn't dance."

"I said, I *don't* dance. Didn't say I couldn't."

"I'm mad at you," she chided as she pretended to pull away.

He smiled as he pulled her in tight. "Where do ya think you're going?" He grinned.

"You were being a jerk earlier, Beaker."

"And you were being a brat."

Rayna looked defiant.

"Listen." He gestured with his thumb. "What happened back there at the table?"

"Let's drop it." Close enough to see the faint white scar cutting through his eyebrow, she was caught off guard by a twinge of sadness. *How could a father hurt their own child, let alone a person as sweet as Beaker?*

She knew he was hurting. She could see it in his eyes, in the way he searched her face for the source of her anguish. She worried he'd think he'd annoyed her again so she offered him a cheerless smile, but it was enough to give him peace.

"Denver mentioned you may be injecting a little photodrama into the event later."

"Well said, Beaker." She smiled with renewed awareness. "A minor production, triumph beats tragedy—hopefully more triumph than tragedy."

"With your talent, I'm sure it will be a hit." His gaze fluctuated between her emerald earrings and diamond pendant. He touched one of her earrings and studied it, as if comparing it to the green in her eyes. "You don't need any of that stuff." He gave her a searing look then moved in closer.

With his face buried in her wavy locks, his deep voice rumbled into her chest when he spoke. In minor increments they skimmed the dance floor, almost motionless. Mesmerized, she nuzzled into his shoulder, and his breath rushed against her neck. The instant she closed her eyes, and let herself melt against him, the music faded away.

Under the dim lights they swayed a second longer, silent. She wondered how many other women he'd held with such interest, and if he'd given them pet names as well. He then graciously bowed and escorted her back to her table, thanked her mother, and said goodbye. She watched as he spoke with her father for a few minutes, then grabbed his coat and left the hangar. It felt like the night was over, yet it was barely ten o'clock.

Two light taps escaped the speakers before her mother's voice traveled through the PA system, pulling Rayna from her trance. "I want to thank everyone for coming. It means a great deal to our family, having everyone present to help us celebrate this momentous milestone and the illustrious Avro Lancaster. I'm not going to go into a long speech. This presentation will confirm the importance of this gala and convey our deepest gratitude." Larissa gestured to a giant screen unrolling above the bomber, her chin tipped down, her eyes cast upward. Her distress was palpable as she waited to see images of Cole.

The lights dimmed as a collage of photographs poured down onto the screen, then fell away to make room for others. The first image showed the weather-beaten Lancaster sitting in a field, with large sections missing and rust eating away at its edges. Another shot revealed it stripped to the metal frame, aircraft parts covering the hangar floor. Like a movie, they told a story by depicting key moments in the restoration. From the morning they towed the battered bomber into the hangar to the afternoon it taxied along the runway for the first time, it was all captured in the thoughtful rendering.

As Cole's smile projected onto the canvas, Rayna watched her mother's face transition from hesitant to grateful. But the pictures denoted the passage of time, and soon enough, images of Cole were absent, and an unfamiliar cast emerged. Her mother's heartbreak was unmistakable.

When the music faded away and the presentation neared the end, the tapestry transformed into an image of a clear blue sky. The room became silent then rustled gently with anticipation. A single violin played a series of haunting notes before mingling with a medley of softly cascading instruments. The last image began to materialize, pixel by painful pixel, as the heart-wrenching melody swelled. At first, only sections of the Lancaster Bomber could be seen, but within seconds Cole was sitting in the cockpit, waving from the side window. Rayna's favorite photograph. For maximum impact, she'd saved it for last.

Rayna didn't have to wait for a reaction, the gasps were instant. Her mother dabbed a tissue to her eye and nodded at Rayna in approval. Her parents were again the highlight of the night when they followed-up with an impromptu and heartfelt message worthy of a king and queen.

By the time the ball ended, Trent still hadn't given her the time of day, not even a smile. But instead of coddling hurt feelings, she boiled with anger. Especially with all she'd done to make the ball a success, which benefited him more than her. She knew Charlotte was behind it, which almost made it excusable. They'd known each other for decades. Their lives were intertwined long before they became a couple. It wasn't like Rayna wanted him back. *Why is everyone trying to erase history?* It was easy for them, their lives had all moved forward. Her future waited, a mystery, while she remained stuck in the past.

Rayna decided she wasn't going to let her imagination spoil it. All things considered, the Winter Ball itself had been flawless. She'd probably never understand why Trent had chosen to ignore her. Beaker, on the other hand, was an entirely different issue. His unexpected attention had given her plenty to mull over.

As she drove along in the dark the questions deepened, and a few of the answers could only come from Trent. She needed to talk to him, and that meant sidestepping Charlotte—and the sooner she could arrange it, the better.

Chapter 36

Unable to sleep, Rayna hauled herself out of bed before the first rays of light settled over the pond. She had two hours of writing in before the alarm rang. After all the time she'd lost to the ball, she was thrilled to have three more weeks' worth of editing complete and ready to add to the laptop. Rayna set the transcribed notes facedown on the proper pile and left for the farm, determined to make amends with her father.

Trent's Jeep backed onto the road as Rayna opened the door of her truck, and he slowed at the end of her driveway then stopped and lowered the window.

"Where're you off too so early?"

"The farm." She answered abruptly.

"Well …" He hesitated. "Enjoy your day."

"I plan on it." She jumped into her truck.

Trent pulled away, bound for the airport, while Rayna headed in the opposite direction. She tried to devise a plan to apologize to her father, but her thoughts kept reversing back to Trent at the hangar, and eventually, so too did her truck. As if it had a mind of its own, her truck rolled onto the shoulder and aimed straight for the airport. *You're not getting off the hook that easy, Trent.*

Ten minutes later, Rayna looked around the airport parking lot, wondering what she was doing there. What did she hope to accomplish by confronting him? He owed her nothing. A number of scenarios fought for her attention as she walked from her truck to the side door.

Once inside the hangar, she was startled by the sight of white linen and chandeliers. Still dressed like a ballroom, the magical air of the previous evening was diminished by the harsh beams of sunlight streaking across the abandoned tables, but even in the large space, on the morning after, the heavy scent of calla lilies remained as potent as ever.

Trent waved from the side window of the Lancaster cockpit. "One minute." He gestured.

She nodded, wandering around the hangar and stopping to smell a white rose from one of the vases. *What am I doing here?*

"Did you forget something last night?" He wiped a screwdriver on a dirty towel as he approached her.

"No. Did you," she said with a pout.

He grinned as he tossed the tool in the air, caught it, and tucked it into his back pocket.

"Trent." She stopped in mid-sentence. "I need to ask you a question."

He wiped his hands on the towel. "Sounds important."

"Cole and Samantha … were they serious? Were they talking marriage?" She could tell she'd caught him off guard.

He walked away from her as he spoke. "Yeah, years ago, for sure. Before he joined the air force." His shoulders seemed to rise as he spoke. "I'm not sure where it would have gone. The relationship became fairly intense in a matter of weeks, but they never had a chance to …" He again moved toward her. "Why are you so consumed with the details?"

Her eyes burned into his, not sure of what to say. "I found a diamond ring hidden in his room." She waited for a reaction.

Trent leaned against a workbench, his hands resting on the edge and his ankles crossed.

"And he was working with an architect, finalizing house plans. They arrived two weeks after the accident." She folded her arms across her chest and cocked her head to the side. "He was going to propose to her. There's no other explanation." She expelled a sigh of relief, a burden lifted.

"Have you thought about contacting Samantha? See what

she has to say."

She rolled her eyes in frustration. "It wouldn't be right to poke around in their past when, for whatever reason, he didn't see fit to share it with us. Any plans they made, or didn't make, have to remain between them." She raised her palms. "Almost three years have gone by and she hasn't approached us, so it's not an option."

"I agree. It wouldn't be fair to Cole to run around investigating his personal life."

"My thoughts exactly. If it was even meant for her. As secretive as he was, the ring could've been for anyone. He always said he'd never bring home a girlfriend, only a future wife."

"Sounds like Cole."

"Anyway, I wanted to hear it from you. It's driving me crazy. At some point, I'll have to discuss it with my parents, but I wanted to wait until after the ball to address it." She raised her hands in frustration. "And it's … after the ball."

"Don't rush. Think it through before you make any decisions one way or another."

"Believe me, I intend to."

"For what it's worth … I think it was meant for Samantha, and long before he ever joined the service. Not sure if that makes you feel any better or not."

Silence.

Her eyes filled. "Cole would've been impressed with the turnout last night."

There was a sadness on his face at the mention of Cole's name. "He would have been happy to know we had the money to finish the restoration and pay off the loans." He looked at the bomber. "He loved the Lanc."

"He did."

Again, they both fell silent.

She looked around. "I should go." She looked into his eyes, hesitating.

He moved toward her before speaking. "Last night … you

know why I couldn't talk to you." He touched her arm and an electric current seemed to travel through his hand, making her thoughts hazy.

She whispered. "I understand, I do."

Rayna watched as Trent turned ghastly white before nodding.

Just as she'd figured, Charlotte was behind it. Unable to tolerate anyone rattling the shaky little fantasy world she'd created. The instant the thought crossed her mind, a pang of regret sunk in as she imagined being on the other end of the scenario. How would she feel if her husband discussed intimate details of their marriage with another woman, a woman he obviously still had a hint of affection for? She stood frozen, her mind reeling, speechless. Deep down, there was a better person that wouldn't approve any of the thoughts going through her head. Rayna wondered if she'd ever catch a glimpse of her again.

"You looked stunning last night."

"Thanks, Trent." She turned to face him, sensing more to come.

"Rayna …" He stepped closer, staring at the floor.

She tried to make eye contact, but he wasn't having any part of it. *Please, Trent, tell me what I need to hear.* She stood quietly, her demons waiting to be fed.

His voice changed to a whisper, mid-sentence. "There are days …" He swallowed hard. "Sometimes … I have regrets, too."

Rayna's heart slammed against her chest.

Tiny beads of sweat appeared across his forehead, his complexion ashen, his reaction coming as a shock, even to him.

When she'd decided to corner him, she never imagined how willing he'd be to throw the truth at her, and his candor revealed what she'd suspected. He may have moved on, but not as easily as she'd once thought. He still cared for her. And it took ten seconds for her to realize the details of his revelation were the last thing she wanted to think about. The blood drained from her face as she felt herself drowning in guilt.

"I better go."

She spun sharply and headed to the exit, but he followed her into the hallway. Someone pulled on the door while she pushed against it, causing it to explode open when the person on the other side let go. She gasped as she fell out of the hangar.

"Charlotte, Mom, what are you doing here so early?" She sat on the ground, brushing herself off, cowering under their intense glare.

"Larissa and I are meeting the decorator."

Their eyes bored into hers as Rayna stood up, trying to formulate a believable lie. "I left my clutch here." Wild-eyed, she gestured toward the ballroom. "I saw Trent on his way here. I knew I could get in to look for it."

Larissa stayed quiet, but her eyes scanned the three of them before staring at the ground. Rayna could only imagine the questions formulating in her mind.

With a clever glance, Charlotte looked for the bag in Rayna's hands.

"But it's not here. I don't know where to look now."

Rayna left as quick as she could, wishing she could start the morning again. While crossing the gravel parking lot, she wondered when their schedule had changed. They were supposed to meet the decorator at lunch. She couldn't help but think that Charlotte had intentionally put her in a compromising position by arriving at the airport early. Their encounter was no accident. Now, Rayna would have to explain the incident to her mother or deal with the shame. She couldn't remember a time when anyone had ever looked at her with such disgust.

She drove back to the cottage with Trent's comments swirling around in her head. She thought about the way he looked at her. It was obvious he still cared for her, and Rayna didn't know how she felt about his disclosure. Part of her gloated. Charlotte thought her world was so perfect when it wasn't. But, in her heart, Rayna hurt for Charlotte, and she hated herself for being reckless and selfish. What a horrible situation to walk into. And now, thanks to her impulsive behavior, she'd put Trent in the middle of a mess.

She'd hurt her father, her mother, even Trent, and now Charlotte. She seemed to be on the wrong side of every issue this week, smashing through her life like a sledgehammer. Mulling her options, she pulled onto the North Road and bolted for the cover of Raspberry Cottage. Unless she left Talsburg, there seemed no other escape route. And she was starting to think that might be a viable option.

Late that evening, while Rayna was writing, she heard a familiar hum from the kitchen. She folded her arms across her chest as she got up to investigate. Walking into the dark she could see the cell phone flashing. It was pressed up against one of the canisters, buzzing. She picked it up, shocked. *Beaker!?*

You okay? it read.

She gingerly set the phone down, as if the slightest movement would alert him that she'd read the text. She held the off button until the screen went dark, unsure why his message alarmed her so.

Chapter 37

Between the cold air, the text message and her conversation with Trent, Rayna tossed in bed for hours. The old furnace couldn't keep pace when the temperature dropped below zero. She couldn't do much about the conversations, but she finally put on her housecoat and scurried to the living room to start the stove.

She grabbed the burn pile off the desk and tossed it into the stove with a handful of kindling. She scraped a wooden match against the stone hearth, lit the pile, and went to the kitchen for a glass of milk. By the time she returned to the stove, a modest flame waved lazily in the firebox. Rayna shuffled through the wood pile, selecting a log large enough to last until the morning. She dropped the hefty chunk on top of the glowing embers, where the flames licked the bark before engulfing it completely. She plunged under the covers and clicked off the bedside lamp.

The cottage was so compact the reprieve from the cold seemed almost instant. Within a half hour she'd forgotten all about the chill in the air and waited for sleep, but it still eluded her. She thrashed around, trying to think of what to say to her mother—who wouldn't be long arriving on her doorstep.

She'd have to call Sage and get her on board with the fabrication, but as logical as Rayna had made it sound, her mother was no fool. And she couldn't use the ring or her brother's death to allay her troubles, it wouldn't be right. No, she'd convince her mother there was nothing to it some other way.

No explanation would sound worse than the truth. *I was furious that Trent ignored me at the ball, so I followed him to the airport to milk a little attention from him.* As ridiculous as it sounded, could it be the truth? Was the ring no more than an excuse to meet with him?

Not only did she feel guilty, she was worried. What did his admission mean? *I'm with Charlotte, but* … Rayna tried to shake it off, unable to believe her mind had jumped so far ahead.

In a shallow sense, it was a relief to learn she hadn't been replaced as she'd thought. He'd never moved forward as easy as he made it appear. She had no idea what she'd do with the information, but it went a long way in repairing her fragile ego, the very reason she hated herself.

Rayna knew she shouldn't have gone to the airport, and she'd coaxed him into the open with her pouty remarks and remember-when comments. She never expected him to be so candid, but Trent was honest—no games, totally trusting to a fault—and it was his most endearing quality.

Charlotte's prospects of having her perfect life with Trent suddenly seemed abysmal. Rayna could sense their futures were about to become complicated if she and Trent weren't careful. Even though she knew, in her heart, there was a line they'd never cross. But when he came to mind, a static charge seemed to snap through the air. She'd be lying if she denied it existed. And the secrecy didn't help the situation. It became the kindling that made it all sizzle.

She wondered if she was lonely, or jealous, or heaven forbid just bored, and she struggled to make sense of it as she prayed for sleep. But while she waited, with her defenses down and the darkness giving way to honesty, she thought about the way he touched her arm. She remembered the sadness in his eyes and the guilty look on his face. She had sensed a shift.

They'd crossed an invisible line, and lying in the safety of her bed, for some terrifying reason, for the first time in years, she felt alive.

* * *

The next morning, Rayna still couldn't concentrate. She made a pot of coffee then poured it over a tea bag she'd already placed in the mug.

Her mother's SUV pulled into the driveway and Rayna's alarm hadn't even gone off yet. "Oh boy." *She is livid!*

Rayna held the door open. "You're early." She closed the door behind her.

"We need to talk." She unbuttoned her coat on the way to the kitchen.

"Tea, coffee?" Rayna stirred the concoction in the mug. "I made both."

"I need to ask you … Why did you meet Trent at the hangar yesterday?" She huffed. "What an awkward situation to walk into. Charlotte didn't look happy, either. She remained quiet the entire time we were there."

"You're reading way too much into this." Rayna paused. "I thought I forgot my clutch at the ball, but apparently Sage has it."

"Sage?" A hint of relief flashed across her mother's face.

"I brought a floral arrangement home from the ball." She pointed to the large spray on the kitchen table. "Leaving the hangar, Sage took the clutch so I wouldn't drop the flowers. She accidently took it home with her." Rayna pushed a key on a tiny ring across the table. "I had to use the spare key to get in the cottage last night."

With a dubious glare, her mother replied, "It looked dreadful, Rayna." She folded her arms. "And I should tell you … Charlotte must have told her aunt, because last evening Myra phoned me 'just to gab.'"

"What a bitch." Rayna tossed her favorite mug into the sink and the handle broke off when it hit the porcelain.

"Rayna!" Larissa picked up a piece of glass, disappointed. "That's the mug Gramma Wescott gave you."

"I'm sorry, but Myra is a mean-spirited woman, and I don't know how you tolerate her. The whole town will be talking by tomorrow if they're not already." Rayna dropped onto a kitchen chair. "Charlotte knew what she was doing, showing up early."

"What?" Her mother looked puzzled.

"Never mind."

"Your father will be devastated if a trashy piece of gossip works its way back to him."

"I know, Mom. I know," she shouted, tired of her mother's support for Charlotte.

"Rayna, I can understand how you might enjoy his attention, and how validating it might be to realize he may not have totally moved on with his life, but I think you underestimate how strong feelings can become."

"Oh, don't beat around the bush, Mom. Say what's really on your□"

"I think you're playing with fire." She raised her chin in the air. "They have a child, Rayna."

Silence filled the room.

"Mom, I wish you wouldn't worry. I'm not. And I don't care what stories the town fabricates because they're bored." She crossed her arms in defiance. "People can say what they want, and Daddy is going to have to ignore it."

"I can assure you … your father wasn't built to ignore anything." They locked eyes until Rayna looked away.

"How long are you going to give this writing venture? I wish you would at least come back to the farm to sleep."

Rayna sprung from the chair. "Mom, I live *here* now." She waved her hand around the room. "Gramma left me Raspberry Cottage, and I've officially moved in. I'm thirty years old. I'd look like a loser still living at the farm with my parents. If I'm going to last in Talsburg, it'll be because I'm here on my own property, living my own life, not sitting at the dinner table with my parents being grilled like a teenager." Her rant ended abruptly.

Her mother sighed. "I understand." She moved the curtain and looked down the road to the Jacksons, concerned, then walked to where Rayna stood.

"Mom, Trent is history. You don't need to worry. Trust me, please."

"Rayna, you don't want him. It's just easier to look back than it is to look forward. It's completely normal to long for the familiar life you knew. It takes courage to dream about the future when you can't see what's out there … waiting for you. I get it, I do. No one likes to think they've been forgotten. But if you wanted Trent, you would have chosen him—and you didn't. You walked away." She lightly touched three knotted locks resting on Rayna's shoulder. "Long before he ever became involved with Charlotte."

Left with much to think about, Rayna waved from the tiny front entranceway as her mother left the driveway. Rayna found it difficult to argue with her mother's insightful words, but she drew the line at the 'playing with fire' comment.

She needed to write. It was her go-to remedy for emotional dilemmas. She grabbed the prized edit pile from the corner of the desk and prepared to enter the three weeks' worth of editing into the final draft. She realized she'd lifted the wrong pile and set it back on the table, facedown. She flipped another pile, then frantically turned over the last stack only to discover the burn pile and not the edited pages. She checked the piles again, looking at the second and third pages of each stack to confirm, but the edited pages were nowhere to be found.

She took a few steps toward the woodstove, remembering that she had started a fire in the middle of the night. It was a major setback. At best it meant four weeks of rewriting. Every detail, up in flames. The story, already more work than she'd anticipated, now didn't seem worth finishing.

Rayna peered through the glass door of the woodstove and stared at the dirty ashes. Her mother's words rang true. She'd spent the night fanning an old flame, and it took her no time at all to get burned.

Chapter 38

Even though Myra had suppressed her desire to gossip out of respect for Larissa, Rayna spent the next few weeks hidden away in Raspberry Cottage. She hated going into town, and avoided it. Even leaving the cottage had become a challenge. There were times she stood by the door, coat on and keys in hand, unable to muster the courage to get into the truck and drive anywhere except for the farm. Whether it smacked of shame or anxiety, she couldn't be sure. But it didn't really matter. The result was the same. She was trapped.

When her need for red pencils and legal pads threatened to derail her book, Rayna realized she could survive without fresh fruit and wine but being starved of writing supplies was not an option. Rayna made her shopping list and prepared to leave for Starling.

But, once again, a sense of foreboding and a heaviness in her chest made her second-guess the need to leave the house. She tried to associate it with a specific event, but it was pointless. She felt a gnawing threat of danger looming when she thought of venturing beyond the front door. The warning caused her such anxiety that it took hold of her plans and controlled her.

Out of nowhere, the objects in the room went in and out of focus, the space felt liquid and the floor spongy beneath her. She sat by the kitchen window with her heart fluttering, waiting for it to pass.

She stared into the yard, sipping a glass of cold juice. The world looked the same, yet all the beautiful little details in her life were missing, as if a strong wind had blown through and taken just the bits and pieces that had made her smile.

Within minutes, she no longer wavered, or felt off-balance. She scooped her purse off one of the vinyl kitchen chairs and filled a travel mug with ice water. Determined, she headed into town.

The open window sent air filtering through her spring coat, instantly reviving her. Thankfully, it didn't take long to get to Starling, but there was more traffic racing around than usual and she seemed to find fault with every empty parking space. They either looked too tight or were too far from the entrance. While circling the town, Rayna was relieved when an angled spot opened directly in front of The Victorian Mall.

In no hurry to leave the security of the truck, she scanned the sidewalk, opened the door, and stepped onto the side runner. But, as her feet touched the ground, a wave of dizziness swept her into a state of panic. With the street spinning around her, and her knees melting into the concrete, she struggled to hang onto the door and pull herself inside the truck. *What's happening to me?*

Her hand reached for the ice water, and she devoured half the bottle as she watched the distracted shoppers smiling and rushing about. Most appeared on a mission, oblivious to the traffic and each other. For them, the afternoon was ordinary. Rayna envied their ability to move about casually, as if they lacked a care in the world.

She sat, overwhelmed, in the cab of the truck. Her symptoms had passed, but for how long? She decided to go home and try again the next day. Whatever caused her unease, would surely pass by tomorrow. Her heart sank when she realized that it was tomorrow. She'd already put the trip off, and more than once.

She set off for the demoralizing drive home. The music failed to distract her, so she changed it to a station offering a livestream interview with a local equestrian. The broadcast held her interest, and the sips of icy water seemed to help. A few miles later, she noticed, as suddenly as her body had turned on her, it had relaxed.

As she got closer to home a sense of relief settled in, and when she pulled in the driveway she felt as if she had averted some unknown disaster. But when she entered the cottage sans paper, pencils, and cream for her morning coffee, she lowered her head in defeat. She sat at the kitchen table, eyeing the open shelf of glass beakers that lacked their usual playful aura. She stared, feeling dead inside, forced to address the watershed moment.

* * *

The next morning, on April Fool's Day, Rayna found herself sitting exactly where she needed to be: in Dr. Parlton's office.

"No one in my family has ever suffered from panic attacks."

He smiled and adjusted his glasses. "There's always a first time."

"I guess."

His reassuring smile offered her instant relief, only to be followed by a twinge of embarrassment for being so needy.

He tore a piece of paper off a pad and handed it to her. "I want you to fill this prescription, but I want you to take this only when *absolutely* necessary. This is the weakest strength. You shouldn't be aware you've even taken a pill. I would've preferred you address this by not relying on medication. If you attempt to manage this with pills alone, you may have an entirely different problem to deal with." He tapped her shoulder. "You're going to be fine, Rayna." He wheeled up in front of his computer station as she left his office.

Rayna went straight to the pharmacy and filled the prescription. The pills were so tiny they barely covered the bottom of the bottle, but the pharmacist assured her if she placed one under her tongue when anxious, the symptoms would magically disappear. She'd decided, if they were so powerful, that she'd keep them close by at all times.

She tried the first one a half hour later, when she was trying to coax her herself out of the truck in front of the mall. The pill bottle shook in her hand as she read the label: Place one pill under the tongue as needed. *Done!*

The first pleasant surprise—they worked. Short of a spontaneous deep breath there were no other signs she'd taken any medication, and the relief was immediate. She looked at the bottle and dropped it into her purse. "Hmm." *These pills are like magic!*

She collected what she needed from town and even managed to shop at the Parchment Press, after she observed a young girl at the cash register filling in for Myra. She walked in and grabbed a stack of legal pads and took them to the cash register. A strip of ten-cent postage stamps sat on the counter, and Rayna picked it up to examine it.

"Did you need stamps," the young girl asked.

"Yes, I do." *Thirty days has September, April* ... "Could I have a roll of thirty, please?"

"The peel-and-stick stamps are sold out. I only have the old style. You have to lick them."

"They'll be fine, thank you." A mischievous grin tugged at the corners of her lips as she dropped the roll into her purse.

She treated herself to a pedicure, and even stopped at a couple of boutiques, before calling it a day. Freed from her prison, Rayna started to see remnants of her old self and savored the moment, feeling strong and happy. She reveled in the pure joy of being anywhere other than Raspberry Cottage. Rayna watched the smiling shoppers enjoying their normal activities. She too, felt back to normal. But for how long?

Rayna ventured from the usual route home, opting to drive by the Grainger farm to be nosy. She coasted down the narrow and desolate road slow enough to take a good look around.

A new steel building had emerged in place of the burned shell of a barn that once filled her with horror—fueling more nightmares than she cared to remember. The new modern structure looked out of place. Her father would never have tolerated such an eyesore on Westcott Farm. With the horses gone, Jordy would be roaming around the farm by himself. Rayna's heart sank at the thought. It looked deserted, lonely, and paled in comparison to her Westcott Farm, which looked so friendly and always seemed full of life. She regretted driving by and pressed on the gas, eager to get out of there.

Following dinner, and basking in the glow of her old self, she decided to take advantage of it. She'd write for a few hours, then reward herself with a trip to the barn. And she did. But as she pulled in front of the stable, she realized she'd forgotten the pills. Rayna wasn't sure how long their effects lasted. She was already feeling an overwhelming sense of dread, urging her to go home. Unable to exit the truck Rayna returned to the cottage, alarmed and disappointed. As she walked into Raspberry Cottage, the truth flooded in: the pills weren't going to set her free, they were going to make her dependent.

Later that night, she was sipping on a cup of strawberry rhubarb tea when she found the spool of postage stamps sitting beside the salt and pepper shakers in the middle of the kitchen table. She took the roll with her to the bathroom. After rinsing her face, she leaned in close to the mirror, licked one of the stamps and stuck it above the bridge of her nose, directly on top of her frown lines. While she added a slight amount of pressure to the stamp and waited for it to dry, she took a swig of mouthwash to rinse the nasty taste away. Within minutes the stamp hardened, like a tiny piece of papier-mâché.

She hoped the patch would smooth her brow over time, and with any luck prevent her from frowning in the first place. A habit she and her mother were more than eager to break. She'd bought enough to last a month. She wondered if it would work on crow's feet as well but opted for trying one experiment at a time.

The stamp annoyed her at first, it was stiff and pulled a little, but eventually she forgot about it. Rayna worked on her story and made a bacon and tomato sandwich, and it even stayed in place during a brief nap. But she peeled it off when it was time for bed, which hurt like heck. She rinsed the area and put on her usual anti-wrinkle serum. She could already tell the lines were smoother, and she was convinced the stamps would prove a better investment than her expensive night cream.

Rayna didn't always remember to apply one, but with her memory the experiment was bound to be hit-or-miss. She did remember to put a half dozen pills in a locket and tuck it into her jacket pocket. The coat went everywhere she did, so it seemed a good place to stash a few. Rayna, confident she'd prepared for every eventuality, left a few in the prescription bottle in her purse.

A few days later, when she was standing in front of the stable and started to feel anxious, she squeezed her pocket to make sure she had the pills. Rayna was mystified to realize that, even being in her coat pocket, the magic pills seemed to calm her through some kind of psychological osmosis. It made no sense. She only had to rub the metal case for them to work, she didn't need to actually take one.

That's weird.

Harvey smiled and dropped his chores when she entered the breezeway. "Rayna! Where ya been hiding?"

A few farmhands joined him in a warm welcome, and she wondered if Beaker would hear the commotion. Sure enough, a few minutes later he surfaced as well. Standing with both hands behind his back, he smiled as he walked to meet her. When they stood close enough to touch, he pulled the willow basket into view and offered it to her, filled to the brim. Just the way she liked it.

"Hey, Brat, it's a little late for you to be here, isn't it?"

"Yeah, I'm late getting here all right."

Over the moon, Rayna savored the moment. And the guys wasted no time topping her up with another kind of medicine she needed, that of love and friendship.

* * *

That night, when she returned to the cottage, Trent was arriving home at the exact same time. He slowed as he passed the end of her driveway but had no idea that she was standing in the shadows. He leaned to get a better look and scanned the house on his way past. She moved beside the cottage and pressed up against the siding, further beyond sight. He pulled into his driveway and went straight to the shed.

No magic remedy existed for what ailed her now. *Guilt.* And, with her anxiety at bay, she had more than enough headspace to wallow in her shame.

Chapter 39

On a warm spring morning, Rayna sat on the steps of the front porch, eating apple slices and cheddar cheese from a petri dish. She watched as Charlotte and Quinn climbed the wooden rungs to his new tree house perched in the willow in their front yard. Staying close behind, she held onto the waistband of Quinn's pants and encouraged him to pull himself up the ladder, one step at a time. The fort measured about six square feet, and the fresh-cut lumber varied in color from white to blonde. When they reached the top, she hoisted him up, nudging him safely inside.

They laid facedown, with their chins resting on their folded arms. Side by side on the floor of the deck, they watched Shivers run around at the base of the tree, barking and whimpering, frantic to join them as he circled the tree in frustration. Rayna smiled as Quinn called out to Shivers, which seemed to rile the feisty pug even more. Minutes later, Rayna looked up to see Charlotte pulling out of driveway, alone.

There was no denying it. Rayna envied the patience and devotion Charlotte seemed to have in abundance. She often thought it selfish not wanting to have a husband or children of her own to dote on, let alone a dog. But there never seemed to be enough time to bring her own dreams to life, let alone to be someone's everything. She wondered what that said about her.

She was determined to live her life minimizing unnecessary pain. But in the process, her strategy left her with an entirely different kind of ache. *One horrible day, Quinn will learn how cruel this life can be, and even Charlotte, with all her love and patience, won't be able to protect him when his world shatters and those beautiful smiles disappear.*

Rayna went into the house and gathered a stack of manila envelopes off the desk and drove to the quaint little post office in Talsburg, a small brick stand-alone between Bart's General Store and Sasha's Hair Salon. Rayna planned on avoiding Charlotte and Myra for as long as possible, on the North Line and at the Parchment Press. And there was no way she wanted them to find out she was trying to get published, or the entire town would find out. *No. This will do just fine.* She parked in front and carried her letters inside.

"Hi, Rayna." The young postal worker smiled, pulling the envelopes across the counter for inspection. "What have we got here?"

She'd seen him once since high school, and it came as a relief when Dillon's name sprung to mind.

He put one of the envelopes on the scale. "Is this your book?"

Rayna blushed. Did everyone know about her book? "It's only the first three chapters." She tried to downplay it.

"Best of luck. The whole town's excited to have a famous author living here. Everyone says, being a Westcott, you'll probably follow the family tradition and make this town even more famous."

"Thank you, Dillon."

Her knees stiffened as she walked out of the post office, never more aware of the weight of being a Westcott and the immense pressure it created. Rayna feared the disappointment she'd face if she fell short of producing a published novel. Now it needed to be a best seller, too!

It had taken her a month to rewrite the sections she'd burned in the stove, but with hard work and determination she'd got through it. Her first submission was a huge accomplishment, and now she deserved to enjoy every second of it. She made a quick stop at the farm to share the news, but with Sage coming to spend the night she had to run a few errands and get back to the cottage to tidy.

Rayna dashed into the grocery store in Starling to shop for a veggie tray and a fruit platter. A couple of bottles of pinot noir managed to find their way into her shopping bag as well. When Rayna walked back to her truck, Charlotte was standing on the stairs of the medical building like she was waiting for a ride, but a few seconds later she walked down the street and got into her car. Rayna was waiting at the corner to cross when Charlotte entered the light. She looked right at Rayna then drove by, as if Rayna wasn't even there.

Her mother had told her Charlotte couldn't cover for Myra at the shop because she'd been sick the last couple of mornings. *Still trying to hem Trent in with a second child, no doubt.* She wondered if Trent had any say in the plan this time.

Rayna got into her truck and headed to the cottage. She'd never understood Charlotte. *How awful it must feel to be so insecure.* With a pang of humility, Rayna shamefully ran her hand over her sweater until she felt the locket.

When she arrived home, Rayna grabbed a few packages from the bed of the truck and made the first trip into the cottage, but on her way back for the second load she spotted a brown van crawling by the front of the house. She walked along the gravel, slowly, not recognizing it at first, but when she read the writing on the driver's-side door, there was no mistaking who it belonged to—Grainger and Son. *Oh boy!* She quickly turned to face the house and kept walking with her bags, pretending not to notice Jordy skulking by.

Was it a warning shot, or just payback for driving by his house? She set her packages on the kitchen table and watched from the window until he drove away. Rayna crept back to the truck to collect the last of her shopping, listening. She kept her eye on the road as she hurried.

Rayna tried not to let her imagination spiral into a dark place. After all, she'd went by his house for no other reason than to be nosy. Her drive past hadn't gone undetected, and he wanted her to know it. *Probably all there is to it.* She hoped.

That night, as she waited for Sage, Rayna barely gave the unnerving visit another thought. The claw-foot tub filled with hot water while she lit a vanilla-scented candle and set it on the black and white penny tiles. She stepped into the bubbly froth, leaned against a foam pillow, and sunk deep into the calming water, admiring the shadows from the dancing flame. Seconds later she drifted off, thanks to the steady drip from the galvanized taps.

Chapter 40

Charlotte had planned on sharing the news with Trent that evening but questioned the timing. He'd been so distant. She didn't know when or how she'd break it to him, but she knew she no longer had to worry that one day he'd leave her.

She climbed the stairs with Quinn and sat against his bedroom door as he played with his favorite toy, a red metal car that fit perfectly into his tiny hand. She stared at the baby pictures on the wall and the bronzed booties on a shelf. A white cotton sleeper, with sapphire embroidery around the neckline, was displayed in a shadow box above his dresser. A blue-and-white beaded bracelet was pinned to the front of the gown that read Baby Boy, Jackson.

Quinn had rarely cried as a baby and was a blessing to raise. She didn't know if all babies were such a joy. Charlotte mused at how fast time had gone by. She'd always longed to have a daughter and had never wanted Quinn to grow up an only child. 'Better to have none than one,' she'd always heard.

Charlotte wondered if Rayna ever regretted the choice she'd made to never marry or have children. Rayna still wanted to travel the world and move back to the city. She'd always been fearless, and Charlotte envied her courage. They were so different. Charlotte had never been adventurous. Everything she'd ever wanted had always been right there in Talsburg.

Rayna was a good person and had probably never hurt anyone intentionally. Unlike herself, who'd manipulated her way through life, always trying to make sure her position improved. And even still, here she was, trying to control and steer everyone to her best end. She convinced herself that protecting her family, the people she loved most in life, erased all sins. For that reason, nothing she ever did felt wrong.

Determined to put maximum pressure on Rayna, she ran the details over in her mind. Charlotte's plans had changed on a dime, and so could Rayna's. Someday Rayna would realize she wanted everything she'd missed out on in life, everything that Charlotte now had. It was only a matter of time.

Chapter 41

Rayna was sitting on the tree swing, waiting, when Sage's yellow mustang veered into the driveway with music booming from the car windows.

"Sage!" Rayna met her at the car, and they hugged.

"I haven't been inside Raspberry Cottage in years. Can I take a quick peek?"

"Sure … I'm done out here."

They wandered in.

"I love this place." Sage smiled. "It looks exactly the same." She pointed to the desk. "Except for the stacks of paper."

"I couldn't wait for you to get here." Rayna tapped her pursed lips. "This morning I sent off a two-page synopsis and the first three chapters of my book to a few publishers."

"What?" Sage bolted to the desk. "Where is it?" She searched the stacks of paper. "You have to let me read it."

"This second?" With dismay, Rayna handed over her manuscript, held together by metal fasteners. "Can we visit first? Don't you want to catch up a little?"

Sage took the bundle and dropped into a floral armchair in the corner of the living room. "Okay but let me read the first page at least. Then I promise I'll set it down."

"If you can just stop reading after the first page"—she shrugged—"I guess I wrote a piece of garbage."

Sage shooed Rayna away with her hand, daring her to take the bundle away. "What are you talking about?"

"The first page provides the story hook, and it's intended to make it impossible for you to stop reading. People often buy a book based solely on the impressions they form from reading the first few paragraphs."

Sage laughed. "Oh, be quiet. You sound like an editor. Give me five minutes. Believe me, I'll set it down after the first page. I'm telling you before I even know whether it's great or not. Feel better?"

"Not much." Rayna placed her palm on her forehead and closed her eyes, waiting for the verdict.

Sage scanned the double-spaced document as if being paid by the line. When she was finished, she slapped the pages against her lap and looked at Rayna.

"Well?" Rayna now paced in front of her, trying to gauge her reaction.

"I love it! I'm so glad you chose to finish this story." She held the pages against her chest. "At last, soon I'll have closure. I always wanted to know how this story ended."

"The bundle on the corner of the desk." Rayna motioned. "Tied with the red ribbon. It's a copy of the complete manuscript. It's yours … to take home."

"What!?" Sage sprang to her feet to inspect the finished product. "It's heavy." She grinned. "I'll be reading it later, in the middle of the night."

"You'll be too wasted." She pointed at the two bottles of wine.

Sage agreed. "So, give me a brief summary."

They discussed the story and Sage shared any suggestions she could think of for attracting an agent, but in no time at all they were on to other things. Rayna unwrapped the fruit and veggie platters, and they were quick emptying the first bottle of wine.

Click!

Just before midnight, a bright light shone into the front windows.

Sage moved to the edge of her chair. "What was that?"

"The motion sensor. The slightest bit of wind blowing

through the trees will trip the lights. The sensitivity level is set too high. The guys are trying to fix it."

"This would be a good time to get my bag from the car."

Sage jumped up and put her shoes on, and Rayna followed. "The guys?" Sage rolled her eyes. "Man, you're lucky. You have *the guys* looking after you."

"Stop it!"

They walked to Sage's car, but as the wine had messed with their heads, they soon found themselves wandering around, and eventually ended up under the oak tree.

Sage stared at the stars, enjoying the gentle sway from the old swing. "You never get this view from the city."

Rayna stared at the Jacksons' house. "I agree. I'm thinking it might be a good time to return to the city. I've made a real mess here."

"I thought Myra kept her tales low-key out of respect for Larissa. Why do you need to go now?"

"I don't want to." She hesitated. "I think being this close to Trent and Charlotte is going to cause trouble. And I've no intention of going back to the farm to live with my parents."

With a pained expression, Sage listened while Rayna unloaded.

"Did I tell you I think Charlotte's expecting again? I saw her leaving the doctor's office and my mother said Myra's shop had to close for a couple days this week while Myra took a long weekend. Charlotte was supposed to cover for her, but she felt sick two mornings in a row and couldn't make it in."

"I hope they planned it this time."

They wandered back into the house.

"I thought she was expecting a few months ago. She was dropping off a morning urine sample way back then." Rayna pulled a couple of multicolored throw blankets from the closet and tossed one to Sage.

"I guess Trent won't be going anywhere."

"Exactly." Rayna hesitated. "Since the incident at the hangar,

I've seen Trent drive by a couple of times and slow down at the end of the lane and look around a bit."

"That's kind of pathetic." Sage nibbled away at the fruit. "When you mentioned making a sudden departure, I knew it had something to do with the Jacksons."

Rayna shivered. "Honestly, it makes me sad, and I feel so guilty. I can't take it. He's in the shed every night almost as soon as he gets home, and he stays there until all hours."

"Maybe it's his doghouse." Sage laughed.

"It's not funny."

"I shouldn't joke." She scanned Rayna's face for clues. "What's really going on with you."

"At first, curious, I wondered how their relationship differed from what Trent and I had, and I sulked over how quickly he replaced me. Knowing they had to get married didn't make me feel any better."

"It should. He never would've stayed with her. Hell, who could? She's so needy."

"When we talked at the hangar, and the sparks zipped between us, part of me wanted him to realize he'd settled for Charlotte or been trapped by her scheming." She paused. "But the second he opened his heart to me, everything I thought I wanted changed."

Sage listened with concern. "What changed, Rayna?"

"I'm over him. And I have been for a long time. I became bored once I moved in here and paid a little too much attention to them to be healthy. Imagining their lives as being perfect compared to the mess I've made of mine. They seemed happy and I got jealous, plain and simple."

"You're right. This is bad."

"When we spoke in the hangar, I finally got the closure I needed. But now I feel like I've left Pandora's box open. I have such a sense of regret … and guilt beyond belief. All I want to do is unwind this mess."

"Listen, Rayna, you may have enjoyed talking to him, but you never intentionally toyed with him. You have no reason to be sorry."

But Rayna knew the truth. She'd flirted with him, changed her hair back to the way he liked it, and splashed his perfume on her neck every day since she'd set up camp across the street. And the evening of the ball she'd intentionally worn his favorite color. She'd toyed with him, in the worst way possible, and she was paying the price.

"I thought it a little convenient when you couldn't move past your relationship with Trent. Not letting go of him kept you from falling in love again, and I often believed that was the entire point. You're terrified of losing someone and being hurt again."

"You might be right." She paused. "I'm going to tour Europe for six months, and when I get back I'm moving to Boston. I broke the news to my mother. She's crushed. Each time I move away then come back it makes it harder for her to let go the next time."

"Have you accepted an offer?"

"No. But I'm looking at one. It's either that or live across the street from Trent and Charlotte for the rest of my life."

Sage gave her a devious smile. "Maybe if you finish your book, it will be a best seller and you can move to Cape Cod where all the prestigious writers live."

"Sure, why not." They laughed.

"Don't make any rash decisions, Rayna."

Rash decisions? If Sage knew how much she'd been thinking about getting away from Trent and Charlotte, she'd understand how badly she needed to go.

Rayna shared the conversation she'd had with Trent at the airport. "Sage, it was pitiful." She put her hand over her mouth. "He broke out in a sweat and his face turned completely white. I thought I may have to scrape him off the floor. His body seemed to react to betraying Charlotte with just his words."

"Sounds like Trent, faithful to the ends of the earth. In mind as well as body."

"True. His moral code points true north."

They managed to change the topic and enjoy the rest of the evening before hearing a soft knock on the screen door.

"Trent!" The inside door rested against the wall, and Rayna could see him through the old-fashioned screen. She jumped up and reluctantly went to the door. "What are you doing here?" She blurted, looking back at Sage, who sat aghast.

He gestured toward the road. "There's a bear on the road out front."

"A bear!?" Rayna flinched, the hair on her arms crawling as she folded them across her chest.

Sage joined her at the door, equally alarmed. "Yikes! We were just walking around the yard."

"You might want to close the big door, and Sage, you better not leave for bit."

Sage and Rayna exchanged a frightful glance. "No worries, I'm staying the night."

"Thanks for coming to warn us." Rayna looked out into the blackness, trembling. "Are you going to get back home okay?"

He raised a can of bear spray in one hand and the shot gun in the other. "Charlotte sent me out well prepared. You can thank her. She noticed the bear walking down your side of the road, in this direction."

Rayna tried to hide her disbelief. "I guess we do have Charlotte to thank. Tell her we appreciate her thoughtfulness."

Trent nodded, then disappeared into the dark.

The women looked at each other in shock as they shut the door. "Charlotte sent him?" Sage rolled her eyes and flopped into the chair. "I have a tough time believing Creeping Beauty is sitting over there worried that we're about to be eaten by a bear."

Rayna rolled her eyes, stunned at the comment. "I get it. You really don't like Charlotte."

"Not even a little bit. She hurt my friend!"

"Please tell me you're not reading the nursery rhymes to your kids while you're making up those names, because that would be really disturbing."

Sage raised her hand in the air and motioned, indicating a little bit.

With a healthy dose of skepticism, Rayna contemplated the likelihood of Charlotte being genuinely concerned for them. "He couldn't even speak to me at the ball because she would have had a fit. She's so jealous."

"There's something else at play here." Sage shot her a serious look. "I don't know what, but there's more to this."

"I agree. But what?" Rayna locked the front door and checked the windows to make sure they were all closed. "This situation gets more confusing every day."

Sage fanned herself. "I forgot how good-looking he is."

"Unfortunately, I never did."

They dimmed the lights and peered through the bay window one last time. A bright light radiated from the Jacksons shed.

"It looks like Trent went back to his doghouse."

Rayna moved closer to the glass. Still shaking, she wrapped her arms around herself as she stared at the glow from his shop window, completely drawn to it.

"I'm sure the bear is gone." Sage looked at Rayna with deep concern. "But … I think you're in more danger now."

Chapter 42

Days later, Rayna arrived at Raspberry Cottage in time to find Beaker in the side yard, stacking armloads of wood from the box of his truck. She pulled in beside him and walked around to the passenger side and opened the door.

"Hey, Brat."

"I hope we're not going to need fire logs any time soon." She scooped the two paper bags from the front seat and threw her hip against the door, slamming it shut.

Beaker pried the heavy sacks from her arms and carried them into the house. He set them on the counter and went back to the woodpile.

Rayna put the cream in the fridge and a bucket of cherry ice cream in the freezer. The rest could wait. From the kitchen window, she watched Beaker move a few blocks of wood and wipe his forehead with the back of his arm as he worked away at emptying the truck. She poured orange juice into a beaker, and with an ear-to-ear grin, she pranced down the stairs of the porch with the chemistry equipment extended toward him.

"Thanks." He eyed the beaker and managed a faint smile.

Dazed and pale, his squinched eyes were the first thing to give him away. He took a couple gulps, then set the glass on the window ledge. Within minutes, he was stacking the last few pieces of wood. He then sat on the open tailgate and finished the juice. With his hands clasped behind his head, he tucked his chin to his chest and stretched the muscles in the back of his neck.

"Beaker, do you have one of your headaches?" Rayna moved closer, studying his face.

"I'm fine."

Rayna took the empty glass and locked her arm around his elbow. She pulled him in the direction of the cottage.

"What're you doing?" He tried to pull away.

"Nice try, but I've seen that look. You're coming inside with me and you're going to lie down for a few minutes. And I don't want to hear any arguments."

"No!" He leaned back in protest, but she refused to let him win. Halfway up the front stairs, when the resistance left his body, she knew she had him. *Your headache must be bad.*

"Your father and I have to make a road trip. We're bringing a stallion home later this afternoon." He tried to convince her. "He'll track me here if I don't get back to the barn soon."

"Let him." She pointed to the sofa. "Don't argue with me. Daddy can wait." She circled the room, closing the blinds and clicking off the lights. Beaker went ahead and stretched out, skipping an argument. One boot hung past the arm of the sofa, the other sat flat on the floor. He had an impressive build and looked enormous lying on the small sofa. Surprised she'd never really noticed; Rayna stole a glance or two. She disappeared for a second, returning with a glass of water and a bottle of pills. She shook two tablets into the lid.

"Here, take these." She dropped them into his palm.

He looked at her, smiling as she cared for him. Following instructions, he swallowed the pills.

Walking on the balls of her feet, she crept into the bedroom and reappeared with a pillow covered in pink tea roses. She watched him from across the room, trying to shield both eyes with his forearm. She held a cloth under cold water and returned to the living room.

"Scooch." She put her hand under his shoulder and gestured for him to raise his head. But when he leaned forward, she slid between him and the arm of the couch and set the pillow on her lap. He stiffened, surprised. She guided his head to the soft pillow. He looked back at her, squinting through one eye. She folded the cloth in half and laid it across his forehead. When his eyes closed, she moved the cool compress over them.

With the pads of her fingers, she traced tiny circles across his forehead and massaged his temples. With a feathery touch, she slipped into his thick head of hair and skimmed her nails lightly across his head. A faint moan slipped past his control, and she knew she'd found the winning touch. With slow, soft movements, she continued to comb through until his breathing became measured and shallow. When his face relaxed and his lips parted, she knew he was sleeping. Rayna sat motionless, reading a few pages from her manuscript, which lucky for her had been sitting close by on the end table.

Surrounded by the cool scent of spearmint, she didn't make a sound for the better part of an hour. She fought every restless nerve in her body and didn't dare move for fear of waking him. Rayna eyed another bundle of notes on the coffee table, frustrated they were beyond her reach. She reread the same pages, determined not to disturb him.

No question, she'd always had a soft spot for Beaker. There were few sorrows she couldn't tolerate; seeing Beaker in pain was high on the list. She found herself wondering about his life as a growing child and as a young teen. She was glad he'd survived his past, and relieved he'd found people who appreciated him.

Beaker flinched and lifted his head a few inches. He pulled the cool cloth away from his eyes and looked around, dazed. When he did get his bearings he tried to sit, but she pressed on his shoulder, easing his head back down to the pillow, and his body melted into the sofa.

He turned his head to look at her.

She smiled, still combing. "Better?"

For a moment, he turned his head back toward her with his eyes narrow and his gaze intense. He had a puzzled expression as he studied her face, as if seeing her up close for the first time. Flustered, she tapped his shoulder, gesturing her desire to stand.

His hand circled her wrist, and he pressed her open palm against his chest and covered it with his. He gave her a sleepy wink, and Rayna slunk into the sofa, unable to speak.

His muscles rolled in his arm as he reached back and touched the shock of chestnut curls tumbling over her shoulder. She watched him inhale as the locks swept past his face. Beaker slipped his hand between the wild curls and the side of her neck, then slowly moved it around to the back of her head. Their eyes locked, neither sure if the next move would prove to be a smart one. She waited to feel a hint of pressure on the back of her neck. But it didn't happen. Beaker pulled his arm away and pushed against the sofa with his elbow until he was sitting next to her. He rolled his head around in circles before turning to face her.

"Man, it's gone. Thank you." Deep in thought, he added. "I can tell you've done that a few times."

"No, actually, I haven't."

In what felt like a pivotal moment, his eyes darted to meet hers. He'd never viewed her as more than a friend. What did it mean? *Why now?*

Beaker's cell phone rang, and he unclipped it from his belt. He checked the display and pointed to the screen, grinning. "Hey, Denver."

Rayna waited, confused and disappointed. He'd be rushing back to the farm any minute. She returned a forced smile, but inside her thoughts raced. It suddenly occurred to her that neither had ever mentioned his text message.

"Yeah, be there in ten."

Before Beaker left, Rayna considered telling him she'd seen Jordy creeping by the house, but decided not to break the spell, certain she probably read too much into the drive past anyway. Beaker and her father paying Jordy a courtesy call of their own was the last thing she needed. Besides, how would she explain being stupid enough to drive by his house first? *Embarrassing.*

Within minutes, Beaker had left, and the screen door

slammed behind him. Rayna burrowed into the warm spot where he'd been moments earlier and squeezed the pillow to her chest. She spotted his white Stetson on the end table and set it lightly on her head, adjusting it in the mirror in the entranceway, humming.

"Hmmm…hmmm." She raised her arms, stroking the air over her head, while her hips rose and fell, teasing her imagination. Her bare feet caressed the hardwood as she swayed. With one hand on the rim of the hat and the other pressed against the front of her hip, she eased into a slow, rolling dip, catlike.

When she'd tired of the tune, Rayna lifted the hat off her head and carefully hung it on the back of the front door. She wondered if Beaker would have enjoyed watching her dance so freely beneath his Stetson.

That night when Rayna went to the barn, she froze, listening every time she heard boots marching along the breezeway. She spent an hour putzing and delivering treats, waiting for Beaker to materialize. But he never did. By the time she returned the basket to the tack room, and his hat to the lounge where he would find it, she'd stopped looking for him.

When she was leaving, Rayna heard a gate slam at the other end of the breezeway and hesitated, wondering if it was Beaker and questioning why he'd suddenly piqued her interest. But wherever he was, she had the distinct feeling … he was thinking of her as well.

Chapter 43

From the kitchen window, Rayna spotted the red flag on the side of the mustard mailbox. There was no mistaking it. That piece of bent metal pointed skyward. She had mail! Dillon saved a bit of time every morning, not having to deliver to the cottage. She hoped to change that.

She raced down the driveway and pulled the flap open, and three large envelopes were stacked inside the tin box. Rayna had no intention of waiting until she got them to the house. She removed the top package, tore the seal open, and peeled off the letter attached to the front of her manuscript.

Dear Ms. Westcolt,

Thank you for your submission, but we do not encourage unsolicited manuscripts. We do recommend that you continue writing and resubmit a new sample of your work when we're actively seeking random submissions.

Regards —.

Why would anyone want to work with someone who can't even take the time to spell a name right? Her face flushed with embarrassment. She looked around, then set the envelope on the ground. The next package, thicker, inspired her curiosity even more. She wasted no time revealing the mysterious contents.

To whom this may concern,

Recently we made the decision to publish historical fiction exclusively, and for that reason we're not in a position to evaluate your work. We've enclosed our submission guidelines for your interest. Thank you for thinking of us.

"Okay. Not so bad." Thunder rolled far off in the distance and a large angry cloud lurched in her direction. She emptied the box and returned to the cottage. Rayna dropped the envelopes on the kitchen table and, with her hands shaking, she ripped the flap on the last envelope.

Dear Rayna,

Thank you for your submission. As you can imagine, we receive thousands of manuscripts and do not possess the staff or time to read each one. However, based on your synopsis, we're rejecting your manuscript at this time. We have offered several suggestions to enhance your writing skills. Best of luck in the future.

Her heart sank as she dropped the discouraging mail into the bottom drawer of the desk and kicked it shut. With her confidence crushed, Rayna swiveled in the chair, despondent. She thought about her story and wondered if she'd ever see it finished. Was there even a point? She had to accept the painful truth: crushing failure was a possibility.

A soft breeze blew the lace curtains upward, and a faint drumming played against the windows. Rayna loved the sound of rain, and if it came with thunder, all the better. Her spirits lifted at the prospect of a summer storm, and she scanned the darkening sky in anticipation.

Rain often made people depressed, but it had the opposite effect on Rayna. Her mother cowered at the first sign of severe weather, and Rayna remembered the many times she'd sat on the spacious front porch during a rainstorm only to have her mother appear in the doorway insisting she come inside.

After a bowl of pasta salad, she dawdled around the cottage. She tried to edit but found the rolling thunder too distracting. Eventually, she had to close the windows to a mere quarter inch but refused to shut them completely. As the thunder eased, she fell asleep on the sofa while rewriting scenes in her head. Rayna saw it as a good sign that she wasn't ready to give up on her book.

Crash!

Rayna bolted off the sofa. It took a few seconds to realize what woke her, but the next thunderous clap helped to clarify. In no time flat, rain pounded off the roof and a loud whistling sound filled the cottage as the air seeped in through the gaps. Rayna darted around, closing windows and pulling the heavier drapes shut. Lightning flashed beyond the lace kitchen curtains at a steady pace, and the flashes of light radiated into the living room.

The wind came in waves and pressed against the front windows. She didn't hear it building at first, but soon enough a hazardous whine surrounded the defenseless cottage. She huddled at one end of the sofa in the middle of the house while branches banged and scraped against the wood siding.

She peeked out in time to see a large branch snap from a birch tree, and the wind carried it across the driveway and wrapped it around the truck. A second limb followed, slamming against the screen door, while others tumbled across the lawn and came to rest against the front of the house. The giant oak swayed, and the limbs bent with every gust. It was the largest tree on the property and awfully close to the cottage, but she remained certain the old oak had survived worse. She caught a glimpse of the tree swing caught around a fence post.

Crack!

She jumped back from the window, not sure what hit the glass. She scrambled to the bedroom for cover. She'd be safer there. Either the wind lessened, or the storm was less noticeable from the rear of the house. Still intense, she watched the rickety boat flip end over end in the pond, but the front of the house continued to take the worst of the beating.

The wind and driving rain battered the wood siding for an hour. She wondered what would be left of Raspberry Cottage after the storm ripped through. Barely able to keep pace with the leaks, she placed an assortment of bowls, buckets, and towels in strategic locations and emptied them as needed.

It was barely noticeable at first, but the heavy gusts started to subside, and the rain changed to a light patter. Within minutes, the storm ended. She left the tiny bedroom to check the damage.

Buckets and bowls had collected most of the water, but the beautiful hardwood floors were soaked. At least half of the birch tree lay against the front of the house, blocking the windows and the front door. Her truck was buried in broken branches and the mustard mailbox lay on its side in the middle of the driveway. Every flower had disappeared; not a trace of color was left in the entire yard. At first, she worried a tornado had barreled across the property, but had it been one, she knew the damage outside would have been far worse.

The branches on the porch started to scratch at the door and she watched them topple onto the lawn. The room brightened and light filtered in between the mass of green leaves. She caught a glimpse of a hand dragging a limb over the railing, and she scrambled around the buckets to open the front door. She was relieved to see Trent removing a branch from the torn screen. He ripped the cord of a roaring chainsaw, and a cloud of smoke billowed around him.

She raised her palms up with a relieved expression.

He mouthed the words. "Are you okay?"

She wrapped her sweater tight and nodded before shutting the door.

The saw rumbled and puffed, but rapidly chewed the last large branch with ease. He shut the tool off and she opened the door.

"Trent, thank you."

He looked around the yard. "Crazy." He shook his head. "It hit the back of our house, but without many trees nearby we escaped this." He pulled the branches into a pile.

"I love a storm, but I have to tell you this one scared me."

She pointed into the house. "There's water everywhere."

"Can I take a look?" He stepped inside the door and instantly slipped on a stream of water.

"Careful!" she yelled.

His hands flew out and pressed against both walls in the cramped alcove. "Damn, I almost broke my neck."

"Sorry, Trent, I saw that mixing bowl overflowing but got distracted when I heard the commotion on the front porch."

He glanced around the room. "You do have a mess on your hands." Trent pulled the curtains back to inspect for leaks. "The windows look dry." He looked at the ceiling. "I can't remember them giving this place a new roof in years. That's likely how all the water got in."

"I appreciate the help, but you probably have damage at your place to deal with. I'll get one of the guys to come and give me a hand." She pointed at the floor. "And deal with the water before it becomes a problem."

"I'm glad Charlotte sent me. You would have been trapped in this place."

"Charlotte sent you," she asked, stunned.

"Yes. Don't look so surprised."

"I'm not□"

He interrupted. "She's a good person, Rayna." He walked toward the back of the house.

"I know." She followed him, flustered, wanting to make amends. "That's not what I meant." She touched his arm, and he stopped walking when they reached the bedroom doorway.

"I've always been able to see the good in her, even when most people refuse to."

"Trent, you don't have to□"

"Yeah, I do." He took a deep breath and slowly released it. "You were gone, Rayna. Charlotte and I, well, things just …" He stared at the floor. "No way in hell did I want to watch another guy playing daddy."

His words were like an invisible force, knocking the wind

from her lungs. She stepped backward in shock.

He looked in her eyes. "I'm finally happy now, but I don't want you to think our life is perfect or magical."

"I did you a favor by leaving, Trent. And I'll be moving on again soon."

"I figured as much. You're not made for small-town life." He scanned her face. "I always knew that."

"Hey, Brat?" Beaker called, walking in the open front door. "Are you still in Kansas? He stepped over a puddle. "Whoa! You need to buy a mop."

"Beaker!" She walked through the bedroom doorway with Trent behind her, still reeling from Trent's admission and certain it showed on both their faces.

Beaker was surveying the damage when they walked into the living room. His hard stare rotated between them, wondering what he'd walked into, no doubt.

"Trent," he said, nodding.

"Beaker." They avoided eye contact.

"Thanks, Trent. Tell Charlotte how much I appreciated the help."

"No problem." Trent gave her a last look. "Beaker." The men squeezed past each other in the entranceway as Trent left.

"Larissa's worried. I said I'd check on you."

Rayna collected a sopping-wet towel and wrung it out above a plastic bucket, unsure of what to say.

Beaker folded his arms across his chest. "As usual, looks like I'm late to the party." He looked at her with a blend of disgust and disappointment.

Rayna hesitated, unable to respond. She looked around the room, pointing to the puddles and buckets, trying to distract Beaker from the fact that he showed up to help her only to find Trent in the cottage.

He moved a bucket with his foot, positioning it to catch a new leak.

She tried to avoid his critical stare. "It looks bad, doesn't it?"

"Yeah, I'd say." His eyes bored into hers.

Instant shame coursed through her blood. He looked completely disillusioned with her. She stood, silent, trying to find the right thing to say, words that she knew would never come.

"I'll tell Larissa you're fine." He stormed into the yard to review the damage. When she checked a few minutes later, he was gone.

Three hours earlier the worst setback in her life had been the dismal responses from the publishing houses, now she was left to face a new regret. She no longer appeared to be his innocent Brat.

Chapter 44

It took the better part of a month to get Raspberry Cottage dried out and cleaned up. Rayna stayed at the farm for a week while they replaced the hardwood in the living room, but she was finally able to work out a deal with the guys. With a bit of coaxing, they agreed to give the dwelling a fresh coat of paint, with her underfoot, moving from room to room as she typed away in the background. Her father had landscapers come in and trim the large trees on the property for safety reasons, but there was no way to bring back the flowers.

The day of the storm, she'd insisted on getting the swing hung and mailbox remounted on the post. And every few days she pulled a manila envelope from the tin box, all bearing tidings of bad news and criticism. But Rayna had made herself a promise early on. For every rejection slip she received she'd send five new submissions. Before long, she was working on filling a second drawer with rejection notices. *One down, three to go.*

With the constant barrage of hits to her self-esteem, most days she found it difficult to muster the energy to write. The publishing houses offered various ideas for fixing the recurring sins—thin plot, shallow characters, the list went on. Bottom line was the manuscript required more of a time commitment than they were willing to invest. Their suggestions were never wasted. Rayna applied every ounce of advice as she polished her story, and the quality of the writing in each manuscript she mailed exceeded the last.

Taking a break, Rayna sat on the porch, eating fresh raspberries from a petri dish, when she caught sight of Charlotte walking down the road with Quinn toddling along beside her. She had one hand in his and a bundle of mail in the other. The shoulder strap from her purse slid down along her arm as she raised the bundle overhead to show Rayna.

With a few flicks, Rayna fluffed her hair around her shoulders, slipped on her flip flops, and started up the driveway. *Of course, I look like a mess.* She smoothed her Henley shirt over her faded jeans, and just before she reached Charlotte, she sucked her stomach in and ran her palm across her now-flat abs. *Won't be holding this in for long.*

"If you're carrying bad news, you can walk right by with it."

"How would I know if it's bad news?" Charlotte asked with a grin.

"It will have the name of a publishing house as the return address."

"Oh, okay." She laughed. "What if it's good news?"

"If it's from a publishing house, you can be fairly sure that it's not."

They met at the road and Charlotte passed her the letters. "It might be a problem with your mailbox. This stuff went into ours instead, so maybe it won't be jinxed."

Rayna tossed her head back and gave a nervous laugh. "Huh! I doubt it. But thanks, Charlotte."

Letting her guard down with Charlotte had never felt comfortable, and she questioned whether she even deserved the honesty. Charlotte seemed to have become unusually welcoming the last couple of months, and Rayna wondered what she wanted. Charlotte always had an end game, every good deed always to her benefit. Quinn entertained himself, looking for unusual stones in the gravel while they talked.

Although certain disappointment waited inside the envelopes, they still gave her butterflies as she stood there holding them. And, like every other rejection, she couldn't wait to tear them open. While they chatted, Rayna sifted through the pile and one letter caught her eye: Clear Word Publishing House.

She set it on the top of the stack.

"I heard rumors you're leaving soon."

"They're not rumors," Rayna said, dreading the conversation to follow.

"I thought you weren't going back to the city until after you published your book?"

"The book might not be done, but I am." She continued in a self-deprecating manner. "It was a pipe dream. Once the rejection slips started arriving, it was difficult to find the motivation to work on it." A painful admission, and to reveal it to Charlotte seemed odd, at first, but for some strange reason it felt especially liberating.

Charlotte rubbed her forehead. "I'm really sorry to hear that."

She assumed Charlotte's sorry referred to the book, not the leaving, but she seemed genuine. "Thanks, Charlotte. It's been difficult to accept the truth."

"I'm planning a six-month European tour. London, Paris … Italy. When I come home, I'll be moving to Boston. I've received an offer from a paper there, and they're willing to work around my trip. I'll probably accept it."

"Exciting." She hesitated. "For me, it would be torture. I hate being away from home."

Rayna had no idea why she rambled on about a trip she knew wasn't in the cards for her, not if her anxiety remained an issue. Oddly enough, saying it out loud gave her a sense of control, even if it represented a different kind of pipe dream.

"You don't seem very excited."

Rayna shrugged, not sure how to respond.

With an animated look of surprise, Charlotte handed Quinn a long blade of willow grass with a fuzzy green tip. Mesmerized, he dropped the pebbles he'd gathered on the way and waved it in the air.

"Maybe you're quitting too easily. The Rayna I knew never backed away from a challenge."

What's with the sudden interest and all-too-nice act? Rayna went into full defense mode. "It's complicated," she reasoned, staring behind her at the road. "There's a lot more to it. I need to go."

She had no doubt Charlotte agreed and was elated at the thought of Rayna bailing on Talsburg. Charlotte would be more than ready for her to be gone. It meant having the North Line□and Trent—back to pre-Rayna normal.

"Anyway." Rayna waved her hands to bring the conversation to quick end, but Charlotte's face forewarned another detail she wanted to add. Baffled, Rayna tried to brush it off.

"Quinn, say goodbye to Rayna." She headed for home.

"Bye, Ray." Aware of little else, he waved the wispy frond toward the sky.

"Thanks again." Rayna held the mail in the air.

She went into the cottage and dropped the letters on the kitchen table beside a plate of veggies and a glass of water. She opened the first package and started reading. Again, the name of the publishing house caught her attention. She read on, certain they had already sent her a rejection.

Rayna,

I love your writing style, and I think your story has possibilities. Sharpen the character motivation and resubmit your manuscript directly to me. I'd like to offer a suggestion. Ask yourself, What is my character most afraid of losing? And, in that answer, you'll find your story question.

Good Luck, Rayna!

Skylar Richmond, Editor, Clear Word Publishing House

Rayna sprung to her feet in disbelief, reading the letter a second time, then a third. The response was exactly what she'd needed. Over the past few weeks, she'd almost lost hope. Staring out the window she pondered making a run to the farm, her smiling reflection staring back from the glass. The sparkle in her eyes soon became tears of relief. She wiped at the constant stream dripping off her chin. Rayna leaned as close as she could get to the glass, grabbed the bridge of her nose, then searched between her eyes. There was no mistaking the hardened patch stuck between her brows.

"No!" She yelled in horror on the way to the bathroom.

As much as she'd hoped otherwise, the mirror verified the embarrassing blunder. Mortified, she rinsed the plaster stamp until it loosened and fell into the sink. *Not in front of her!?*

With the letter in hand, she grabbed her keys and headed for the truck, no longer puzzled about Charlotte's cryptic behavior.

With the exciting news, it was easy to push the incident out of her mind. She drove straight to the farm and her mother met her on the porch.

"This is amazing!" Her mother read the letter. "What are your plans?"

"I need to make the changes and polish my manuscript."

"This will affect your trip to Europe. You will need to concentrate on your story now that it's generating interest."

Rayna silently agreed, but for her mother it presented another excuse to keep her from leaving. "I can write from anywhere." But she knew that traveling around Europe was out of the question. Truth be told, it spared her the embarrassment of having to admit it. Regardless, the publishing house would want to meet with her if the revisions went well.

She kissed the letter. "Hello, gorgeous."

"If you and your father were speaking …"

"Mom, I got it." The happiness drained from her body. Beyond common courtesy, he'd barely spoken an extra word to her in weeks. He tried, but it always seemed forced. He would be so proud, and she couldn't share it with him.

"This might be a good way to break the ice."

"Soon, Mom, I promise." She didn't have the mettle to approach him only to be rejected again. It hurt too much.

Her mother stared at the floor, then back at Rayna. "Beaker left last night."

What!? "Left?" A shot of heat spread inside her chest and

settled into her knees. She leaned against the doorframe.

"Left the farm. He handed in his notice a week ago. We never mentioned it. We were hoping he might change his mind."

"Where did he go?"

"The Bentley Farm. He never said why. Beaker hasn't been happy the last month or so. Maybe he needs a change." She shrugged. "You know what Beaker's like. He keeps things to himself."

"Yeah." Rayna was quiet. Her response from the publisher wasn't enough to chase away the heartache. How would her father get by without Beaker? How would she? It never occurred to her he might not be around forever.

"Don't let this dampen your spirits. I wish I had waited until tomorrow to share the details of his leaving. I'm afraid my news has ruined your celebration."

"Of course, it hasn't. Why would it?" Rayna hated that his leaving bothered her so, and she questioned why she thought it might be her fault.

Chapter 45

Rayna hung around Starling longer than she'd intended. The fall fashion displays were being swapped for winter apparel, offering twice as much to explore. Between the well-dressed window mannequins in Tweed & Cashmere, Rayna caught a glimpse of the disappearing sunlight and hurried to the counter to check out. Driving in the dark had never been an issue for Rayna, but it seemed to be lately. It made sense to run her errands during the day.

The sun set behind the mall as she pulled away with a new pair of jeans, a few groceries, and enough writing supplies to last a lifetime. The truck seemed a bit sluggish, so she pressed a little harder on the gas to get it going as she left Starling. Halfway home, the slow-moving truck meandered, and she struggled to control it.

Since her anxiety issue had surfaced, she had a habit of getting off the main roads as soon as possible in favor of the quieter back roads, and unfortunately, that afternoon was no exception. The back road was deserted! She hadn't passed a single car. When she found a safe-looking open area, she coasted to the shoulder and stopped. Rayna dumped her purse on the passenger seat, searching for the cell phone her mother had brought from the farm, already aware it had never left the counter. *I'm such an idiot!*

The truck was leaning on the driver's-side back end, and Rayna started to get nervous. She pinched her blazer pocket until she found the locket. "Thank goodness!" At least she had her magic pills. Rayna looked around before opening the door, grateful she'd at least chosen a good spot to break down. If there was such a thing.

Her knees softened when she stepped from the cab to have a look, and she felt like she was breathing through a straw. The rim on the back tire sat on the pavement and the rubber lay beneath it like a flat loaf of pumpernickel. She got back behind the wheel and tried to drive onto the road, but the rear end dragged and slipped sideways. The tire was completely flat. She was stranded.

Rayna held the locket in her hand, wondering if the pills worked on real fear or if they only offset the fake stuff. She slipped one under her tongue for good measure. But, Rayna knew, to counteract legitimate panic she'd need a concrete plan. Pills couldn't touch this problem, but they did help her to think clearly and stopped her body from shaking. As the sun set behind the trees, she tried to relax so it could work its magic. She counted a dozen left in the case, snapped it shut, and tucked it back into her pocket.

When she looked to her left, a brown van was sitting on the road right beside her□a foot from her window. Grainger and Son was printed on the side door. Her hand flew to her chest. "Oh, boy!" She rolled down the window as her heart jumped into her throat. Jordy Grainger was slouched in the driver's seat, with a death grip on the steering wheel. Rayna tried to appear calm.

"Looks like you have yourself a flat tire there, Rayna."

Trembling, trying not to look terrified, she spoke in a nervous whisper. "Yes, yes I do."

"I've never fixed a flat." He mashed the side of his thumb into his mouth and chewed on the skin.

This isn't good. Trying to sound as nonchalant as possible, she asked, "Can you call the farm for me, Jordy?"

He snorted between laughs. "Nope." He stared at the road straight ahead. "I don't have one of those carry-around phones." He looked at his watch. "It'll be dark in an hour."

"Yes, yes it will be." She cowered, wondering how it would

end. *If he asks … you're not getting in there with him.*

"Do you want me to drive to the farm to get Denver? It would only take me ten minutes. Be quicker than going back into town for a tow."

Her body started to vibrate. "Yes, please. Thanks, Jordy." She could still hear him talking while she closed the window.

"Okay." He gave a single nod. "Keep your doors locked, there's a lot of weird people around here," she heard him mumble through the closed window. He tipped his baseball cap and sped away.

"Oh, thank goodness," she blurted with a huge sigh of relief. The story was already formulating in her head. *You'll never believe what happened! The person I least wanted to see in the world came to my rescue.* You couldn't write stuff like this; publishers would say the plot was too far-fetched.

In less than twenty minutes, her father rolled in with one of the farmhands and she leaned against the back quarter panel while they stepped from her father's Suburban. The farmhand grabbed a jack from the back of the SUV, and they walked toward her.

"Beaker! I didn't see who …"

He gave her a nod, but little else.

"I must have run over a nail. I was sitting here about five minutes when Jordy came to my rescue."

They squatted by the back tire and Denver ran his hand around the rubber.

"Denver, look." Beaker pointed to a fine line on the side of the tire. "That's it."

Her father slid a pen-like metal tool into a faint line and the rubber opened. He stood, put his hands on his hips, and looked around at the deserted road. He gave Beaker a stern look, then turned to Rayna. "Were you scared, sweetheart?"

"I'm fine, now. But I was terrified." She folded her arms. "Never again will I leave the house without a cell phone□ever."

Beaker rolled the spare tire to the back of her truck. "Forget the nail theory." He looked at Denver for approval before pointing to the tire. "There's a gash in the sidewall."

"What!?" She leaned in to see it for herself.

Her father studied the road in both directions. "I don't think it was a coincidence Jordy happened by when he did."

"Want to make a run by the Grainger farm, Denver? Pay him a courtesy visit."

"No!" She grabbed her father's arm. "I don't like this. Notify Sheriff Buck, Daddy."

"Rayna's right." He started jacking the truck. "We don't have much light left."

She meandered over to her father's SUV, hoping Beaker would wander by, but he never came near.

That night she still couldn't get Beaker off her mind. Why was he at the farm? Had he come to her rescue, or had he just been riding shotgun when they got the news? She walked over to the canisters and picked up the cell phone, disappointed to discover there were no missed calls or messages.

From the bay window, Rayna could see Quinn waddling around on the front porch with a blue, helium-filled balloon floating behind him. Trent marched ahead of the bouncing tot, and Charlotte seemed to be directing the parade from their porch swing. Rayna watched Quinn as he tugged on the ribbon and the unusually shaped mylar balloon pitched in the air above him. It took a few minutes for Rayna to realize it was shaped like the number two. "Aww … it's his birthday." She smiled and watched him bounce around for a few minutes.

Rayna grabbed her agenda and looked for the year-at-a-glance calendar. She stared at the squares representing each month and marked an "X" on September 18th. She tapped her pursed lips with her index finger, then placed it on the month of September. Her finger slid backward to August. *One.* She moved it on to July. *Two.* Rayna continued to move backward through the months—June, May, April—and stopped when her finger hovered above the month of December. *Nine months.*

The Jacksons were going into the house when she looked up from the calendar, pleased with herself for solving one mystery. She tapped her lips. *Charlotte's winterberry red dress had been worth every penny.*

Chapter 46

The evening after Rayna's flat tire, she pulled up in front of her parent's house to find Sheriff Buck sitting in his cruiser talking on the police radio.

While she waited for him to finish, she enjoyed the almost musical sound of acorns bouncing off fence posts and the hood of his car. Hoping to catch one, she raised her hands as if it were raining. He smiled at her antics as he stepped out of the cruiser, adjusting his gun belt and tucking in his shirt.

"Hi, Sheriff." She turned to the porch and gestured for him to follow her. "My parents are expecting me for dinner. Are you hungry?"

"No, but I wouldn't turn down a cup of hot coffee." Short and barrel-chested, he didn't look like he'd be much protection, although he had a fierce reputation for keeping the worst characters in check. He was a classic example of the power of mental brawn over physical.

Her parents met them on the porch and her father shook his hand. "Buck." They walked into the house as they spoke.

"Denver, Larissa. I wanted to update you on the tire incident from the other day. I'm glad I met up with Rayna here, as well."

"Come sit. Coffee?" her mother asked as she led him into the kitchen.

"Sure, thanks."

Rayna waited patiently as they caught up on the local news then pivoted to the reason for his visit.

Her mother set the four cups of piping hot coffee on the table. "I'm so upset. This is not the Jordy I knew."

The sheriff pulled a pen and a small notepad from inside his vest. "We'll figure out what went on."

"Thanks, I feel horrible." Rayna watched him gulp down half of his coffee before theirs were even cool enough to drink.

"Listen, I talked to Jordy, and he owned up to the entire charade. And he wants to apologize."

Her mother waited for her father's response, but he remained quiet.

Rayna jumped into the conversation "Did he say why he did it? I know he's upset with me. I take full responsibility for this." She pushed on her temples and closed her eyes. "You were right, Mom, I should have left that door closed."

Her father joined in. "You were just doing your job." He cleared his throat. "Sort of."

Rayna's eyes darted to meet his. She could tell he wasn't impressed.

"Denver, I don't believe he had any intention of hurting anyone or doing any damage. Unhinged over this whole thing, he acted without considering the consequences. But he could have caused Rayna to go off the road, so we can't just act like it's not a big deal. He needs a reminder that the law is the law."

"I agree, Buck. Rayna could've been hurt."

Relieved to hear his concern, she knew he was softening. Rayna looked his way, but he avoided eye contact.

The sheriff swilled down the last of his coffee. "I'm not concerned that he presents any kind of danger. I'll tell ya why. Jordy told me that, when he slashed the tire, his immediate concern turned to Rayna. He said he, 'didn't want her stranded on the back road and running into some lunatic.'"

They all looked at each other, shook their heads, and smiled.

Rayna laughed. "Thank goodness *that* didn't happen."

Larissa got up from the table. "He has a few issues, Rayna, but he's not a lunatic. His father kept him on the farm too much and didn't encourage him to have friends. He's socially awkward more than anything else."

"He didn't think this one through very well." Her father pushed himself up from the table.

The Sheriff stood by the door. "At least he had the sense to try to remedy the situation. He told me, after he punctured the tire, he knew he had to make sure Rayna got home safe. So, there you have it."

"Well, I feel better." As a second thought, Rayna added, "Hopefully, he has it out of his system now."

The sheriff sighed heavily as he walked along. "There was something else though … a detail he wanted to get off his chest. I've watched people make confessions and I know how they act right before. The way their demeanor changes." Bemused, he continued. "He had that distinct look. Not guilt, but there was something." Sheriff Buck tucked his notepad into the palm of his hand. "He said he 'worried stuff would come out' and it would make us 'not like him.' But I couldn't get any more from him." He walked onto the porch. "He won't give you any more trouble."

Rayna followed them. "Sheriff, have they determined what really went on over there yet? Do they still consider the farmhand's death an accident?"

"I don't know, Buck. Brimstone was a hell of a rough horse but …"

"Denver, I fully agree. They don't have any new evidence, one way or the other. And unless Jordy tells them what he's hiding, they're not likely to ever learn the truth."

"You don't think Jordy was in any way responsible, do you?" Rayna's skin crawled at the notion.

Sheriff Buck reacted quickly. "No, no. But I sensed there was more. There's something he's not telling anyone."

Denver walked down the stairs ahead of them. "Maybe you and I could take a trip there this week. I'm sure he'd like to apologize and get it off his chest, and I think we should leave Rayna out of this going forward. What do you think, Buck?"

Sheriff Buck adjusted the spotlight on the side of the cruiser.

"I think that's a good idea. We can pass his message along to her. Okay, night everyone." He waved from inside the cruiser.

The Westcotts went back inside for their ham dinner. Rayna dreaded the conversation about to take place at the kitchen table, but as soon as they finished eating her father got up and left for the barn.

"Your father will come to you when he's ready. He's one stubborn man, and we're not going to change him now." She handed Rayna an apron for good measure. "It works for me."

Rayna wiped her hands on the apron and gave a mock heavy sigh of relief. "Hey, it does work. I'm feeling much better, and I can't even remember what I was just worrying about." They laughed. Her mother was right about her father as well, but it didn't make the distance between them feel any less painful.

* * *

When Rayna arrived back at the cottage, in the dark, she walked around with a sense of dread. She couldn't shake it. She'd left her journalism career to be free of the sinister vibes and constant foreboding, to forget the stories haunting her, but it hadn't happened that way. Even now, between the Grainger case and the groundwork for her delinquent Darklend investigation waiting for her in the desk drawer, her old world still had a grip on her.

Rayna lifted the key from the cup hook and stood in front of the desk. As soon as she slipped the key into the lock and turned it, the drawer ominously rolled forward on its own and came to rest against her legs. It was the last thing she wanted to be doing, when the night already seemed menacing enough.

Rayna inserted the red flash drive into the port on the side of her laptop and waited for the image of a file folder to appear. And it did: Confidential, Darklend. She clicked on the icon and scrolled through the documents. She scanned a requisition for sixty industrial sewing machines and an assortment of dressmaking tools. She rotated through a collection of pictures: hollow-eyed Mexican women boarding a matte black bus, a dingy basement workshop with bars on the filthy windows and racks jam-packed with knockoff designer apparel ready for the black market.

The story, almost ready to reveal, had a major piece missing. It could all be connected to Darklend, but so far, she lacked the tie connecting it to his boss. Rayna knew she had to move the evidence along. Give it to a reporter who'd at least have the guts to resolve the case. A person she could trust, or it would all come back to haunt her.

Chapter 47

Charlotte stuffed another bundle of mail into Rayna's mailbox and started walking back home with Quinn in tow.

"Swing, Mommy. Swing!" Quinn pointed to the oak tree. He pulled on her hand and leaned away from her in protest as she tried to walk back home with him.

"Let's go home to get an apple, and then we can play on our swing."

She tried to coax him away from the cottage, but he wasn't about to give in without a more tempting offer. Charlotte studied the cottage. The truck was there, but Rayna's blinds were still pulled down and the front door was closed. *Is she even awake?* Not everyone had reason to be alert at the crack of dawn. Quinn could probably get in a short swing ride and Rayna be none the wiser.

"Swing, Mommy." Quinn had no plans of giving up easily.

Charlotte reminded herself how difficult it must be when you're little, how frustrating to have every move controlled. She scanned the yard before entering. "Okay, Quinn." She let his hand go and he darted ahead to the swing. "Only for a few minutes," she called after him.

Charlotte laughed at the sight of Quinn lying facedown on his tummy atop the wooden seat. She picked Quinn up and made herself comfortable on the swing, and he quickly settled into her lap. After taking a few steps backward, she lifted her legs and the swing moved forward.

"Wee, Mommy," he giggled. "Wee." He leaned back into her chest and his wispy hair tickled her face.

"Do you want to go higher, Quinn?"

"Quinn wants high."

"What do you say …"

"All da way up, Mommy. Up to da sky."

"Yes! All the way up. Up to the sky." She pumped her legs, and the swing went higher and higher. "Hang on, Quinn."

For the next few minutes, she closed her eyes and Quinn melted against the safety of Charlotte's chest. The way he leaned into her, limp, with such trust, touched her heart like nothing ever had. Charlotte opened her eyes when the screen door slammed, spoiling the moment.

"Hi, Quinn, Charlotte." Rayna greeted them from the porch.

Great! She wished Trent had remembered to bring the mail over the night before. She stopped the swing. "I hope you don't mind. Quinn wouldn't take no for an answer. Say, 'Hi, Rayna.'"

"Hi, Ray."

"Of course I don't mind. Why would I?"

"We have our own swing, but he prefers this one."

"This is a great tree." Rayna leaned in close to him. "I think this swing is magical, too."

"Up to da sky, Mommy." He pointed. "Up to da sky."

"Okay, Quinn. Okay." She rolled her eyes and pumped the swing a little higher. "I left a couple of letters in your mailbox."

"Thank you." She eyed the box. Charlotte had even raised the flag to make sure Rayna knew she had mail.

"I haven't a clue what's going on with our mail. It's leaving our Starling Post Office bundled properly." Charlotte gave a nervous smile. "Dillon's asleep at the wheel in the morning, delivering this stuff."

The women smiled while Quinn called out to Shivers, who was barking on the other side of the street, encouraging their hasty return.

"Did you get the mess from the storm cleaned okay?"

"I did, and I wanted to thank you for□"

Charlotte raised her hand and stopped Rayna mid-sentence. "There's no need. You would have done the same for me."

"You're right, I would've."

Charlotte needed the tension and issues behind them, and Rayna seemed more than eager to oblige.

"Quinn looks so comfortable, with his wispy hair floating around your face."

"I know, and it tickles." She beamed. Charlotte touched his little button nose and ran her hand through his fluffy head of hair and kissed his ear.

"Thank you, Mommy." He bent sideways and kissed her wrist while she hung on to the rope.

"Aww." Rayna pressed her hand to her heart, touched by the tender scene she'd witnessed. "So sweet."

"As a mother …" She swallowed hard. "A moment like that makes you feel … invincible."

"Invincible. I can see that."

They were quiet, taking in the gravity and warmth of the tender gesture. She set Quinn on the ground, and they started walking toward the road. Rayna grabbed Charlotte's purse by the tree and handed it to her.

"Look." Quinn stopped to show her a brown suede satchel tied to a loop on his teeny jeans. He held the bundle, shaking the contents with a smile.

"What's in there?" Rayna knelt beside him and widened her eyes in mock excitement.

Quinn stretched the draw strings open at the top of the bag and offered it to her.

Rayna tried to put her hand inside but could barely get more than two fingers into the tight opening. "My hand is too big. You'll have to show me."

Charlotte watched her talking to Quinn. She couldn't help but notice how attentive Rayna was, and how Quinn always seemed to enjoy the time Rayna spent with him. She could tell he'd touched Rayna's heart as well and she knew, deep down,

Rayna would have made an amazing mother.

Quinn slipped his hand in easily, and it disappeared inside the satchel. His expression serious, he rummaged around, and the women smiled at each other while they waited. Seconds later, his closed fist popped out of the bag.

"Oh my goodness. Let's see what you've got there." Rayna covered her mouth in exaggerated anticipation.

With a glowing smile, Quinn held his fist closed between them and slowly unfurled his fingers. Her head snapped back when she saw the little brown acorn rolling around in the palm of his hand.

Rayna's face revealed her shock. She stared at Charlotte for what seemed like an eternity, commenting, in an ominous tone, "Acorns." She stared at the small nut, frozen. "I love acorns." She studied his smiling face. "They're my favorite treasure in the whole world, Quinn."

Charlotte knew something had clicked, and she tried to scoot Quinn off as quickly as possible. "We have to go, Quinn. Say goodbye."

Rayna looked up, searching Charlotte's face. "Oh, don't rush off, Quinn. Let me look at you. You're getting so big." She took him by the hand and moved him back a foot, as if to get a better view. "You're growing into such a big boy." Rayna was laser-focused, her eyes darting from Charlotte to Quinn and back again.

Charlotte struggled not to react. She watched Rayna scan his face and look deep into his eyes, like she'd never seen him before. Rayna had a distant look when she stood, and without a doubt, Charlotte knew what it meant.

"Enjoy your day, Rayna." She looked back as they walked away. A blank stare settled over Rayna's face and Charlotte began to shake. Her secret was exposed. Beads of sweat prickled from every pore in her body as she rushed to get home.

She staggered up the driveway, feeling off-balance, and reached for the front of her car. It would be the last thing she remembered.

Chapter 48

Rayna's mind reeled. Could it be possible? Was Quinn Cole's child? She sat on the tree swing, trying to decipher what it all meant.

A soft growl came from behind her, and a wet clump nudged her heels. She looked back to find Shivers, who'd appeared as if from thin air. She twisted, trying to grab the toy he had in his mouth, but he kept pressing it against the back of her legs. She stood to take the wet toy, only to realize he was chomping on a woman's purse. Charlotte's purse.

What? She flipped it over. It was hers, all right. Rayna walked up the road to the Jacksons, but when she turned into the driveway, she found Quinn crying, sitting beside the hatchback. As she moved closer, she could see Charlotte's twisted legs on the ground by the front of the car. Rayna raced to her side, finding her facedown on the gravel like a rag doll.

"Charlotte!" She rolled her over and scraped a tiny rock out of her nose. She shook her a little, then tapped her cheek, and she seemed to rouse.

"Rayna?" She looked around, confused.

"Did you fall? Do you hurt anywhere?"

Charlotte rolled her eyes. "I am so embarrassed. I made myself dizzy spinning around with Quinn. I lost my balance." She labored to sit, as shocked and confused as Rayna.

"You must have fainted and knocked yourself out."

Charlotte rubbed her head. "Ouch." She looked at Rayna. "I think I banged my head on the bumper."

Rayna ran her hand across the side of Charlotte's head. A

warm, soft lump was forming. "You already have a bump there." Rayna tried to stop her from getting up. "Let's sit for a minute."

But Charlotte insisted on standing, Rayna could only help steady her.

"I'm fine now. Really, I am." She stood, rolling her neck around. "So stupid."

"At least let me help you get into the house. We better call Trent."

"Yeah, that might be a good idea." She gave Rayna a worried look. "You don't mind?"

Rayna gave her a reassuring smile. "Charlotte, of course I don't mind."

Rayna helped her to the couch and handed her the phone. She gave Quinn a few of his toys to distract him. He climbed on the sofa and sat by Charlotte's feet, holding a red car, his tears a distant memory.

Rayna studied the friendly living room while Charlotte spoke with Trent. She hadn't been in his house in years. *It certainly didn't look like this.* Charlotte had replaced the old furniture with stylish pieces and painted the walls in modern colors. Rayna looked around, absorbing how cozy putting down roots could be. Family pictures of Trent, Charlotte, and Quinn were scattered around the room, and a tall bookcase held aircraft manuals, women's fiction, and needlepoint magazines. She noticed a white crocheted square on the coffee table, with a single strand of wool circling it. A metal hook pierced through it, holding it all together.

Charlotte hung up the phone. "Trent's on his way." She laid on the sofa with her eyes shut, stroking the back of Quinn's head with one hand as the back of the other rested across her forehead.

"I'll stay with you until he gets home." She smiled at Quinn. "Is it okay if I stay for a visit, Quinn?"

Rayna poured Charlotte a glass of juice and encouraged her to drink it. She pulled a bentwood rocker up to the coffee table and drew the outline of a red truck on a piece of paper. Quinn happily colored it, with broad strokes from one edge of the sheet to the other.

In a pitiful whisper, he asked Rayna, "Mommy seepy?"

"Yes, Quinn, Mommy's sleepy."

Rayna heard Trent's Jeep pull into the yard and walked to the door to meet him. "Trent's here, Charlotte."

"Thank you for staying with me," Charlotte said in a soft whisper.

"Let me know if there's anything else I can do." She watched Trent take the porch stairs two at a time.

"What happened," he asked as he bolted toward the door.

She shrugged and gave him a worried look. "When I got here she was out cold, lying facedown on the driveway."

He leaned toward Charlotte. "I'm taking you to the clinic."

"I'm fine," she protested.

He looked at Rayna. "Can you stay with Quinn?"

Before Rayna had a chance to answer, Charlotte got off the couch and went into the kitchen to put her glass in the sink. "I'm not going anywhere. You're worrying for nothing."

Rayna walked to the front door and looked back at Trent. "I'll be home."

Trent nodded. "Thanks, Rayna."

"No worries." She waved goodbye to Quinn. "Call if you need me."

She looked back at Trent's chiseled jawline and smiled at Quinn before the door shut. It was true. Her skin flushed at the realization they looked nothing alike.

Chapter 49

Rayna walked back to the cottage in a daze, reliving her dream. She recalled the acorn rolling around Cole's palm, and how it had changed into a shimmering crystal. Seeing the acorn in Quinn's hand happened by chance, but she believed it was a sign. Quinn was Cole's son.

She wondered what to do with the information. If Quinn was her nephew, she had every right to be part of his life, and so did her parents. If he had a drop of Westcott blood in his veins, they deserved to know. But there would be another battle royal between the Westcotts and the Jacksons if her instincts proved right. Taking it further, without solid evidence, would be a disaster. She needed time to think and plan a strategy.

Sitting on the swing, she closed her eyes and pictured the little guy smiling, his breath smelling of bubblegum. And she thought about the look of horror on Charlotte's face at the realization that Rayna suspected something. *Charlotte couldn't scurry away fast enough.*

The truth always comes out. Trent would be devastated, and the situation would end badly when it did. How could she ever be sure Quinn belonged to Cole? An admission was not likely to come from Charlotte, and Trent obviously had no clue.

Rayna ran the timeline over in her mind. She thought about the Christmas party. Trent strutted out with Charlotte at the end of the night, and Cole left with Samantha at the exact same time. "Ahh …" She freed the air lodged in her chest. *They met somewhere … and switched off.* It all started to make sense.

Rayna went back to the farm that evening and grabbed the

box from under the dresser, holding the ring between her thumb and index finger. It was tiny, like Charlotte. *If Quinn belonged to Cole, did the ring belong to Charlotte?* She didn't have her brother, but she had a nephew. She was sure of it.

With so much trouble in her life, she didn't dare risk starting more. Rayna still needed to make amends with her father, Trent had told her way too much, her story still required one hundred percent attention to get published and, worse yet, Beaker was gone, and his life no longer involved the Westcotts. She could struggle through, but she felt sick at thought of not having Beaker on the farm. He'd been a security blanket—for them all.

Her mind reeled. Her new predicament was so badly timed. It would be impossible to concentrate on her story. She considered returning to her apartment in the city to do the rewrite, get away from everyone. Rayna slipped the ring into her pocket and headed back to Raspberry Cottage.

That night, Rayna went to bed drowning in reality, but luckily for her, she woke in a convenient state of denial. The next morning, as she'd often been promised, the sky was, indeed, still there.

* * *

She spent the next two months immersed in rewrites. She'd wavered on her commitment, but in the end, she'd slayed her own personal antagonist: self-doubt. Editing scene after scene had been overwhelming at first, but discipline and hard work had prevailed. With the revisions complete, her story was ready to resubmit.

It was surreal to hold a polished manuscript in her hand. Rayna cherished the moment. Although relieved and delighted to move on to the next step of the adventure, saying goodbye to the characters proved painful, like letting go of old friends who'd been a welcome distraction when she needed one the most.

Following a year of shuffling mountains of paper across the

writing desk the dark wood surface gleamed, visible once again. She'd discarded piles of sticky notes and whizzed unnecessary hard copies through the shredder to be recycled. Free of the clutter and the endless reminders of countless details, she could finally take a deep breath, her mind clear to obsess about any matter she wanted … or not.

Wrapped in protective packaging, Rayna's manuscript sat squarely in the center of the writing desk. Special delivery would ensure Skylar had it in her hands by the end of the next business day.

It had been quiet on the road. Trent continued to redirect the occasional letter, and Charlotte seemed to fabricate excuses to send him to the cottage. He brought Rayna baked goods and freshly creamed honey, jars of homemade strawberry jam, and items for her mother. Since she scraped her off the driveway, Charlotte had become a different person. Rayna was happy and ready to make amends, but she wondered if Charlotte would be as eager to share Trent if she was aware of his confessions? It would be devastating to learn his decision to marry her had been based on Quinn's well-being, not his own, and especially not Charlotte's. But there was no doubt in Rayna's mind he had come to love Charlotte. Rayna was relieved their rivalry and cold war was finally over. She hated to admit it, but Charlotte was kind of your growing on her, too.

For weeks, writing had occupied most of her time. She hadn't been aware of anything going on beyond the surface of her desk, including the comings and goings of the Jacksons. It seemed to happen all at once. One minute they were there, and the next Rayna was deeply involved in her new world, living her own life with little awareness of their day-to-day activities. She recognized the progress. Finally, in her head, the Jacksons were gone. And her manuscript finished.

Chapter 50

From the moment Charlotte's eyes opened that morning, she knew it was going to be a bad day. She'd noticed the subtle changes for months: a dizzy spell here or there, her strength deteriorating, and the seismic shift in her energy level that had happened almost overnight. Every warning sign Dr. Parlton had discussed with her.

Quinn played with his toys in the middle of the kitchen floor while she breathlessly struggled to open a can of creamed corn at the kitchen counter. Charlotte's plan hadn't worked as she'd imagined, and with every day she weakened. Her time was dwindling, all while Rayna packed and prepared to move on.

Shivers circled her legs with a toy in his mouth, but she walked past and around him as if he wasn't even there. He dropped the toy and crawled into his bed. Frustrated, Shivers let out a soft growl and a snort of air. He kept one eye on Charlotte as she moved around the kitchen.

"No milk, Mommy. Juice."

"Mommy's tired, Quinn. Let's have milk now and juice with your supper."

He shook his head and pushed the glass away. She looked at the fridge for a second, deciding whether she had the energy to cross the room. She pushed herself up from the table and hung on to the counter as she poured the juice. Such a simple task had become a challenge, a reality she could no longer hide.

She could hear the phone ringing, but by the time she got there it had stopped. She remained on the couch until a knock came to the door.

"Charlotte! It's Rayna."

Charlotte answered the door, then staggered back to the couch, breathless.

"Trent asked me to come and check on you. He's worried. He said you seemed a little off this morning, and you weren't answering the phone."

Charlotte grabbed for the arm of the sofa when it was within reach.

Alarmed, Rayna followed her, staying close behind. "You don't look well."

"Call him. Please!" Charlotte pointed to the phone and recited the number.

With one eye on Charlotte, Rayna dialed.

Expecting her call, Trent answered right away.

"I'm at the house. One second, I'll put her on." She handed the receiver to Charlotte.

"Charlotte, how are you, sweetheart?"

"Trent, please come home." She whimpered, relieved to hear his voice. "I'm not feeling well."

"I'm on my way. Put Rayna on the phone."

"Rayna." She passed her the phone.

"My flight leaves in fifteen minutes, and I won't be home for at least two hours. Can you stay until I get there?"

"Of course I can stay." Rayna walked away from the sofa, but Charlotte could still hear his desperate voice as it traveled through the phone. "Trent, I'm worried," Rayna said under her breath. "She's resting on the couch. I'm shocked by how pale she looks. She's breathing a little heavy, and she's awfully tired. You better hurry home," she whispered before hanging up the phone.

Rayna gave Quinn his coloring book and crayons and settled him in front of the coffee table. She went into the kitchen and returned with a glass of juice and encouraged Charlotte to take a few sips before resting her head on a throw cushion Rayna tucked under her.

"Thank you, Rayna." She was grateful Trent had sent her over. They exchanged a heartfelt smile.

"Charlotte, should we send for an ambulance? I'm not sure it's smart waiting for Trent to get here."

"Rayna, we need to talk." She tried to sit, but Rayna motioned for her to stay lying down. "When Trent gets home, he's going to find out … I'm sick."

"He knows you're sick, Charlotte. That's why he's rushing home."

Her glassy eyes met Rayna's for what seemed like an eternity, and leaning back against the sofa, she looked up at the ceiling before closing her eyes. One after another, tears pushed their way passed her closed lashes. With her head tipped to the side, she raised her shoulders up in acceptance, then dropped them in despair.

Rayna's body went limp. "Charlotte, no!" She covered her mouth. "You can't be."

"Show Mommy, Quinn." He held up the book and showed her the picture of a tree with red apples. She forced a beaming smile and widened her eyes in amazement, earning a hug from the grateful toddler. Charlotte selflessly went through the motions, mustering the inner strength to soothe Quinn and managing the courage to smile on cue.

"I thought you were … and then I saw the blanket …" She shook her head. "Never mind." She sighed. "Oh, Charlotte."

"He's not going to take it well." She searched Rayna's face for a reaction, but a blank stare had settled over it.

"Charlotte, I'm so sorry."

"I've had a few months to get my head around it. If that's even possible." She paused. "I won't see the spring."

Rayna's hand flew to her chest, grabbing a handful of her sweater in a tight fist.

"I want to be here, in our home, for as long as possible, especially when I tell Trent." She scanned the room. "I have so many beautiful memories of this room, this house."

It still didn't seem real. How could she possibly be gone one day and everything around her stay just as it was.

"This can't be happening," Rayna whispered. "This is too cruel to believe."

Charlotte faced Rayna and took a deep breath. "In case an unexpected event happens … suddenly, I have to tell you something." She combed her fingers along the tiny cowlick in Quinn's bangs. The same unruly feature Cole had cursed his entire life, and Rayna had probably never noticed until now. "You know, don't you, Rayna?" She twirled a ringlet at the nape of his neck.

"I think I do." Rayna paused. "Quinn is Cole's son, isn't he?"

Charlotte nodded. "Promise me you won't tell your family."

"I can't promise you that!"

"Rayna, I'm begging you!" Her voice was frantic.

"I can't, Charlotte!" She shook her head.

Charlotte stared at Quinn as she spoke. "I loved your brother. All I ever wanted was a life with him. I knew if I waited long enough, we'd be together. The signs were there. He was always so secretive and private, but I didn't mind being kept under wraps. I would have gone along with whatever he wanted. The night of the Christmas party, Trent and I left together but we were meeting Cole. We had it planned. Your brother and I had been seeing each other for months." Charlotte smiled. "And … we were going to be married." She looked at Rayna, defiant. "I Know your family will find that difficult to believe … or accept." She twisted her wedding band.

"No … not at all, Charlotte. My mother adores you. She always has."

"Trent and I never got together until after Cole's accident." She smiled at Quinn. "I was already expecting at the time. Everyone in town thought he had to marry me, even Trent. I've always gotten through life being devious, and it's served me well." Her gaze pierced Rayna's. "I could have taken this with me." She touched Rayna's hand. "Please keep this one secret for me."

"Why did you even tell me, Charlotte? You're asking me to …" She folded her hands together in despair. "Quinn has grandparents …"

Charlotte handed Quinn a crayon. "I was desperate. I thought I could push you and Trent together, then when things happened and I … well, Quinn would be part of all your lives. The trips to the cottage, delivering jam and pie, the mail runs, Trent helping when the storm hit … and there wasn't any bear." She looked at Rayna. "All part of the plan. I was sure the feelings between you two were just below the surface and, with a little nudging, I could get you to realize."

Rayna lowered her head. "It's starting to make sense."

"But I could tell it wasn't going to work." She paused, smiling in disbelief. "I hadn't counted on Trent falling in love with me. And I never had to pretend to be anyone other than myself for it to happen."

Rayna discreetly dabbed at the tears in her eyes.

"Trent is so shy, such a loner. He'll never marry again. He will be alone with Quinn forever. I was raised without parents, and I can't describe how sad I've been my whole life. I don't want Quinn to suffer the way I have." *And he won't if I can help it.*

Rayna sat on the floor in front of the couch. "Charlotte, I'll do anything else, but please, don't ask me to keep this a secret."

With Charlotte's spirit broken, a steady stream of tears poured down her cheeks. Her face was expressionless, as if her mind was resigned to the horrible news but her heart had yet to accept it. She had laid her pain bare at Rayna's feet, willing her to go along. To hide the truth□forever.

When Trent appeared in the driveway Charlotte gave her one last look, imploring her. "Rayna?"

"*I promise.*" She mouthed the words, then slipped past Trent in the doorway as he rushed to Charlotte's side.

Chapter 51

As the last rays of sunlight filtered through the sheer curtains, Rayna paced from room to room trying to find relief, but there was none to be had. Charlotte couldn't be sick. She thought about Quinn, the hazel-blue eyes, the tiny cleft chin, and the cowlick in his bangs. How had they missed it?

Whoop, Whoop!

Rayna reached the window in time to see them load Charlotte into an ambulance. Myra was doing her best to hold Quinn's hand, and when he dropped to the ground she lifted him to his feet. At the sound of Quinn's hysterical sobs, Rayna chest writhed with pain so intense she buckled forward. She watched as Trent hugged him, then crawled in behind the stretcher. The lights flashed as the ambulance drove away, and a few seconds later she heard the faint whoop of the siren as it ran the stop sign.

Rayna bolted to the truck and headed for the farm. With limited memory of driving there, she thrust the truck into park. Harvey stood shaking his head as she pulled in front of the barn.

"Where's my father?" She headed for the entrance.

"He's with the new colt in the stall beside the lounge." He pointed to the truck. "Denver's going to give you the devil for leaving your truck parked here."

In a state of panic, she charged through the breezeway and pushed the gate open on her father tending the newest colt. "Daddy, we need to talk."

He froze, a look of concern on his face. "Rayna, what is it?" He put his arm around her back.

"I'm so sad." She looked at him. "Charlotte's sick, Daddy. They just took her by ambulance." Rayna told him what'd happened and watched his shoulders drop. He, too, was brokenhearted.

She rested her forehead in her palms. "Daddy, I …" She faced him. "I am so sorry." She wrapped her arms around him, pinning his elbows to his sides.

"Whoa!" He looked at her and smiled. "No. I've done a lot of thinking. I'm programmed to go by the book. It would have been wrong to report the accident, and I see that now. And I'd give my left arm to go back and make things right with Harland."

"You have no idea how many times I've wished I could take that comment back."

"Sweetheart, don't give it another thought. It's in the past." He shook medicinal powder into the colt's feed bin. "I wanted to come to you first, but I couldn't. I wish I could explain why."

"Is he sick, Daddy?" With long, soft strokes, she smoothed the colt's shiny coat between his trusting eyes and along his face.

"Not sure." He studied the colt with an eagle eye.

"He's lucky to be here if he is." She paused. "How are you managing without Beaker?"

"I knew he did a lot around here. I'm starting to realize how much." He set the medicine can on a shelf above the feed bin. "It's a lot to get used to. I think about him."

"I'm sure you do. Beaker is one of those rare people you can't help but miss when they're not around."

He took her hand in his. "Stop at the house and talk with your mother."

"I can't, Daddy. I need to be alone. I'll talk to her tomorrow."

"It's late." He gestured toward the gate. "Come on, I'll walk you back to your truck."

She hooked her arm in his, leaning into him as they walked. "Have you heard from Beaker lately?"

"No." He was silent before adding, "Beaker knew how to handle whatever the farm threw at him." He turned to face her. "And he had a way of keeping everyone off my back." He smiled.

She listened, sensing more to come.

"As far back as I can remember, Harland was my best friend. How many people can say they've been best friends since their playpen days?"

"A long time."

"Our families have been close for generations. Beaker and Harland are the only two people I've ever fully trusted who weren't kin." He looked down at his boots.

"And for good reason." She touched his arm. "They earned it."

"I have an image in my head of Harland cutting across the back field that separated our houses. I can still see his blond hair bouncing above the towering grass, or the tip of his fishing rod bobbing up and down because it was taller than he was. Later, he would make the trip with a steaming cup of coffee in his hand. You could see him coming from the porch."

"The damage between the families can never be set right. I see how difficult this is for you, Daddy."

"I think about him a lot. Every morning he wakes up on someone else's property makes him even more bitter."

"Making it even less likely that one day this will be behind us." She sighed.

"It's hard to believe … but until a few years ago, Harland only drank with the boys and never more than a beer or two."

"Hard to believe. He's a complete wreck now."

"You never know what life's going to throw at you, Rayna."

"Like Charlotte."

"Yeah." He hugged her and kissed the top of her head. "Like Charlotte."

"Daddy, I had no right to insinuate any of Harland's troubles were your fault." Rayna hated upsetting her father. She could handle her own heartbreak, but she couldn't take watching people she loved suffer theirs.

"No. You were right to say what you did. It brought me to my senses. And your trip here tonight, even more so." He stared at her for a moment, his thoughts elsewhere. Seconds later, he made an abrupt departure.

The breezeway was dimly lit for the evening and appeared deserted. She put her hand against each pocket, searching for the locket, disappointed when she remembered leaving it at home in another sweater. If she had the pills she was fine, but the minute they weren't available a panic attack would ensue. She'd come to accept the nature of the beast. But it didn't much matter. Since Beaker left, she had little interest in her evening walks through the barn. They offered little pleasure and had become few and far between. With a heavy heart, Rayna returned to Raspberry Cottage.

* * *

With her final manuscript mailed off to Skylar, Rayna had nothing left to distract her from the misery to come. In early November, the Christmas trees were already being harvested on the Jackson farm so they could be shipped across the country for the start of the holiday season. Fighting the short daylight hours, Harland's groomers tried to bale as many as they could. Rayna watched the flatbeds haul one heaping load after another past the cottage. Every hour a different truck passed the house, like the ticking of a clock. It was a daily reminder Charlotte's time was running out, as well.

One late November night, Rayna's denial was breached when she looked up from her computer to the flashing lights of an ambulance. By the first of December a team of caregivers had circled around Charlotte, trying to make her comfortable at home and ensuring she was in need of nothing. The Westcotts were at the heart of the effort.

Chapter 52

Charlotte enjoyed a hot cup of apple cider while she watched Larissa decorate the Jackson's house for the holidays. The Christmas tree was eight-feet tall, full of shimmering white lights and covered in red, gold, and silver ornaments, a generous amount placed deep within the tree. Sparkling silver sprigs and pine boughs with frosted white needles sat on the tips of the branches, giving the appearance of freshly fallen snow. As with every Westcott Christmas tree, it made the room feel heavenly. And having the meticulously decorated tree tucked into a corner at Charlotte's house was no exception.

Swags of garland adorned the white railing on the front porch, and every six feet it was caught up with a red velvet bow. The summer planters were transformed with holly, and bittersweet berries nestled into a fountain of cedar and cypress boughs. Sprigs of twinkling lights and birch branches sprayed skyward from the center. The arrangements were highlighted by shiny silver Christmas balls and ruby red metallic mesh. The garden lanterns had tufts of snow sitting on top and resembled giant ice cream cones, the magic illuminated by strategically placed white spotlights, creating a winter wonderland.

When they were finished decorating, Charlotte insisted on a tour, ending up on the front porch swing in her housecoat and slippers. Larissa tried to convince her to get back in the house before she caught her death of cold, but Charlotte was quick to remind her it was a little too late for that diagnosis.

Larissa had been spending a lot of time at Charlotte's, minding Quinn and helping her with small chores. Before long

Charlotte found herself unable to do the most basic things, a humbling experience. Every evening she'd ask Rayna if her mother was coming the next day, and she'd be disappointed if she learned Larissa was not. She told Rayna she liked it when Larissa came for a visit, saying it made her feel safe and taken care of. Rayna started telling Charlotte her mom would be visiting even when she wasn't sure. Charlotte knew it was just so she'd have something to look forward to when she closed her eyes at night. Having had no mother of her own, she craved the nurturing she'd never received. The basic comforts Rayna had taken for granted; Charlotte was certain Rayna never would again.

Even a softened version of Aunt Myra emerged from under her cold and bitter façade. She was a different person, a real person, remorseful and far sweeter to Quinn than she'd ever been to Charlotte.

Most afternoons, Harland would take Quinn outside to build snowmen and toss balls of the white stuff through a rubber tire. He'd spent a few days in bed, sick, and he shook a little, but he was now stone-cold sober. He had to be.

Trent brought Charlotte flowers and perfume. He brushed her hair and made her laugh, and in the evenings, he'd make promises. She made him swear he'd let himself fall in love again, and he vowed to find a new mother for Quinn.

* * *

One night, while Trent flew a late charter, Charlotte nestled under a billowy lace duvet, with Shivers sleeping on her feet. Rayna sat in the bentwood rocker beside the sofa, inches from her shoulder.

Rayna leaned into the sofa as she spoke. "Secretly … I've always envied you, Charlotte."

"I can't imagine why." She stared at Rayna in disbelief.

"For many reasons, but you always knew what you wanted,

and you never wanted much." Rayna picked up a red metal car off the coffee table. "One of life's big questions I could never figure out."

"You will." Charlotte smiled reassuringly.

"Maybe."

It wasn't easy for Charlotte to let people see her true feelings, but she was determined to try. "Funny. I envied you, too." She rolled over to face Rayna. "I've spent every waking hour trying to bend fate to suit my needs, manipulating every situation I could." *Clawing for everything.* She moved onto her back and stared at the ceiling. "You let life unfold naturally because you're sure of your worth, and you have the courage to believe that you can handle whatever comes your way." With her eyes glistening she looked at Rayna. "You're fearless."

"I'm sure it looks that way, but you had to fight hard for what you needed. I never had to."

"You know, I thought I'd be terrified of what's happening to me, but I'm not, really."

Rayna bit her lip and leaned closer, listening.

"It's being gone that tortures me. Quinn and Trent need me and …" She picked at the lace blanket. *I won't be there for them.*

Rayna nodded, unable to speak.

"I can't explain what it's like not to have a mother. It's worse than you could ever imagine. No one to tell you you're smart or funny." *Or pretty.* "It's like you're drifting … without an anchor."

"Don't, Charlotte. Don't do this to yourself. They'll be fine, we'll all see to it."

She looked deep into Rayna's eyes. "You'll be here. Will you promise me you'll watch out for them until they get through this?"

"Quinn is my brother's son. He's family. I'll do whatever I can. And my mother will keep an eye on them. A team of wild horses couldn't keep her away from Quinn now. She's so attached to him."

"I can see Larissa falling in love with him. Being around

Quinn is like touching the powdery wing of a butterfly. It's impossible to do without a little staying with you." She looked at the collection of family pictures Rayna had moved to the foot of the sofa where she could enjoy them. She didn't have the heart to tell Rayna that her vision was too blurry to see them, and she could only enjoy the memory of them.

"Let's get you beautiful before Trent gets home." Rayna held the flatiron in one hand and a set of hot rollers in the other. "Curls or straight?"

Charlotte wavered as she sat at the end of the sofa, regretting the friendship she'd rebuffed her entire life. She pointed to the rollers, grateful.

"Curls it is." Rayna shook the cord loose and leaned over the end of the sofa to plug them in. She was fumbling for the outlet when Charlotte pressed her hand against her arm.

She'd never felt as close to Rayna as she did at that moment, and she wanted to let her know. *Don't crumble, Charlotte.* She willed herself to not to cry.

"Thank you," Charlotte whispered. It was everything she needed to say, and a sense of peace settled over her.

Rayna's body seemed to slump forward under the weight of the tenderness. She took a deep breath and slowly turned toward Charlotte, managing only a comforting smile as their watering eyes met.

Chapter 53

Rayna ignored every piece of mail she received from agents and publishers. Even letters from Skylar, where a deal seemed certain, were collecting dust on the kitchen table. Her mother was quick to inform her they were calling the farm as well. But Rayna had no desire to respond to the messages, amazed at how little interest she had in her book or in getting published. It seemed like it had been on the wish list of a carefree young girl. Would she ever again enjoy such trivial pursuits with a light heart?

Charlotte had no interest in seeing her ring. She put her hand on the box to keep the lid shut when Rayna pulled it from her purse. The same for the house plans. She said Trent had given her a good life and she owed him as much out of respect. Then one afternoon, in the quiet, Charlotte offered a different version, saying she was just over it, and that it would be a bit like rethinking your choice of swimsuit color when you're drowning. It made perfect sense.

There were good and bad days for Charlotte. She loved the sound of people chatting as she drifted in and out, the comforting voices a reminder she wasn't alone. And she said it took a burden off when she didn't feel the pressure to be bubbly. She slept more and more, although sleep must have been a blessing. Every moment she slept spared her from thinking about leaving Quinn without a mother. *After a certain amount of grieving, even death must be a relief.*

One evening, Charlotte opened her eyes while lying on the sofa. She licked her lips and swallowed hard, staring at Rayna.

"Charlotte, take a sip of nice, cold water." Rayna touched the straw to her lips, and she took a sip and wiped her mouth with the back of her hand. Rayna sat back in the bentwood rocker across from her.

Charlotte rolled on her back and looked at the ceiling, quiet, thinking. "Does anyone ever hear from Beaker?"

Rayna was too shocked to answer the question at first. "Yes, yes, my mother and father hear from him all the time." She paused. "Beaker is fine. He's working on the Bentley farm."

She rolled on her side to face Rayna, waiting for more details.

Charlotte wasn't going to have one care in leaving this world if Rayna could help it. She elaborated. "They're incredibly good to him. I hear he's quite happy there. The Bentleys have a daughter, and she's quite beautiful. I'm sure they're an item by now."

Charlotte seemed to be listening to every word so Rayna went on, fabricating details. She looked deep into her eyes until Rayna looked away. She rolled onto her back and stared at the pictures of Quinn and Trent. "Poor, sweet Beaker."

Charlotte hadn't fallen for a word of it. "Rayna, remember, you promised me."

"I did, Charlotte, and your truth will never come from my lips. I swear."

Within seconds, she'd fallen asleep.

A lump settled in Rayna's throat. Even if she could speak, there were no words. She wished Beaker had been there to comfort her in the same way. She wondered where he was, and if he was alone.

* * *

A few nights passed, and once again, Rayna was sitting on the floor beside the sofa, fluffing the blankets. Her heart sank when she spotted the white, knitted squares piled up on the coffee table, another labor of love left unfinished.

"Are you awake, Charlotte?"

She stirred but didn't respond, her skin pale and damp, not a lock of hair out of place.

"Charlotte, do you remember the day you were on the swing at Raspberry Cottage?"

"Raspberry Cottage …" Charlotte whispered with a smile, but she didn't open her eyes.

Rayna leaned in closer. "Do you remember being on the swing with Quinn?"

"The swing?" She looked confused as she struggled to remember.

"You were on the swing at Raspberry Cottage, with Quinn sitting in your lap." She listened for a response. "His wispy little head of hair blowing on your face."

Charlotte smiled. "It tickled." Her eyes remained closed.

"Yes, you said it tickled your face." A paralyzing ache settled into Rayna's throat, and she pressed on the painful lump.

"Aww … the swing." She sighed before slipping into a deeper sleep.

"Charlotte."

No response. Her breathing became more rapid, and her lashes fluttered.

"Do you remember what Quinn would say to you on the swing?"

Her head twitched left, then right, as she searched for the answer. "No." She became agitated.

"All the way up," Rayna said in a singsong voice. "All the way up." She watched Charlotte's brow furrow as she struggled to remember. "All the way up," Rayna repeated.

"Yes … to the sky, Mommy." She exhaled deeply. "To the sky."

"That's right." Rayna swallowed hard.

"Yes … I remember. Up to the sky." A hint of a smile

touched the corners of Charlotte's lips.

Rayna sat straight, taking a deep breath before continuing. "You said it made you feel something very special. Do you remember, Charlotte?"

Her eyes remained closed. "No." She squeezed her eyes tight.

Rayna waited.

No response.

"You said it made you feel … invincible."

Charlotte smiled. "Yes."

Rayna struggled to hold back the tears. With her eyes closed and her splayed fingers pressed against the unimaginable weight in her chest, she continued. "Charlotte, your love for Quinn will always be … *invincible.*"

"Yes …" She sighed heavily. "Invincible."

Charlotte rallied long enough to enjoy a beautiful Christmas morning, but the doctors were right—she wouldn't see the spring, she wouldn't even see New Years. Trent buckled, wracked with tears, when Charlotte passed three days after Christmas, Quinn in her arms and Shivers by her feet.

Chapter 54

Winter had disappeared, and with it, so too had their innocence. And after less than a respectful amount of time, spring had the audacity to return—and without Charlotte.

The season had officially arrived over a series of three pivotal days: a blanket of warm air settled over Talsburg; the last stubborn piles of snow melted; and on the third, the ditches ran high with water.

Devoid of ceremony, the modest trees released their promising buds and unfurled their leaves, while the spring flowers paraded their colors. The side garden filled with daffodils first, then tulips, followed by mounds of weeping bridal veil. Beyond the bedroom window there were lilac bushes and patches of hyacinth, and the June breeze twisted their scents together, dispersing the heavenly fragrance throughout the cottage.

One spring day, Rayna crisscrossed the yard, cutting any flowers able to meet her mother's standards for an acceptable shade of purple. A cluster of white lilacs and alliums caught her attention, and she snipped a few to add to the mix. To keep them hydrated until the Family Day Celebration of Life at the cemetery, she laid the stems in a gathering basket lined with wet paper towels ready to wrap the ends.

Fighting every instinct to do otherwise, Rayna inched her way to the front corner of the yard closest to the Jacksons. Heartsick, she stood facing the house where Charlotte had hoped to raise a family. Trent's Jeep had driven by earlier, but Charlotte's car had been moved to the garage, leaving the driveway empty. The curtains were pushed open and hung straight down, not the usual tied-back look Charlotte had been fond of. The wooden swing sat void of its comfy cushions, and the floral planters were empty. The front door was barren. She remembered the fall wreath Charlotte had once lovingly hung, and with a hint of shame Rayna acknowledged how it had, selfishly, upset her so.

As painful as it was to confront the reality of it, Rayna appreciated the quiet moment. Staring at the empty house, she cataloged the changes while she tried to process what had happened. It seemed unreal that people just vanished, and that life went on without them. She had an overwhelming sense that Charlotte couldn't possibly be gone. Her mind knew it to be true, but her heart would never accept it.

Rayna's mother wore a solemn expression when her SUV rolled into the driveway. Rayna picked up the basket and walked to the driver's-side door.

"Do you like any of these?" Rayna offered the flowers, and her mother touched the dewy petals. "I just cut them."

"I love them all." Her mother picked a dark purple strand of hyacinth, her favorite flower—she loved the tiny, bell-shaped florets. "These are one of the most fragrant flowers in my spring garden. I miss them when they're gone." She looked back at the Jacksons front porch, connecting the two thoughts.

"Sad, isn't it, Mom?"

"So young. I still can't believe it." She closed her eyes and pinched the bridge of her nose. "It's a mother's worst fear, being taken from your children, especially when they're young and need you the most." She swallowed hard.

Rayna edged toward the front fence, studying the house. "At a glance it's not obvious, but when you look close …" She shuddered. "The signs are everywhere. Empty gardens, no car□"

"No wreath." Her mother sniffed and wiped away a tear. She sat straight and checked her face in the rearview mirror. "Let's not torture ourselves." She cleared her throat. "Charlotte wouldn't want us to be mournful."

Rayna agreed. "Look at the shade of this dark purple." She moved the flowers around in the basket. "I'm glad we're bringing flowers from our own garden. A little piece of home."

Her mother buried her nose in the bouquet and inhaled deeply. "Oh my, they smell lovely."

Rayna climbed in beside her. "The entire cottage smells like a flower shop."

As her mother backed from the drive, Rayna scanned the road. She noticed the curtains on the Jacksons side-patio door moving slightly, and she questioned it at first. Rayna flinched in her seat. *What? The house is empty.* She lowered the tinted passenger window, almost afraid to look. As they pulled forward, Rayna could see Shivers standing on his hind legs, with his belly pressed against the pane, barking and pawing at the glass. She cradled herself as a quiver rolled across her bare shoulders.

With a hint of concern her mother looked at Rayna, tapping the flowers on the console between them as she drove. "Thank you, sweetie."

Still rocked by the tragic vignette, Rayna could only nod.

* * *

There were at least a dozen cars in the cemetery parking lot when they arrived, her father's being one of them. Her mother touched Rayna's hand and gestured in its direction. "Your father seemed quite troubled this morning and didn't plan on attending."

"He knew Harland would be here." Rayna gathered the bundle of flowers.

"Just what I was thinking." Her mother smiled at Harland as she parked beside his battered flatbed. "They probably haven't shared more than a simple greeting."

He raised his hand and nodded.

"Look at him. He's still sober." Rayna glimpsed Trent and

Quinn off by themselves. The toddler was busy chasing a wiry squirrel or whatever interesting bits the wind managed to toss about. When Rayna and her mother joined the group, Trent encouraged Quinn to wave hello. With a toothy grin capable of melting a popsicle, the tot raised his tiny hand high above his head.

Her mother separated the purple and white flowers and placed a few of them on Cole's grave and the rest on Charlotte's. Trent thanked her mother as she walked from one site to the other. Rayna was saddened by the new lines on her mother's face. They seemed an awful reward for a winter's worth of worry and sorrow.

Grieving families gathered for the inspiring memorial service, and they were in no hurry to disperse when the service ended. Her parents left together, and she agreed to drive her mother's SUV back to the farm. When Quinn finished hiding behind the headstones, Trent made his way back to the parking lot and joined her.

"Okay, big guy. Time to go."

Quinn turned and hopped to the Jeep. "To da big plane?" His eyes widened.

"Sure. Do you want to see the Lancaster?" Trent squatted beside him and flashed a smile at Rayna as he encouraged the excited tot. "Hey, Quinn, can you say Lancaster?"

"Ancasser." He clapped his hands and raised them in the air. "Big Ancasser."

Rayna laughed as she watched the pair. He certainly gave the impression they were managing fine. "Was the brave face for the service?"

He strapped Quinn into his car seat and closed the door. "It's tough." His voice softened. "I have to leave every door in the house open. If I forget and shut a closet door, Quinn knocks on it and pulls on the doorknob, thinking Charlotte's hiding in there."

Rayna touched her throat, swallowing hard. "Trent, I'm so

sorry you have to go through this. Believe me, I know how tough it is."

"We have some rough times, but we're managing." He stared at her, as if he wanted to say more but didn't dare to.

They shared a few minutes of light conversation before both squirmed with discomfort, Rayna ever mindful of spilling the secret Charlotte had forced her to keep.

"Well, I should go." She started walking to her mother's SUV.

"Rayna, I know about Quinn."

She stopped in her tracks when the words tumbled from his mouth. Her head was spinning. *I know about Quinn.* The words echoed. "What are you saying?"

"You've done a lot for us, for Charlotte. You deserve the truth."

She turned to face him. "What truth?" She played along with his vague tease, unsure whether to confess or deny.

"I think Charlotte must have been afraid of what would happen if it got around that Quinn belonged to Cole. I never forgave Denver for us losing the farm. She couldn't trust what your parents would do if they learned he was a Westcott. She may have thought they might try to take him."

Rayna stormed away. "I'm not hearing this."

He followed her. "Rayna, you witnessed what happened to my father when push came to shove with Denver."

Rayna's breath caught in her chest as she struggled to reconcile his truth with Charlotte's. "Did you talk to Charlotte about this?"

"No. And from the beginning, that's the way I wanted it. Over the years I've looked at this from every angle, and playing stupid seemed like the best option for everyone."

How were they ever going to see their way clear of the mess they had made? *So many lies.* And, worse yet, she worried he might be right about her parents. "So … what now?"

His shoulders slumped. "I guess it depends on you."

"Oh no. This is on you, Trent. Don't try to put this on me." She closed her eyes and tipped her head back. "I'm already being forced to live with one lie."

"Charlotte expected a lot from you, and now I'm making it worse."

Glancing around she opened her arms wide. "Trent, look at this damn place! There are purple flowers everywhere! My mother is hurting. She can't stop grieving." Rayna climbed into the SUV and rolled the window down as she put it in reverse. "Don't tell me you kept this a secret from Charlotte and still expect me to be silent."

"What are you going to do?" He looked worried as he walked along beside her.

"Maybe I'll keep that a secret from you," she huffed. "Then we'll all be complicit."

She watched in the rearview mirror as he took one last look around the cemetery before getting in his Jeep.

Her mind reeled. How did she get in the middle of this, and what did he expect her to do with this new information? What *could* she do with it? She was still locked into a pact she had made at Charlotte's death bed, regardless of what Trent had revealed.

The closer she got to the farm, the more agitated she became. *What had Charlotte been so afraid of?* Her parents were good and kind, they would have seen to it she and Quinn longed for nothing. And Trent knew that as well. Who was he kidding?

Not wanting to face her parents, she parked the SUV and decided to cut across the field to get back to the North Line. Rayna's mind darted from one unsettling thought to another as she trudged through the lofty brush to a chorus of chirping grasshoppers, swatting them as they jumped in front of her. By the time she noticed the spongy ground, she was already too far in to go back.

Rayna was surprised to find her pants covered in burrs from the knees down when she climbed onto the North Line. She didn't remember seeing a single thistle, yet they'd had no problem finding her. The nasty brown thatch stuck deep in the threads of her white pants, and it seemed a futile battle as she picked away at them.

Getting coated in burrs had been a once-a-year occurrence when they were young. But always the wiser from previous misadventures, they would try and avoid getting into them. Until one sunny afternoon much like this one, they'd haphazardly risked an unfamiliar field and all bets were off.

"Ugh!" She flung her hands in the air. Rayna smiled at the distant memory and made her way back to Raspberry Cottage.

* * *

That night, lying under the covers, Rayna tossed about until the chenille spread tangled into a knot. She finally gave in and stepped onto the cool hardwood to spread the blankets and fluff the pillows before climbing back into the bed.

In the soft glow of the moon with a gentle breeze blowing through the window screen, a rush of thoughts swirled around in her head. As she lay under the white shiplap ceiling she wondered about Quinn's future and the promise she'd made to Charlotte. *How can I fix this mess?* Rayna closed her eyes and massaged her temples, certain the right blend of pressure and concentration would conjure an answer, but the solution eluded her.

Deciding that no good decisions were ever made after midnight, Rayna tried to concentrate on her book. She thought about the publisher's promising advice, brainstormed an alternate ending, and devised creative new dialogue. And to her frustration she thought about Beaker … and how much she missed him.

As her body relaxed into the mattress and the last sleepy thought drifted from her head, Rayna finally understood what Charlotte had wanted her to do.

Chapter 55

The next day, beneath a warm, sunny sky, Rayna's bare feet skimmed the cool grass under the tree swing. On three hours of sleep, she mulled over her conversation with Trent. She wondered how he'd known about her promise, and she thought about how she planned to honor it. The swing twirled in circles as she sipped on crackling iced tea from a mason jar. She tipped the drink forward, siphoning off slivers of ice, and like her options, she chewed through them one after the other until they were gone.

The instant she closed her eyes and slid the sweaty glass across her forehead, Rayna's father pulled into the driveway unannounced. He walked across the side yard with his head down, a large brown envelope tucked under his arm.

"Hi, Daddy." Curious, she leaned toward the envelope. "What are you hiding under there?"

He tapped it against the palm of his hand a couple of times before passing it to her.

Sturgess, Parklan, and Morton
Transfer of Deed
Denver Alec Cole Westcott
To
Harland Gordon Jackson

She gave him a puzzled glance while opening the mysterious envelope. *Transfer of Deed.* "I don't understand." She slid the documents out and fanned the pages. *Deed Transfer?*

"It's the title transfer for the Jackson homestead." He rubbed the back of his neck.

"All this time *you've* been the mysterious owner of Harland's property?" The papers shook in her hands as the reality of it sunk in.

He stared at the ground. "Yes." He stuffed his hands into his front pockets, like a child scolded.

"Daddy, I …" She lowered the envelope to her side and stepped away for a few seconds.

"When Harland was forced to sell his property to cover the debt, I made the decision to buy it." He paused. "If he had to lose the farm, I needed to be certain he could, at least, spend the rest of his life there. And if anything happened to me, I left details in my estate to will it back to him."

With watering eyes, she asked, "So, he's been renting his property … from us?" A million questions swirled in her head as she searched the sky for answers but only found more questions. How would their lives have been different if they'd avoided all of this?

Too guilt-ridden to speak or even look at her, his silence confirmed it.

"I don't even know what to say." The deal had soured the relationship between the families. She watched him twitch with shame while waiting for a response. She'd never seen her father look as vulnerable as he did standing there before her, devoid of words, asking for her forgiveness.

When she couldn't stand it any longer, she said the first thought that entered her head. "You're doing the right thing, Daddy." Even though part of her remained angry, and worried that it might be too late.

"I should've done it sooner. I've agonized about this, day and night, for years. After we talked in the barn, the evening they took Charlotte, you helped me realize what needed to be done."

There was no hiding the pain in his eyes, and the way his shoulders rolled forward she braced for more bad news. Rayna passed the envelope back to him.

"There's more to this, isn't there?"

He wiped his hands on the sides of his pants. "Rayna … I had a suspicion the horse might have been sick. That's why I had him sleeping away from the others, but I wasn't sure. It was too early to know, but I had a feeling." He glared at her as he continued. "But I want to be clear, the contest was fair! If I'd drawn that horse, I would've lived with the consequences."

She spoke quickly. "I believe you. I do." She squeezed his arm. "There isn't a person around who thought it wasn't fair." She pointed at the papers. "When are you going to tell him?"

He gestured to the Jackson Tree Farm. "Right now. Are you busy?"

"Let me get my shoes." She slipped on her sandals and moved the mason jar to the base of the tree before leaving the yard.

Her father scanned Trent and Charlotte's on their way past the house, and a long puff of air escaped his chest before he looked away. Rayna laced her arm around his elbow and leaned her head on his shoulder. They passed the lifeless property in silence and continued walking next door, to Harland's.

"Is this about Charlotte?" She gestured to the Jackson home as they passed.

"Random events have a way of shining a spotlight on our burdens." He tapped the envelope. "It has everything to do with Charlotte."

Rayna knew exactly what he meant. She, too, struggled with her own moments of clarity.

They stopped under the large homestead sign at the top of the laneway. Harland was busy closing in a small play area in the side yard, unrolling temporary wire fencing around a red swing set with a matching slide.

"Quinn must be spending a lot of time here." Rayna turned to face her father. "You should talk to him alone."

Her father squared his shoulders and started down the long

gravel lane.

Rayna got a surprise when she glimpsed Quinn shuffling around inside a nearby chicken coup, sprinkling seeds from a sand bucket. Tiny yellow birds were running in every direction, waddling behind him and circling his ankles. She smiled as he squealed with delight. Rayna wished she could see his cute little face. It was all she could do not to walk into the yard and join the tiny flock as they jockeyed to be near him.

Trent was determined to avoid late charter flights, so it had been weeks since she'd spent time with Quinn. She gleaned a little relief from the occasional details she managed to coax from others. Standing in the driveway, she found it impossible not to imagine how different their lives might've been.

Shivers started barking at the base of the oak tree that marked the property line between the old Jackson house and Harland's new bungalow. She could see what appeared to be every toy he owned piled in front of him: an orange ball, a length of rope attached to a bright green rubber ring, and an assortment of colored shapes. After rooting around in the pile, he bit into a toy then dropped it for another. She found his behavior curious. For a few seconds he'd sit quietly, bark, then lay flat on his belly and let out a frustrated growl.

"Aww … yes," she whispered. *He wants to play.* In his own pitiful way, Shivers was grieving the loss of Charlotte. She watched him as he sat bolt upright, staring at the wooden tree fort. *What's he doing?* His little ears flopped as his head tilted left, then right, as he stared up at the tree house. *Oh my God … he thinks Charlotte is in the treehouse.* It made perfect sense. Of course he would. *It's the only place he can't check for her.*

Rayna covered her mouth and closed her eyes. When stopping the tears was no longer an option she blinked rapidly, willing the droplets to vanish into the air. Her father needed her. *You can't fall apart now.* She turned her thoughts to Quinn, still running in the coup with his little sand pail. The chicks were flapping their tiny wings as they swirled around his feet. He bent forward and an excited ball of fluff jumped into his pail. He dropped it and ran away, squealing. In that instant, when she least expected it, a faint smile rose from the darkness.

The sound of crunching gravel pulled her from the abyss and alerted Harland that he had a guest. He stopped working long enough to notice Denver, then abruptly turned his back. But her father's stride never changed. Not even when he walked twenty feet from Cole's beautiful boy, his own grandson.

Harland leaned back with his hands on his hips, but within seconds his posture softened. He glanced at her father, then back at the envelope Denver had in his hands. She watched her father put one hand on Harland's shoulder and offer him the envelope. Shaking his head, Denver faced him as he spoke.

Harland didn't take the manilla folder at first, and he stood there with his arms at his sides. He glanced to the top of the laneway, where Rayna stood, and waved. He took the envelope and read the large print and didn't look up for a solid minute. Denver was halfway back to the road when Harland called to him.

"Den!" Harland hurried along the drive and caught up with her father. He muttered a few words and neither man moved.

Denver offered his hand and Harland wasted no time gripping it. With a peaceful smile, her father walked back to the road.

Rayna watched Harland flip the pages in the middle of the laneway. He pulled a white handkerchief from his overalls, scanned the farm, and put the hankie to good use.

When her father reached the top of the laneway, Rayna gestured for him to turn around. "Daddy, look."

Denver turned to see, but his head snapped back around when he caught the tender image of Harland wiping his face, the moment revealing her father's undying regret.

"You did the right thing, Daddy?" She linked her elbow with his.

He studied the clear blue sky. "It's been a painful few years."

When they arrived back at the cottage, Rayna rested her arms on the open passenger window as he got in the truck. She spied a second envelope on the seat, but he flipped it over before she had a chance to read it.

She mumbled under her breath as he left the driveway. "What else are you hiding, Denver Westcott?"

* * *

Her father's visit had triggered Rayna, reminding her of her own unfinished business. Later that night, she pulled on the narrow drawer in the center of the desk to confirm it remained locked. The shadowy keyhole seemed to stare back at her as she swiveled in her once-favorite chair, the place she'd spent so much time. The dark wooden desk glistened. The surface bare from corner to corner.

With a shaking hand, Rayna fumbled under the desk, removing the bronze key from the cup hook. She slipped the key into the lock, opened the musty-smelling drawer, and confronted the red flash drive.

Life had gone from tragic to busy. It had been months since she'd even given the memory stick a second thought. The time had come to deal with it, and she knew exactly what she needed to do. Finally, she could accept the truth. She wasn't cut out to work in a dark world, she needed to be in the light.

The cell phone had worked its way behind a canister on the kitchen counter, and she stared at it for a moment before dialing.

"Nalan Shalar, please."

"Thank you. One moment."

Rayna waited for the firm but feminine voice.

"Nalan speaking."

"It's Rayna Westcott … are you working on anything right now? I'd like to send you a few documents I think you'll find interesting."

The package would be sent early the next morning and would arrive at a private post office box in the city by dark. Rayna never had a chance to experience the true courage she would have savored by seeing the investigative report to completion, but a tremendous weight had been lifted from her shoulders. And for now, that had to be enough.

Chapter 56

The next day, Trent was standing on the Westcott porch, talking to her parents, when Rayna pulled into the driveway. She watched from inside the truck as he stared at the deck, talking.

"Please tell me you're here to do the right thing." Rayna shook as she waited.

Seconds later, her heart pounded when her instincts were confirmed. She watched in disbelief as her mother's knees buckled beneath her, like she'd been hit from behind. Rayna's father was the only thing keeping her on her feet. It took her parents mere seconds to digest the news. With help, her mother staggered to the top of the stairs, and with one hand buried in her hair she waved Rayna up with the other.

Rayna raced, breathless, straight into the arms of her mother. She looked at Trent for direction, not sure what truth he'd decided to tell them.

"Rayna." With a look of confirmation, he smiled.

"Thank you, Trent."

In shock, she hugged her parents. After carrying the burden for so long, their impasse had resolved so swiftly she didn't dare believe the nightmare had ended. For an instant, she had the strangest sensation; her body tingled and seemed to float into the air, stars blinking all around her, dream-like.

"Rayna, I …" Her mother sobbed, wiping her eyes.

"Mom, Daddy, I'm so sorry. I promised Charlotte□"

Her mother interrupted. "Enough crying. There'll be no more tears spilling onto this property." She pulled a folded tissue from her pocket and dabbed Rayna's cheeks. "Trent told us everything. You have no reason to be sorry." She turned back to Trent. "Next time bring him with you, please. We miss him already." She smiled before adding, "We've already gotten attached to him."

"I will, and soon, I promise."

"I have a few toys in the front closet. They were on their way to your house."

"Well, I guess you're going to need them here now."

Far off in the field, a dark object, moving slowly toward the house, caught Rayna's attention. "Daddy." She pointed.

Leaning back against the railing, his arms folded across his chest, her father turned and glanced over his shoulder. Watching the figure cut through the long grass, Denver moved to the top of the stairs and stood at the edge of the porch, squinting as he stared into the field amidst a backdrop of afternoon sun.

"What is it," her mother asked.

Denver stepped off the porch and slowly descended the first few steps. "Is that …" When he cleared the bottom step he gathered speed, heading to the field.

Rayna squinted, leaning forward. "There's someone walking through the field."

"Harland." Her mother gasped and stood for a better look. "It could only be Harland."

They waited for confirmation, and when Rayna could see him clearly, she blurted out, "It is Harland!" And there was no mistaking the small figure walking alongside him. "Quinn's with him!"

"Rayna, are you sure?" They dashed to the top of the steps and waited.

Her father met them at the edge of the pasture. Harland let go of Quinn's hand and reached for her father's, who used it to pull Harland in for a hug. Without hesitation, her father then squatted beside Quinn.

Trent pointed in the direction of the field. "Looks like we're going to need those toys sooner than we thought."

Larissa disappeared into the house and returned within minutes, carrying a cardboard box. A butterfly net and the silver wing of an airplane jutted above the flaps. She beamed as she set it on the floor of the porch and shuffled through the contents to free the model plane. Turning the aircraft to view it from several angles, Rayna could see a flash of sadness as her mother eyed the toy with renewed nostalgia.

Holding Harland's hand, Quinn climbed the towering staircase one step at a time. When he reached the top, he spotted the shiny metal plane and his face lit as he dashed toward Larissa.

Already on her knees, Larissa made a soft whistling sound as she flew the model plane overhead and passed Quinn's ear. *"Whoosh."* She banked the plane onto its side and brought it down between them in a slow, rolling dive, all the while his fingers twitched in anticipation. She pitched the wing as the tiny plane performed a final dive, and the family treasure flew right into Quinn's hand. *"Whoosh."*

"Dis for Kwen?" His eyes sparkled as he held the model plane.

"Yes, Quinn. This belongs to you now."

He moved past her, heading for the treasure chest. "What's dare, Lissa?" He rifled through the toys and cherry-picked a black plastic horse with a cowboy on its back. "Mo toys for Kwen?"

Larissa laughed. "Yes, more toys for Quinn."

He struggled to loosen a bright red toy from the box as Rayna knelt beside him. "Can I help?"

"I do it." He pulled harder on the toy.

Trent spoke up from behind her. "Tell Auntie Rayna what you want Quinn."

Rayna slumped forward, frozen. Tears filled her eyes, and she batted her lashes, willing them away, too emotional to even turn around.

"Wow!" Quinn freed a red wooden truck and rolled it across

the porch.

Harland joined them for a closer look. "What have ya got there, Quinn?"

"I got dis!" Quinn handed him the red truck and Harland studied the toy before handing it back to the excited toddler.

"Show Grandma Larissa and Grandpa Denver what you found hiding in there."

Rayna shook when she heard a weak sob escape her mother's lips. With glassy eyes, Rayna slowly looked up and smiled at Trent and Harland. "Thank you," she mouthed as she pressed her hand to her heart.

"I'm glad you're back, Harland." Her father's bloodshot eyes spoke more than any words could say.

They enjoyed each other's company for a few hours and, when everyone left, Rayna dropped onto the porch swing. The same envelope from her father's truck was lying on the seat of the swing. She spun it around to get a better look. *Deed - Lone Pine.* "Hmm."

Her mother joined her with two steaming cups of tea, and Rayna set the envelope on the side table. She patted the thick green cushion beside her. "Come sit here, Mom."

She handed Rayna one of the mugs and sat, resting her head on the back of the swing. They glided back and forth in silence.

"Rayna, you sure do love swinging, don't you?"

"You know, they say swinging or rocking is like an internal massage."

"Really?" Her mother opened her eyes and studied Rayna's face.

"It's true. They say the rocking motion is healthy because it promotes blood flow and good circulation."

Her mother smiled. "I can see that. So, technically … a rocking horse would fit the criteria."

"Yeah, I guess so." Rayna looked at her, puzzled.

"So, I wonder if horseback riding is considered a circulation booster?"

"Not if it's on Aragon."

They laughed. "I think most people would agree." She looked at Rayna like she hadn't seen her in forever. "Did I tell you I like your hair like that?"

"You did." She smiled.

Rayna leaned into the swing, and her eyes closed. The air seemed fresher, the sun brighter, but it was a day like no other. "Having Quinn in our lives is like having Cole here with us."

"He *is* here, Rayna. He's always been here." Her mother sighed. "From the very first time I visited the house to care for Charlotte I sensed a familial bond with Quinn, instantly. Our flesh and blood, I should have known." She stared at the sky.

"I hope Charlotte would be happy with the way things turned out." Rayna sipped her tea.

"I think she would be." Her mother stared at the toys strewn across the porch. Quinn couldn't part with the model plane and the red truck, but the rest sat waiting for his next visit.

"Rayna, did you want to take one last ride with me tomorrow? I really need to go to the garden." Her mother's voice trailed off mysteriously.

"Yes. I'd love that."

Rayna sat silently, rehashing every detail of the last few hours in her head. The look on her mother's face revealed she was clearly doing the same.

Chapter 57

When Rayna arrived the next afternoon, her mother was fussing at a workbench in the weathered garden shed. An assortment of clay pots and hand tools cluttered the counter. Milk paint coated a partitioned box filled with colorful seed packets, and a pair of floral rubber boots sat under an antique sign. Grandma Westcott's Garden. Wearing a wide brimmed straw hat, her mother was taping closed the flap of a kraft paper sleeve filled with flowers when Rayna walked in.

"Darn. I left a bundle of dark purple hyacinth sitting on the counter at the cottage."

"No worries. I have those in my garden as well." Her mother hung the straw hat on the back of the door and plucked the paisley garden satchel from a peg board. She lifted the heavy package of flowers off the bench. "Oh dear, this is quite the bouquet."

"You picked them. I'll carry them." Rayna took the heavy bundle.

"Gentle, don't squash it." Her mother's eyes twinkled in a way Rayna hadn't seen for a very long time. She looped her arm around Rayna's, and they strolled between the white fencing as they made their way to the barn.

"You must hate staying at Raspberry Cottage with all that's happened."

"I'm not staying there, Mom." She smiled and spoke softly. Any other time she would've jumped at her mother and needed to apologize afterward. "I own Raspberry Cottage. If I come back to Talsburg for any reason, I'll be living there. In my own place."

Her mother bit her lower lip and stared at the ground as she spoke with care. "Rayna, I can imagine what it would be like looking across the street and …"

"It did bother me, being so close to the Jacksons, but I felt different the instant my eyes opened this morning. Now that I'm not burdened with secrets, and Quinn is in our life, I'm fine there."

With the publishing house putting pressure on her to make a trip into the city to finish with Skylar and the legal team, she didn't plan on hanging around much longer anyway. Telling her mother wouldn't be easy. She'd gauge the right time to drop the bad news.

"You'll let us know if it starts to bother you? It's a big property. We can get you settled in somewhere else. If you ever decide."

"Right away. I promise."

It was quiet when they arrived at the barn to collect the horses. The guys had left them tacked up and tied to a rail in the main breezeway, ready to go. Aragon scrapped with his cross ties as he waited, kicking up bits of sparkling hay into the air, while King waited patiently, his tail swishing from side to side.

Rayna looked around to see if Beaker might be nearby, though it was pointless. Another habit she needed break. She wondered if he was happy, and if he missed them as well. As great as things were at the Bentleys, the Westcotts had been more than an employer; they were his family and had been there when he'd needed one the most. With his life elsewhere, she knew his new world revolved around other people. A harsh reality she had no choice but to accept, and the sooner the better.

Larissa and Rayna rode side by side across the pasture, quiet at first. But rehashing the events of the previous day soon dominated the ride. They counted their blessings as they made their way to the garden.

"Your father has an important week ahead. He secure'd a deal for three mares and four stallions from the Hardsand estate. The paperwork alone will occupy most of his time, let alone getting them assessed and settled in. With Beaker gone, he's not going to have the support he's always been able to rely on."

"It's been a big transition for Daddy, but he seems to have settled into the changes."

Her mother sighed. "Beaker had a rare talent. He never needed direction. He always knew exactly what needed to be done."

In silence, Rayna thought about his more endearing gifts. "I'm sorry Beaker's gone, Mom. I can't help but think it's my fault."

"Your fault!?" She flinched. "Nonsense, you had nothing to do with his leaving." She scowled. "The Bentleys have had their eye on Beaker for a long time. Why, they've been trying to steal him from Denver for the past five years!"

"He probably needed a change. You know he appreciated everything you and Daddy did for him over the years, right?"

Her mother nodded. "When are you meeting the publisher in New York?"

"In a few days." She stared at her mother before continuing. "I might stay in the city." She waited for her mother's long face, but she smiled instead.

"Rayna, you do what you need to do. It's your life to live, sweetheart." She closed her eyes and tipped her cheeks toward the warm sun.

When her mother turned to look at her, Rayna noticed the serene expression and a softness in her eyes. She hadn't seen her mother so content in years—three and a half years, to be exact. The darkness had disappeared, leaving her free of fear and foreboding. Rayna sensed an invisible tether had been cut between them, and another weight had been lifted for them both. Not a word needed to be spoken.

Warm rays of sunlight poured over them when they arrived

at the garden. Her mother retrieved the satchel and the flowers from her saddlebag, and they walked on to Cole's and Charlotte's markers. Rayna removed her blue jean coat and laid it across her arm. Her mother tapped the jacket pocket as she slid her hand around Rayna's waist.

"What's in there? I can feel a box."

Rayna's eyes glistened as she stuck her hand into her pocket, withdrawing the black velvet ring case. "Mom …"

Her mother's eyes opened wide with excitement.

Rayna snapped the lid open, revealing the ring, and watched her mother's face as the sun caught the diamond full-on.

"What!?" Puzzled, her eyes darted back and forth between Rayna and the dazzling diamond.

"I found it under Cole's dresser." She paused before adding, "It was intended for Charlotte. I'm sure of it."

With shaking hands her mother plucked the ring from the box. She stared at the sparkling jewel as tears streamed down her cheeks and her breath hitched in her chest. Her mother studied the tiny band. "Yes." She nodded. "There's not a doubt in mind he had this ring designed for Charlotte's slender finger."

Rayna shared every detail of how and when she'd found it, and how it had tortured her keeping it a secret. Her mother couldn't stop looking at it. Rayna gave her time to absorb the news.

Rayna then pulled the locket from her pocket. "I forgot I tucked this in here."

Her mother leaned in closer, surprised. "Gramma Westcott's locket. Does it still hold the picture of you in front of Raspberry Cottage?"

"It does indeed, fuzzy hair and all." She clicked the locket open and showed her mother.

"Aww … I love it."

"Seriously!" Rayna puckered her face.

"I do like your hair better now, though." They laughed and looked at the pills floating around inside the tiny space. "I had forgotten about these." She smiled, unable to recall how it felt to need the magic pills.

"A distant bad memory, I hope."

"Yeah. None of this has even crossed my mind since I learned Charlotte was sick." She'd been so consumed with Charlotte's welfare; she'd taken no time to think about herself.

"You know …" Her mother dumped the tiny pills into the long grass and closed the locket. "Life seems so beautiful and hopeful. It's like, with Charlotte being such a good person, she took all the bad stuff with her when she left this world."

"I'm sure she did." Rayna smiled softly at her mother.

They stood in front of Cole's stone. Rayna set the bundle of flowers on the ground and watched her mother's grooming ritual, waiting patiently while Charlotte's marker and garden received the same attention to detail. Her mother gathered the wilted purple flowers from both sites.

When she was satisfied with the clean-up, she carefully ripped the tab open and slid her hand into the paper sleeve to retrieve the fresh flowers. Rayna's breath caught as a spray of sunshine yellow tulips and daffodils, mixed with white lilacs, burst from the package. The brilliant flowers were matched only by her mother's radiant smile as she admired them, but the two images together rivaled glancing at a sunbeam.

"Mom!" Rayna stood frozen from the minute they were unwrapped. The intense yellow petals were almost blinding, and there wasn't a purple flower to be seen.

They split the cheerful bundle between the two gardens and stood back to admire their handiwork.

"Rayna, they smell glorious."

Whether the after-effect of the joyful news, or the passing of time … Rayna knew her mother had reached the light.

Chapter 58

Larissa had passed Aragon's reins to one of the farmhands and went back to the house. Rayna led King to his stall, where she lovingly brushed him, a welcome treat for both after their long, warm ride. It would be her last grooming until she next returned home, and she had no idea when her new schedule would accommodate a visit.

Harvey stuck his head in the door. "Rayna, your dad wants to see you in his office. Sheriff Buck's with him."

Sheriff Buck? Rayna looked at her watch. "Can you tell him I'll be there in five?"

"Sure." He stepped forward. "Want me to finish here for ya?"

"No, I've got it, thanks." She filled King's trough with water, added a scoop of beet greens to his bin, and returned her riding gear to the tack room. With King settled in, she closed his stall and hurried through the breezeway, humming. Looking in the office window she could see her father, relaxed, sitting on the corner of his desk. The sheriff's arms were crossed tightly in front of his barrel-like chest, and he stood with his boots spread two feet apart, like he was preparing to frisk someone.

"Hi, Daddy. Sheriff."

"Hello, young lady, and congratulations! Your father filled me in on the good news."

Congratulations. It had such a nice ring to it, and having her father brag meant more to her than the book deal. "Thank you," she said as her father beamed with pride.

The sheriff moved onto the balls of his feet, then dropped on his heels as he spoke. "This is going to come as a shock." He glanced at her father. "We still can't prove it, but we've good reason to believe Grainger was on the horse when it stomped his farmhand to death."

"What!?" Rayna moved closer to her father. "Beaker was right. He actually said, 'There's no experienced handler that stupid, and no horse that mean.'"

"I agree with him. This news is shocking, but not surprising," her father added. "Mean bugger."

The sheriff pulled his notebook and scanned a few pages. "I had a long visit with Jordy earlier this week, and he had an interesting tale to tell."

Rayna's father listened to the sheriff and watched a few farmhands pass by the window.

"Do you remember when the Grainger barn mysteriously burned to the ground? Jordy would've been …" He checked his notebook. "Fourteen at the time."

"Larissa and I both thought Jordy became a different kid after the fire."

"Well, the fire ties into this."

"It does?" Rayna looked at her father, puzzled.

The sheriff adjusted his stance as he spoke. "When Rayna had the case reopened, Jordy feared the interest would draw attention to the fire."

"Why would it?" She locked eyes with the sheriff.

"He thought the truth would come out. People would learn the fire was his fault."

"His fault!?" Rayna's mind jumped three steps ahead. *How does a fire in the barn fit in with the cold case?*

"Jordy confessed that, one night, he was sneaking a smoke in the barn and heard the old man coming, so he crushed the butt into the ground and tossed hay on it to hide it." The sheriff slipped the notepad into his vest pocket. "He set the place on fire."

"This is worse than I thought." Her father walked to the window and stared into the breezeway. "No wonder Jordy didn't want any more eyes on this."

"Grainger always blamed it on a lightning strike. But Rayna's reporting already uncovered one important fact. He'd never filed an insurance claim for damages. He probably didn't want to draw any more attention to it."

"Grainger acted true to form—mean, but honest," her father commented as he walked back to his desk.

The sheriff hesitated. "It had nothing to do with being honest. And it gets worse."

"I can't imagine how." Rayna stood next to her father, waiting for the rest of the story to drop.

"Jordy said the farmhand knew he'd set the fire and threatened him, saying everyone would know the truth soon, and what a bad person Jordy was. I guess he tormented him until Jordy finally fessed up to his father. Grainger told him he didn't have to worry about anyone ever discovering what happened. And he made sure of it. With Grainger's help, the next day, Brimstone stomped the hand to death."

"What!?" Rayna struggled to believe it. "Are you insinuating Grainger was capable of a deed so horrible to protect Jordy from facing, worst case, a little scrutiny or embarrassment?"

"We'll probably never be sure, but I think it looks like sparing Jordy the ridicule became top of mind for the old man. It might not have been planned. Maybe they got in the barn, started arguing, and in the spur-of-the-moment, he reacted." He pointed to a glass water cooler. "I'll have a swig of that?"

"Sure, help yourself." Denver folded his arms as he spoke. "Do you think Jordy is aware that you suspect his father might have been behind all of this?"

"He hasn't got a clue." He guzzled the water from a miniature paper cup, then refilled it. "The saddest part … Jordy's only concern is making sure no one realizes he started the fire. He thinks people will 'hate him.' His words."

"So … when I filed the story on the unsolved death and they reopened the cold case, Jordy believed the investigation was focused on the fire?"

"I think so." He crushed the cup and tossed it into the wastepaper basket.

"Daddy, I feel horrible picturing Jordy tied in knots over this."

"Sweetheart, it's not your fault."

"It was all so pointless." She leaned forward, burying her face in her hands, her mind reeling. "I don't even want to update the story now."

Her father put his arm around her. "Why would you think you had to? You're not at the paper anymore." They walked the sheriff to door.

"Denver's right. This story will get buried away again, where it belongs. There's no way we can prove any of it. Technically, the details we've discussed here are just theories, not facts. Tell you what … the minute I have newsworthy information to report you'll be the first one I call for an interview."

Her father walked the sheriff to his cruiser. They did present a reasonable argument. Deep down, Rayna knew they were solely interested in making it easier on her, and she decided she'd let them.

Chapter 59

Rayna couldn't miss the jovial banter coming from the staff lounge when she left her father's office. She walked over to investigate, waving as she passed by the window. Harvey was holding the door open for a few of the guys, and when they walked past her, she could see Beaker left standing in the middle of the lounge. Alone.

And not at all surprised to see her. He must have known she was in the barn. Rayna's head was spinning as she stood in the doorway of the quiet room.

"Rayna."

Ouch. Not long ago, she'd appreciated him referring to her by name. Now, she hated it. "I'm surprised to see you here."

"I check on Denver from time to time … hang out with the guys." He took her hand and lead her into the room, closing the door behind her. "I still enjoy wandering through the barn. It helps me think."

"Someone told me once: 'It's the perfect place to clear your head.'"

"Smart guy." He winked. "Hey, congratulations on your story."

"Thanks, Beaker."

He walked to the leather sofa and tapped the cushion beside him. "Come sit."

She sat, with her knees touching his leg. "There's a lot of work to do on the book. A team is waiting for me in the city. It needs to be edited, and we have to work on a title and a cover. All time-consuming, I'm sure." Moist heat surged beneath her clothes.

"I guess you'll be leaving soon."

"First of the week. I never intended to stay this long." Rayna had no idea when she'd see Westcott Farm again, but knew she needed to make a clean break. She'd had her fill of making promises and refused to suggest she might not stay in the city.

"It's what you've wanted. I hope you're really happy there," he said, his voice reserved. He leaned against the sofa and looked around the cozy room. "I was happier to find this place than I was to leave it."

"Then why did you go?"

"It was time. The same way it's time for you to follow your dreams. You have no idea what doors are going to open for you. Your life will change in ways you can't even imagine."

Exactly what she was afraid of. "Not too much, I hope." It was all she'd dreamed of. Why didn't she want to leave?

With a grin, he ran his thumb across her furrowed brow. "I'll miss that worried little expression of yours. It's so adorable." Then he was gone.

She sat, frozen. He loved her furrowed brow. *Impossible.* Rayna felt like her body weighed three hundred pounds as she dragged herself off the couch and walked to the feed room. She grabbed the pole to get the basket, but the hook above the door sat empty. She looked around, opening one cabinet door after another. There were no carrots or apples, and the peppermint shaker was gone.

"This place is going to heck, guys … and in my handbasket, apparently." *Where's my stuff?* She could smell the mint. It couldn't be far.

Rayna dashed into the breezeway, looking for one of the farmhands, when she bumped right into Beaker, smelling of spearmint and waiting for her just beyond the door.

"Oh!" She jumped back, breathless.

He stood holding the basket, filled to the brim. Carrots at one end and apple slices at the other, just the way she liked it.

"You won't get too far without this." He held the basket between them.

She walked toward him, focused. "It's not the basket I need."

"What do you need, Rayna?" He swallowed hard returning her stare, the skin tightening under his eyes.

"For starters, I need you to see me, Beaker, as a woman. I'm not a kid anymore."

"See you? Since I left the farm, I've looked for you everywhere. Hoping to see you in a crowd or a store, pass you on the street … or find you in the barn." He closed the distance between them. "I've been wanting nothing more than to see you … for too long."

He put his hand on the back of her neck and leaned in, his forehead touching hers, whispering, "Stay … please."

"I have to go Beaker." Her voice quivered. But as the words tumbled out of her mouth Rayna realized, she'd been trying to live between two worlds, and she'd been unable to find happiness in either.

"I know you have your heart set on leaving, but are you planning on returning?"

Beaker had waited for his mother to come back, he'd waited for his father to stop beating him, and now he stood before her, humbled and crestfallen, waiting for her to love him. For months her heart had been broken, but in that moment, as he stood before her, she felt all her shattered pieces falling away.

She pulled a carrot from the basket. "How would life change if I said I'm only going to remain in the city for as long as they need me to be there?" Her commitment to return came easy, and her sudden change in plans made her heart race.

His eyes glistened. "I wouldn't say goodbye, I'd say … welcome home."

"But I'm still going, though," she quickly added, daring him to protest.

He set the basket down and his shoulders dropped.

She tucked her chin to her chest, smiling, and looked at him in a forgive-me kind of way.

"What?"

"I like 'Hey, Brat' way better than Rayna."

"Ohh … really?" With a serious look he picked up the basket and started walking through the breezeway.

She nodded with satisfaction as she followed him.

"No. Sorry, you're too late. I can't call you Brat anymore."

"What!?" She looked at him with mock horror as she walked along beside him.

"You see … there's this little bratty boy on the Bentley farm, and I might start calling him Brat."

"You can't do that."

"Oh, I can't? And who says?"

"Beaker?"

"Ryder." He kept walking.

"You want me to call you Ryder? Why now?" She trailed beside, trying to keep up.

"It's my name."

Beaker slowly turned to face her. He took her hand in his and kissed the back of it, then pressed it to his heart. He looked deeply into her eyes and softly kissed her lips, and she covered his cheeks with feathery kisses. He hooked his arm around her waist as they strolled through the barn. Their heads tipped toward each other, touching.

"What would you have done if I never came back for the basket?"

"It's my basket. I guess, it goes wherever I go."

"Beaker!"

"I told ya, it's Ryder."

"You gave the basket to me. It should stay here—with me."

"Now, I like the sound of that." They stopped walking.

"So, my basket stays?"

"If you are." He kissed her furrowed brow. "And why do you have to be such a brat, eh, why? You're right, no other name suits ya."

"I agree."

"Hey, you never told me what your book is about."

She pressed her face into a warm spot on his neck. "It's a story about a woman who finally realizes what she wants and is fearless enough to just let life happen."

As they walked through the breezeway, Beaker wrapped his arm around her shoulder, tugging her in close. She circled his waist with hers, hooking her thumb through his belt loop. When something scratched her forearm, she leaned behind him to check the cause. Rayna's heart soared when she recognized her father's envelope, the deed for Lone Pine, sticking out of his back pocket.

Beaker, too, was coming home to Westcott Farm.

A message from Raspberry Cottage

We hope you have enjoyed spending time with the Westcotts and snuggling up on the sofa, with a fluffy warm blanket, inside Raspberry Cottage. From the pink and white, checkered tile floor to the Lancaster Bomber tucked into the corner of the hangar at the Winter Ball, Lara spent thousands of hours bringing A Branch in Spring to life.

Please take a moment to leave a review.

Rayna & Beaker

Discussion Questions

1. Rayna originally had a dislike for the nickname "Brat". What was the significance of her change of heart about the nickname as the story unfolded?

2. Rayna's relationship with Trent was complex. Was Sage right? Did he serve a purpose in Rayna's life, and if so, what purpose?

3. We all have fears that hold us back. What do you think was Rayna's biggest fear, and why?

4. You could feel Beaker and Rayna trying to sort out their true feelings for each other. Can you explain the progression of their relationship? Was there a pivotal moment for them when everything changed?

5. Throughout the book, Rayna delt with a severe anxiety disorder. Have you ever suffered from anything similar, and how do you think you would deal with it if you did?

6. Figuring out what we really desire in life can be abstract; often we pursue superficial goals that have no ability to make us genuinely happy. What was Rayna actually searching for? What did she think would give her life meaning, as opposed to what she truly needed?

7. Charlotte and Rayna had constant misgivings where the other was concerned. What do you think was at the root of their star-crossed relationship?

8. Motherhood is a main theme throughout A Branch in Spring, represented in both positive and negative characteristics. Can you recognize the various differences between the mothering styles depicted in the story?

About the Author

Lara Meredith writes touching stories that revolve around flawed but loveable characters who break readers' hearts. She dreams of having her own Raspberry Cottage, where she could while away the days writing her next tearjerker.

When she's not writing, she enjoys spending time in the beautiful provincial parks of Ontario, lying in her gazebo sipping hot rhubarb tea, or crying over an old black-and-white movie she's now watched for the fifteenth time.

A Branch in Spring is Meredith's debut novel, although in 2021 she published a children's book on the pandemic called *Almost the Same … but Not Quite*, which has been described as a 'timeless keepsake'.

laramerdith.ca

laramereditwrite@gmail.com

Follow me on Instagram @ laramereddith_writes

Acknowledgments

To Crystal, my daughter-in-law, for her tireless editing and support; David, my son, for his invaluable business acumen and technical skills; Ashley, my daughter, for her wisdom and guidance; my beautiful grandchildren, who inspire my stories; Julian for encouraging me to write; Sharon for encouraging me to be fearless and to keep my eye on the big picture; the loving pugs who share my life, Charlie Brown and Harvey; Afra Amin Orony, for her beautiful cover illustration; and Jennifer Dinsmore, whose patience and dedication helped to make me a better writer—thank you for making my priorities your priorities!

Last, but not least, to my amazing team of beta readers for the endless hours they sacrificed to bring my books to life. They are there for every major decision, and I am lucky to have them on my team. Their contributions have made my stories richer and my writing experience more gratifying: Anne, Cathy, Catherine, Cynthia, Heather, Janice, Jean, Julie, Kim, Lindsay, Lindsey, Patrice, Patti, Shannon, Sheila, Stephanie, Tracey and Virginia. I could not have accomplished this without you.

Manufactured by Amazon.ca
Bolton, ON

25159690R00182